EMMA ROUS

THE
PERFECT
GUESTS

PIATKUS

PIATKUS

First published in Great Britain in 2021 by Piatkus
This paperback edition published in 2021 by Piatkus

1 3 5 7 9 10 8 6 4 2

Copyright © 2021 by Emma Rous

The moral right of the author has been asserted.

A CIP catalogue record for this book
is available from the British Library.

ISBN 978-0-349-41912-1

Typeset in Goudy by M Rules
Printed and bound in Great Britain by Clays Ltd, Elcograf S.p.A,

Papers used by Piatkus are from well-managed forests
and other responsible sources.

Piatkus
An imprint of
Little, Brown Book Group
Carmelite House
50 Victoria Embankment
London EC4Y 0DZ

An Hachette UK Company
www.hachette.co.uk

www.littlebrown.co.uk

Praise for *The Perfect Guests*

'The ultimate house party mystery ... old secrets and new dangers collide in this deliciously thrilling tale' Lisa Gardner, No.1 *New York Times* bestselling author

'Anyone yearning for a page-turning gothic story with a big house – and a shocking family secret – at its heart should gatecrash *The Perfect Guests* immediately!' Eve Chase, *Sunday Times* bestselling author

'A richly atmospheric time-slip mystery with the pulse of a thriller, *The Perfect Guests* is deliciously evocative and absolutely spellbinding' Christina McDonald, *USA Today* bestselling author

'A fabulously atmospheric setting, a cast of intriguing characters, and layer upon layer of mystery – this is a brilliant read' C. J. Cooper, bestselling author of *The Book Club*

'A large, old house with a tragic past; a murder mystery weekend turning sinister; strange games of pretend being played within a family ... What's not to love? Gripping from start to finish' Helen Cooper, author of *The Downstairs Neighbour*

'A page-turning tale full of suspense, secrets and shocking revelations ... *The Perfect Guests* is a deliciously compulsive read' Saskia Sarginson, bestselling author of *The Twins*

'Twisty and utterly engrossing, I raced through it in one sitting and didn't stop until I reached the jaw-dropping ending' Lindsay Cameron, author of *Just One Look*

Emma Rous is a Cambridge University graduate who spent eighteen years working as a veterinary surgeon before switching to writing fiction. Her first novel, *The Au Pair*, was a *USA Today* bestseller. Emma lives in Cambridgeshire with her husband and three sons, and she now writes full time. *The Perfect Guests* is her second novel.

By Emma Rous

The Au Pair
The Perfect Guests

You are cordially invited
to play a Game
at Raven Hall

PART ONE

Beth

The house sat on a gentle rise in the otherwise flat landscape, as if it considered itself a castle in this kingdom of marshy scrubland and water channels and rustling green fields. Pale grey walls, broad steps rising from neat gravel to the front door, row upon row of gleaming square windows, and—

'Is that a *turret*?' I craned my neck through the passenger window. 'Is this whole place really just for three people?'

'Four, if you behave yourself.' Caroline jerked the steering wheel to swing us on to the driveway, bumping me back into my seat. 'Remember your manners, Beth. Stop gawping.'

The driveway was longer than the road I used to live on when my parents were still alive, but someone in the house must have been watching for us, because already the front door was swinging open. Three figures emerged, and they waited, side by side on the top step, like a proper welcoming committee. Even from this distance, I recognised Leonora's golden curls and Markus' thick, straw-coloured hair.

I'd met Leonora and Markus only once before, a week earlier,

3

when they introduced themselves to me at the end of my summer concert. Markus had congratulated me on my performance, while Leonora studied me with an intense, sympathetic gaze. Then, somehow, Leonora had coaxed more details out of me about my life at the children's home than I'd ever shared with anyone.

Standing between them now, on the top step, was a slender teenage girl, and I knew this must be their daughter, Nina. Nina was the important one. She was the reason I'd been invited here. I wasn't close enough yet to read her expression, but I crossed my fingers and tried to do the same with my toes inside my too-tight jelly shoes. *I hope she likes me.*

The car came to a crunching halt on the sun-baked gravel and, for a long moment, nobody moved. Leonora, Markus and Nina squinted down at us from the top step. Caroline, for once, offered no spiky words of advice. I squeezed the door handle with clammy fingers, holding my breath, gazing back at Nina. She wasn't smiling. Did she hate this idea of her parents? Would Caroline end up driving me – her jaw tight, her knuckles a furious white on the steering wheel – straight back to the children's home before today was over?

A disdainful squawk made us all glance up as a goose flapped overhead, and the tension was broken. I scrambled from the car, and Leonora's gaze locked on to mine. Then she started down the steps, her arms outstretched.

'Beth! Caroline. We're so glad to see you. Welcome to Raven Hall.'

I leant into Leonora's hug. Her perfume was powdery rose

4

petals, soft and comforting. When she released me, Markus shook my hand heartily, and then he glanced over his shoulder to where his daughter still hovered on the top step.

'Nina, come down and say hello.'

All I knew about Nina was her age. When I'd asked Caroline for more information in the car, she'd snapped at me to let her concentrate on driving. So I'd turned my gaze to the blurry fields and tried to recall the conversation I'd had with Leonora and Markus – I'd been entirely oblivious to its significance at the time. Leonora had mentioned that their daughter had recently turned fourteen, but that was it – that's all I remembered. It meant we'd be in the same school year, since I was only a few months older, and of course, we might have all sorts of other things in common . . . But as I watched Nina skip down the steps and land lightly on the gravel, I felt a lurch of doubt.

Not only was she shorter than me, she was also much skinnier and younger-looking. Her pixie-like face wore an expression of detached amusement, and I tugged at my T-shirt self-consciously, not knowing what to say. No one had explained what was expected of me here; I didn't even know how long the arrangement might be for. All Caroline had said was: 'You can go and be a companion for their daughter for a while, until I'm ready for you to move in with me.'

Nina and I studied each other. The adults watched us in silence, as if we were specimens being introduced in a zoo. The conviction that she was going to reject me swelled in my chest until it was physically painful. Then she gave me an unexpectedly shy smile.

'Hi,' she said. 'I'm Nina. I really hope you're going to like it here.'

Relief rushed into my lungs.

'Me too,' I said. 'I mean, thanks.' I gestured awkwardly at the imposing grey house behind her. 'I'm sure I will.'

Leonora stepped between us then, and she placed one hand on the back of my head – she was barely taller than me herself – and the other on Nina's dark hair.

'Look at you two,' she murmured. 'Like chalk and cheese.'

I stiffened. Nina seemed happy enough to meet me; surely Leonora hadn't changed her mind? But Leonora sounded wistful rather than disappointed, and Nina sidestepped away from her and gave me an apologetic grimace.

'Can I show Beth up to her room, Mum?'

Leonora blinked, as if dragging her thoughts back from somewhere else.

'What? Oh yes, of course.' She turned to Caroline. 'Will you come in for a cup of tea? Or you're welcome to stay for dinner . . . '

But Caroline was already reaching into her car boot and setting my bags and violin case down on the gravel. 'No, no, I've got to get back. Long flight tomorrow, you know.' She slammed the boot shut, walked around to the driver's door and fixed me with her sharp stare. 'Be good, Beth.'

I ground my teeth. When had I ever not been good? I'd never complained about Caroline putting her work before me, even though we were the only family each other had left. Each time she'd promised vaguely that I'd be able to move in with her soon, I'd smiled as if I believed her. Even this morning, when she confessed – out of earshot of the children's home staff – that she wasn't quite ready to take me in herself, but that she'd found me a private foster placement, I'd merely nodded politely.

Now, she raised her eyebrows at me, waiting.

I gave her a tight smile. 'I will, Aunt Caroline. Thank you for driving me here.'

I stood between Leonora and Nina as Caroline's car accelerated away down the drive, and I knew this was my last chance to change my mind. If I ran now – if I sprinted after her car, waving my arms – Caroline would see me in her mirror, and she'd stop for me; she'd take me away from these people – these strangers. She'd take me back to the children's home, before flying out to Istanbul or Sydney or wherever her work was taking her tomorrow. I glanced left and right at Leonora and Nina. But why would I want to leave, when these people seemed so welcoming and this house so entrancing?

'Not even a cup of tea,' Leonora muttered, staring after the car, but I knew her disapproval was for Caroline and not for me, so I didn't mind.

Nina swivelled to face me. 'Come on. Let's take your things upstairs, then I'll show you round.'

'One more thing, Beth,' Leonora said, also turning her back on the receding car: 'make yourself at home.' She searched my gaze and nodded, as though she approved of what she saw there. 'I mean it. We want you to feel like you're part of our family here.'

It took me a moment to find my voice. 'Thank you.'

Leonora's gaze slid over my shoulder to the house, and her voice took on that distant tone again. 'It can get lonely at Raven Hall for an only child. It'll be lovely for Nina to have someone to play with . . .'

I scrunched my toes in my jelly shoes and tried not to let my smile slip. We were fourteen – a little old to *play*, I thought. But I didn't want her to think I was ungrateful.

'Mum,' Nina said impatiently, shielding her face from the sun's glare with her hand as she squinted up at Leonora.

Leonora gave her head a little shake and blinked back at us. 'Okay, run along now, girls. I've got things to do. Dinner at seven. Stay out of trouble till then.'

Sadie

JANUARY 2019

Sadie shoves the front door repeatedly to dislodge the pile of junk mail and newspapers wedged behind it. The narrow hallway feels even colder than the street outside, and there's a damp patch on the carpet where the doormat used to lie. Her mother always kept the thermostat turned up high in the winter; Sadie used to peel off layers and complain it was like an oven in here, and her mother would grumble it was what her cold bones needed. But the central heating hasn't been on for weeks now, and the air has acquired a musty, abandoned smell that makes Sadie miss her mother more than ever.

She scoops up the post and adds it to the considerable amount already collected in a cardboard box in the corner. With a bit of luck, this will be the last trip she needs to make here – the whole process has taken longer than she'd expected. Most of her mother's possessions have been cleared out, and only one more vanload of furniture remains to be picked up by the charity shop.

The new tenants are due to move in next week – a young couple with a baby, apparently. Sadie hopes the landlord will warm the house up for them before they arrive; and, more pressingly, she hopes he'll return her mother's deposit promptly once she's handed the keys back. Sadie has lost two part-time jobs in the last twelve months, and the income from her acting is erratic. She desperately needs that deposit money.

If her mother was still here, she'd be snatching up the local newspapers as they fell through the letterbox, circling job adverts for Sadie with her black marker pen, pressing them into Sadie's hands as soon as she stepped through the front door . . .

Sadie sighs and wanders through to the living room, where an old sideboard and two faded armchairs are the only pieces of furniture left. A half-empty bag of her mother's favourite toffees still sits on the mantelpiece, and she scoops it up and stuffs it into her coat pocket before checking around the room for anything else she might have missed. Her gaze is drawn back to the sideboard.

It's scratched in places, but it's solid wood; an object so familiar from her childhood, she's never properly examined it before. She runs her gloved fingers over it, searching for other damage, and her heart thuds guiltily; her mother was adamant that all her furniture should go to a particular homeless charity, but what might this fetch on eBay? Enough to cover the shortfall in her rent next month? Her phone buzzes under the toffees in her pocket, and she snatches her hand from the sideboard as if she's been scorched.

Her agent's name glows on the screen, and she jabs to accept the call.

'Wendy, what did they say?' Sadie presses the phone to her ear. 'Have I got it? Did they like me?'

She knows it's a no from the delicate sigh at the other end.

'Sadie, I'm so sorry. They *loved* you, but they want someone with a bit more ...'

Disappointment churns in Sadie's stomach. Will she really have to tell the charity collectors they can't take the sideboard after all? And what about next month? Will she have to give in and sell her one piece of good jewellery – the charm bracelet her mum gave her on her sixteenth birthday?

'Someone with a bit more what?' she says dully.

'A bit more gravity, they said. But, listen—'

'Gravity?' Sadie spits out the word. 'For a mermaid in a toy commercial?'

'Toys are serious business.' Wendy's voice is surprisingly upbeat. 'But listen, I've got much better news – a fabulous job offer for you. It's a murder mystery company, just starting up, and they want to act out a trial run of the game so they can take photos for their website – glamorous costumes at a posh dinner party, that sort of thing. It's out in a big old mansion in the Fens – gorgeous-looking place, full of dark history ...'

Sadie straightens, the mermaid commercial already forgotten. 'Sounds interesting. When's the audition?'

'That's the best bit, Sadie. There's no audition. The job's yours if you want it, and the money is *excellent*.'

Sadie's eyes widen, but her attention is caught by movement

11

outside the window. The van from the homeless charity has arrived and it's blocking the road, its hazard lights flashing while the driver looks for somewhere to park. Directly opposite the house, a dark-coloured Audi eases away from the kerb, and Sadie peers into it; she's seen it parked around here several times recently. But the driver shields her face with her hand as she passes, and Sadie glimpses only a white sports watch, a matching white hairband around the bun on the back of her head. Immediately, the charity van manoeuvres itself into the vacated space.

'Hold on, Wendy,' Sadie says. 'I'm at Mum's. The people are here to collect the last bits of furniture.'

'Oh, sorry,' Wendy says. 'I can wait.'

Sadie greets the senior charity volunteer at the front door with an apologetic wave of her phone. 'Sorry, just on a call, are you okay to . . . ?' She gestures towards the living room.

'You carry on, my dear.' The woman gives her a sympathetic pat on the arm, and she and her assistant tug on their thick work gloves as they make a beeline for the sideboard.

Sadie speaks into her phone again. 'So, how much, then?' She listens to Wendy's reply and laughs. 'Seriously? For one weekend? Of *course* I'll do it.' She hurries up the stairs, embarrassed to be overheard sounding so desperate for money, but relieved she'll be able to pay next month's rent now, and the month after, without a problem. 'So, tell me everything. What does it involve?'

'Well, I've got the actual invitation card right here.' Wendy sounds a little breathless. 'I'll forward it on to you, you'll love it – it's all embossed and everything. It says on the front: *You are cordially invited to play a game at Raven Hall . . .'*

Downstairs, the charity workers load the last of Sadie's mother's furniture on to their van, and they close the front door softly behind them.

She shouldn't be here. But, oh, how she's missed her beloved Raven Hall.

She hurries up the driveway, on full alert, prepared to be challenged at any moment. She used to feel so proud of this long, open approach – the way it shows off the grand beauty of the house to any visitor from a quarter of a mile away. But now, the lack of cover feels like a hostile security measure. No matter how tightly she wraps her arms around herself, or how low she shrinks inside her jacket, the new owner could glance from a window at any moment and spot her approaching.

And what would they do, if they knew who she was?

As soon as she's crossed the last drainage ditch, she veers off into the scrubby grass towards the side of the house, heading for the high wall that borders the back garden. She quickly passes out of sight of the front windows. Only someone peering down from the turret bedroom would be able to see her now.

When she reaches the garden wall, she places her palms against its sun-warmed, wind-softened surface, and it doesn't feel like stone at all, it feels almost like a living thing. Home, she thinks. Have you missed me?

But she can't waste time being sentimental.

She hurries alongside the wall and around its corner, and she smiles with relief to spot her beloved old treehouse peeping out from among the leaves at the back of the garden. A little further along is the familiar curving branch that used to give her a route out into the fields to go looking for hedgehogs and badgers. Now she climbs up and over, dropping into the laurel bush on the inside of the garden wall. She wiggles through, scratching her face and hands, until she can see the lawn, and then the garden chairs, and then the back of the house itself. Her gaze skitters from window to window, and back down to the veranda, but the only living creature in sight is a small, white, fluffy dog, apparently asleep, just outside the open French doors.

Slowly, cautiously, she creeps along the garden's border, ducking behind bushes, parting branches, keeping her gaze fixed on the back doors. The little dog lifts its head and scratches itself behind the ear, then settles down again, and she releases a shuddery breath. She finds a dry spot behind a red robin bush and checks the view across to the back of the house, then she settles in to wait.

Beth

Nina picked up one of my bags, and I grabbed the other and trotted up the broad stone steps after her, through the front door, and into a huge, wood-panelled hallway. I slowed my pace as I gazed around. The ceilings were twice as high as in a normal house, and old-fashioned portraits decorated the walls at regular intervals. The air felt cool after the July sunshine outside, and the house smelt of wood polish and lavender and safety. I peered left and right, but there were too many half-open doors and ornately carved side tables for me to work out what each of the many rooms could possibly be used for.

'Come on,' Nina said, already halfway up the wide central staircase. 'This way.'

My bedroom was up one floor, at the front of the house, and I dropped my bag by the elaborately made-up double bed and hurried straight to the window. Caroline's car was long gone. The driveway was empty. And there wasn't another house to be seen, just fields and water channels and—

16

'Is that *your* lake?' I asked. On the far side of the parking area, the grass sloped gently down to a band of feathery-headed reeds. Beyond this, an expanse of water sparkled hypnotically in the afternoon sunlight, silver on blue.

Nina joined me at the window. 'Yes. Avermere, it's called. After my family, you know – the Averells.'

I gave her a sideways look. 'I thought your parents were Mr and Mrs Meyer.'

'No, they're Markus Meyer and Leonora Averell, actually. Mum says they always meant to get married, they just never got round to it.' Nina swivelled on her heel and studied me. 'Were your parents married?'

I blinked in surprise. 'Yes.' I pushed away from the windowsill and retrieved both my bags, lifting them on to the bed and unzipping them noisily.

'I'm sorry,' she said. 'I didn't mean to be nosy. I just … I wondered, you know, what happened to them, but Mum said I shouldn't—'

'A car accident.' I pulled my hairbrush from the first bag. 'They were rushing my brother to hospital, he was having trouble breathing. It happened sometimes. They went through a red light, in front of a lorry.'

'Oh, Beth.' Suddenly she was beside me, tugging my wrists to make me sit on the bed. 'I'm so sorry. That must have been awful.' She gave me a moment to compose myself. 'So you had to go into the orphanage?'

'The children's home. Yes.'

'Your Aunt Caroline didn't … ?'

17

I shook my head sharply. 'She travels for her job all the time. She's hardly at home at all, some months.'

Nina put on a disapproving voice. 'Wouldn't even come in for a cup of tea.' She sounded so much like Leonora, I felt my mouth twitch despite myself.

'Exactly,' I said. 'Your parents inviting me here is like Caroline's dream come true – she can stop coming up with excuses now; she'll be driving home with a clear conscience.'

'No more niece locked up in an orphanage.' Nina tilted her head. 'Is it really that bad there? What's it like?'

I searched her expression. Did she really want to know?

'They try to make it nice.' I sighed. 'Some of the adults are lovely. But you can never relax for long, there's always someone doing something . . .'

Nina shifted on the bed. 'Like what?'

'Like . . .' I shook my head. 'Like there's this boy who gets to visit his mum once a week – she's like a drug addict or something. And when he comes back, he's always really angry, yelling at us for tiny things. And we try to be understanding, you know, because it's not his fault, but then he takes it too far. He smashes something, or last week he shoved his wheelie chair out of his room and it went down the stairs and hurt another kid. So they called the police, and he spent the night in a cell, and he's younger than me . . .'

'Oh, Beth.' Nina squeezed my hand. 'Don't cry. I'm sorry.'

I swiped at my eyes. 'Bet you wish you hadn't asked now, hey?'

But Nina looked stern. 'No, not at all. You can tell me anything. We're going to be best friends, aren't we?'

I blinked at her. 'Really?'

'Really.' A second later, she was back on her feet again. 'Come on. I know what'll cheer you up. Follow me.'

She was at the door before my mind had caught up. I glanced at my bags – shouldn't I unpack first? But Nina had said we were going to be best friends, and I wanted to hold on to that promise. I scrambled up and followed her.

There was no sign of Leonora or Markus on our way out of the house, and I supposed that wasn't surprising considering how vast a mansion it was. I hurried to keep up with Nina, trotting across the gravel and down the grassy slope, until we reached a wooden dock and a little boathouse half-hidden amongst the reeds. Nina sprang down into a small blue-painted rowing boat, and it rocked alarmingly on the otherwise placid water. She looked up to where I stood, hesitating, on the dock, and she gave me an encouraging smile.

'It's perfectly safe,' she said. 'Here, you sit this end, and I'll row first.'

I glanced back at the house – were we allowed to do this without adult supervision?

'Come *on*, Beth.' There was a crack of impatience in her voice.

I did as she instructed, and within seconds she was unhooking us and pulling on the oars, and we were leaving the reeds behind us, carving our way through the glassy water. At the centre of the lake was a small island, dense with brambles and stunted-looking trees. Halfway across to it, Nina made me swap seats, and she showed me how to dip the oars into the water, and how to synchronise my arms to keep us moving steadily towards the island's stony shore.

'You see?' she said. 'You're getting the hang of it already.'

By the time we scrambled out into the island's shallows, I was ready for a rest. We sprawled in the shade with our feet pointing at the water, and I gazed up at the cloudless blue between the branches and remembered that this was the first day of the summer holidays. Would I still be here on the last day, in six weeks' time? I had no idea whether the adults had a specific time period in mind for my stay at Raven Hall, but I knew I'd rather be here than tiptoeing around Caroline's apartment or stuck back at the children's home.

I turned my head and squinted at Nina. Her arm was draped over her face, but she chose that moment to lift it off and look straight back at me.

'What are you thinking?' she asked.

I was hot and sweaty, and had no energy left to skirt around the truth. 'I was wondering why your parents picked *me*.'

She said nothing, just watched me, waiting for more.

'And,' I said, 'I was wondering why you need a companion, anyway. What about your school friends? What about the kids in the village?' I'd spotted a group of teenagers messing around in the park in the last village we drove through before reaching Raven Hall. It could only have been a couple of miles away; not far to cycle.

'I don't go to school.' Nina allowed that to sink in, and then she added, 'Not at the moment, anyway. I used to. And I might try it again, one day.'

'Are you sick?'

She grinned. 'No. I just didn't like the school much, so I talked Mum into letting me learn stuff from books at home instead. She treats me like I'm sick half the time, so it didn't take much persuasion.' Her face became serious. 'I'm sorry, that was tactless. You said your brother was ill?'

'Yeah, Ricky. He had cystic fibrosis.' I turned my head away. I didn't want to talk about my family. 'So, what about friends in the village?'

Nina took her time replying. 'I do know one boy, but he's always busy in term time. He'll come over this week, though, now he's off school – you'll see. Why are you frowning? Are you wishing you hadn't come here?'

'No!' I gave her an earnest look. 'Honest, I'm not. I'm just . . . it was so nice of your parents to ask me, I guess I just wasn't expecting it. Caroline says they were looking for a companion for you, and she's going to sort out me going to live with her in the longer term, but—' I swallowed a sudden lump in my throat. 'The thing is, I don't think Caroline'll ever be ready to take me on permanently. So . . .'

'Then you can stay here as long as you like.'

'But you don't even know me yet.'

Nina pulled a face, considering. 'I know. But I've got a good feeling about you, Beth. Do you know what?'

I shook my head mutely.

Nina grinned. 'We should swim.'

And just like that, the conversation was over. She sprang up, slipped out of her shorts, and splashed into the shallows. The

21

bottom of the lake fell away steeply, and within seconds she was swimming, heading away from me before curving around and calling out my name. I hauled myself up and hovered at the very edge of the water, flinching as it lapped over my toes, sending goosebumps up my limbs.

'It's so cold!' I shouted.

'Only at the start,' she called back. 'Oh, come *on*, Beth. It's amazing once you're in.'

And again, in response to that note of impatience, I gave in. I copied her by discarding my shorts, and then I waded into the weedy water, only just suppressing a shriek as the biting chill crept up my legs. And I discovered Nina was right. Despite the shock of the cold, it *was* invigorating to wash the sticky sweat from my skin – to hurl myself forwards and feel the tingle of lake water on my shoulders, my face, my scalp, tugging at my hair, snatching my breath away.

Gradually, my muscles warmed as we raced each other out into deeper water and back to the shallows. It was nothing like the chlorine-fumed swimming pool my dad used to take me to on Saturday mornings; this was slimy underfoot and smelt of swampy wildness. It was exhilarating.

We stayed in until our fingertips wrinkled, and the cold of the lake seeped into our bones. Then we pulled on our shorts and rowed back to the dock. The sun was already drying our hair and our T-shirts, and by the time we'd strolled back to the house, we'd warmed up again. When we reached the front door, Nina caught hold of my wrist.

'Probably best not to talk about swimming at dinner.'

I was surprised. 'Why not?'

'Oh, Mum's a bit over-protective – she worries about me getting ill, you know? It's ridiculous.'

I pressed my hand over my stomach, remembering the mouthful of chilly water I'd accidentally swallowed. 'Is the lake water dangerous?'

Nina laughed. 'No, it's fine. Honest. It's just . . . it's easier not to mention it. Come on, I want to show you *my* bedroom. Best room in the house.'

Again, there was no sight or sound of Leonora and Markus as we jogged upstairs, and I hoped the faint damp patches we left on the hall floor would dry quickly. This time, Nina turned the other way on the landing, and she led me to a door at the very end of the corridor that opened on to another staircase. This rose in a spiral, and I realised we were inside the turret. At the top, she pushed open a heavy wooden door and we stepped into a bright, circular room.

A high double bed with a curved headboard nestled against the opposite wall, its sheets and blankets rumpled, scattered with ornately embroidered cushions. Clothing was strewn over furniture and books were piled everywhere, but something in my peripheral vision made me turn slowly, and I found myself gazing at row upon row of eerie faces, all staring unblinkingly back at me.

They were like dolls, but animals. Furry heads with coloured glass eyes, their necks disappearing into the collars of waistcoats and ball gowns. A fox, a leopard, a badger, a walrus – there must have been two dozen of them at least, and every single one set the hairs on my arms rising. How did Nina sleep with all these unearthly creatures watching her?

'My dad brings them back for me,' Nina said casually, 'when he goes travelling. He goes diving sometimes, or climbing mountains. When I'm older, I'm going to go with him.'

I turned my back on the nightmarish faces. 'What about your mum?' I wasn't sure myself whether I meant – does she go on her own travels, or does she go with him?

Nina shrugged. 'She'd rather stay here. She says it's a precious gift, this house. She doesn't like to go away even for one night.'

'Huh.' I strolled from one of the four tall, arched windows to the next, pretending to admire the views of fields and drainage channels and the walled back garden. Really, I was buying time, puzzling through my feelings about this strange house and the intriguing, lonely-seeming girl behind me. No school friends, an over-protective mother, a sometimes-absent father – I could see why she might want a companion.

'Beth?'

I swung around. 'Yes?'

'Do you believe in Fate?'

I frowned, thinking of my parents and my brother; thinking of the lorry that just happened to be crossing the junction when they shot through the red light.

'No,' I said shortly.

But Nina scrambled up from her bed and came to stand directly in front of me, and she caught hold of one of my hands.

'I do. Mum says everything happens for a reason, and I think

24

you came into our lives for a reason. I really do think we're going to be best friends.'

I couldn't help but return her smile. 'Yeah, well, that sounds good to me.' I glanced at the alarm clock on her bedside table. 'But, um – can I have a bath before dinner? I feel a bit ...' I picked up a lank strand of hair and dropped it again.

Nina laughed. 'I'll show you where your bathroom is.'

I followed her back down the spiral staircase with a cautious, unfamiliar sense of optimism unfurling inside me. Perhaps it was true – perhaps Nina and I might end up being best friends, after all.

Sadie

Wendy is as good as her word, and the Raven Hall invitation is delivered to Sadie's flat the next day, along with an incredibly chic, old-fashioned suitcase with *Sadie Langton* printed on the luggage label. Sadie studies the front of the heavily embossed card: *You are cordially invited to play a game at Raven Hall.* She flips it over to read the details: *Saturday 19th January. Chauffeur to collect you 5:00 p.m. Drinks in the drawing room from 7:00 p.m. Dinner and the Game to commence 7:30 p.m. in the dining hall.*' Beneath this is a handwritten line in looping blue ink: *Thank you so much for agreeing to join us – it will be a weekend to remember!*

Sadie carries the case through to her tiny sitting room, and she blinks around, looking for a clear surface to lay it down on. The coffee table is covered in paperwork – lists of auditions, bank statements, budget plans, job adverts, a half-written letter . . . She plucks a couple of empty mugs out of the way and sets the suitcase down on top of the layers of paper.

She's hoping the case contains clothes, and she's not

disappointed. There's a choice of three vintage evening dresses, each in a different shade of cream or off-white, for the dinner on the Saturday night. A cream woollen skirt suit and a blouse, for wearing at breakfast on the Sunday morning. Two pairs of ivory shoes, one with high heels, the other low. A string of lustrous pearls in a velvet-lined box. A silver brooch shaped like a bird in flight. And, to top it all off, a beautiful, white faux-fur coat. She examines each item in turn before laying them out on the sofa behind her.

Underneath all that is a folder of instructions, which begins with a character description for Sadie's part in the game. She will be Miss Lamb, 'newly arrived in the area and seeking employment at Raven Hall'. The mystery central to the game won't be revealed until the guests sit down to dinner, the folder tells her. Miss Lamb's preliminary alibi is enclosed in a separate envelope, but Sadie is instructed not to open this envelope until after she's arrived at Raven Hall, just before she goes down to the drawing room for the pre-dinner drinks.

Sadie hesitates. She's never been good at obeying rules, but this tendency has lost her two jobs in the past year alone, and on each occasion, she vowed to herself that she would turn over a new leaf. A memory of her mother's pained expression flashes into her mind – *Not again, Sadie. What did you do this time?*

Reluctantly, Sadie sets the alibi envelope to one side. She still feels perfectly justified in what she did, as it happens. She'd hated pestering customers at the department store to take out the store's credit card, and her refusal to try to improve her

take-up figures led to sharp words in the manager's office, followed eventually by her being told not to bother coming back.
And then, the corner shop job – all that out-of-date food she
was supposed to throw into the bins when there was nothing
really wrong with it . . . When the owner realised she was leaving some of it out by the back door for hard-up locals to help
themselves to, she was instantly fired.

Sadie sighs.

On the other hand, this murder mystery weekend isn't an
ordinary, rule-bound job, is it? At its heart, it's just a game, and
she's pretty sure the other guests will cheat too . . .

She squeezes her eyes shut in a silent apology to her mother,
and then she snatches up the envelope and tears it open.

A small, square card informs her: *Miss Lamb, you spent the
morning alone in your bedroom, writing letters. You took a walk
around the garden with Colonel Otter before lunch. At some point
between two and three o'clock in the afternoon, you visited Lord
Nightingale in his study. You can't remember the exact time, but
you were in there for less than five minutes.*

Sadie smiles to herself. This is going to be fun.

She tries on each of the dresses in turn, twirling in front of
the full-length mirror by her front door to assess their fit. Most
of Sadie's own clothes are second hand – she loves hunting
down bargains in charity shops – so she has an idea of what
these vintage items might be worth, and she feels flattered to
be trusted with them. They're all beautiful, but the ivory silk
dress is the best; it's so smooth against her skin, she could close
her eyes and forget she's wearing it. The pearl necklace adds

the final touch of sophistication. Rather more upmarket than the mermaid costume, she thinks wryly.

She sends a quick text to Wendy to confirm she'll accept the job. Then she starts up her laptop, and types in 'Raven Hall, Fens'.

Within seconds, she's gazing at a grainy photo of a neglected-looking country house with a tower at one end. Ivy hugs its walls, and for a moment she envisions it being surrounded by a thick forest, like a Sleeping Beauty castle, and it makes her smile. But a second view from further away shows only a bleak, empty landscape all around, with a glint of dark water in the foreground.

She skims down the other search results, but there isn't much. A ramblers' group blog entry from a couple of years ago describes the house as having been 'abandoned and uncared for since a tragedy befell a local family in the late 1980s'. Sadie clicks back to the photo and peers at the hazy smudging on the pale walls around one of the upstairs windows. It looks like soot – perhaps there was a fire there. How awful. And how sad that the house then sat empty for thirty years – but what a perfect location it makes for a murder mystery event.

If the glossy invitation and the attention to detail in the suit-case of clothes is anything to go by, the company has the funds to have turned Raven Hall back into a comfortable, welcoming place, Sadie thinks. But even if they haven't – even if she turns up and discovers it's still a crumbling wreck – she'll follow through with the job anyway. Her mother's landlord hasn't yet returned the house deposit, and Sadie can't push her overdraft any higher; she doesn't have any other options. She'll cheerfully camp out in a soot-blackened room in a mansion heaving with ghosts, if it means she'll get paid this month before her rent's overdue. Besides, the game sounds like it will be fun.

Beth

Nina gave me the beginnings of a house tour before dinner. We started downstairs, in the drawing room, and I could have spent ages in there alone, looking at the paintings and the grand piano and the black marble fireplace. My fingers itched to stroke everything, but I clasped my hands firmly behind my back. Nina was already marching back out to the hall, and I hurried to follow her.

The dining room felt as big as the entire ground floor of my old house. The kitchen was similarly huge, with a rich aroma drifting from the enormous oven. I could see no evidence of meal preparation on the long, wooden worktops, and I wondered fleetingly whether the Raven Hall family did the same as the children's home, buying in meals that had been prepared off-site. Nina went straight to the open French doors and stepped out on to the terrace, and she gestured at the wide lawn in front of her.

'What would you like to see first? Do you like raspberries? We could go and pick some.'

My stomach rumbled, but Leonora bustled into the kitchen behind us and interrupted.

'Dinner in ten minutes, girls. Leave the raspberries till tomorrow, okay?'

So, instead of heading outside, Nina led me down a short corridor from the back of the kitchen to a long, narrow room that I guessed was meant to be used for laundry. A wooden worktop ran all the way along one wall, with a huge double sink at one end, but there were no clothes or drying racks to be seen. Instead, the whole of the work surface, and much of the tiled floor, was covered in piles of paper. Drawings, paintings and sketches were stacked haphazardly on every surface.

'Mum's an illustrator.' Nina picked up a few of the sketches at random. 'Have a look – they're good, aren't they? She doesn't sell much, but ...'

I admired drawings of fantastical beasts and fairy-tale castles and tropical islands. 'Yeah, they're great. And what does your dad do?'

'Oh, he runs a landscape gardening business,' Nina said. 'Based in Cambridge. He took the day off today to welcome you.'

I felt flattered, but also bemused. I thought of my own parents' former full-time jobs at the council, and the modest family home we used to live in, and I marvelled that a gardener and an artist could make enough money to own a house like Raven Hall.

'So ...' I plucked up my courage as we returned to the kitchen. 'Do you know where my violin went? Only, I like to play it every day, especially since ...' I bit back the rest of the sentence. My violin was the one constant in my life; the one activity that kept my grief at arm's length. Nina looked surprised, but Leonora was removing a casserole dish from the oven and she turned around with a delighted smile.

'Markus put it in the drawing room, just now, Beth. Please, play it whenever you like. We're all looking forward to hearing you.'

This had to be a good sign. My newfound optimism glowed a little brighter. Nina and I hurried off to set the table in the dining room, and then the four of us sat down to enjoy the most delicious chicken casserole I'd ever tasted.

'So, Beth,' Markus said, offering me a second helping of vegetables across the table, 'did you have a nice afternoon? You don't want to go home yet?'

I flinched at the word *home*, but I didn't blame Markus for being tactless. I'd lost count of how many well-meaning people had said similar things since my parents and brother died; they spoke without thinking. Leonora, however, shot me a look brimming with sympathy, and then she frowned at Markus.

'Give her a chance to settle in, poor girl. She's barely had time to unpack.'

Nina didn't quite manage to suppress a smirk, and I dipped my head and focused on my food, conscious of the ache in my arms from the rowing, and the tingle of sunburn on my shoulders from swimming in the lake.

'I'll tell you what,' Markus said, 'I'm sure we've got a bike the right size for Beth in the stables. I'll have a look after dinner and I'll check everything's roadworthy, and then maybe the two of you can cycle around the lake tomorrow. What do you think?'

Nina shrugged and looked at me.

'That sounds nice,' I said. 'Can we ride into the village?'

There was a moment of silence, and I sensed I'd made my own faux pas. Leonora appeared to choose her words carefully.

'We don't tend to encourage that, Beth. But ...' She tried to catch Nina's eye, but Nina had her head lowered. 'Nina has a little friend who comes out here to play with her, don't you, Nina? Jonas, whose mother runs the B&B. He's a nice boy.'

Nina's eye-roll was so dramatic, I felt sure either Leonora or Markus would tell her off, but neither did. Leonora turned back to me instead.

'Perhaps you could play something for us after dinner, Beth? Would you mind? That piece you played at the concert last week was lovely. It might inspire Nina ...'

I nodded eagerly. 'Of course. If you like.'

Leonora smiled. 'Thank you.' She turned abruptly to Markus. 'Oh, did you ring the caterers? The party's so close, and I've got so much to do ...'

I could see where Nina got her rapid changes of subject from.

After dinner, I played my violin for them, and then we all carried our drinks out to the terrace – white wine for Leonora and Markus, lemonade for Nina and me. Nina and I played cards and chatted lazily as the sun went down, and I felt more tired than I had in a long time. When Markus picked up his guitar, Nina and I settled back in our chairs, and we gave him our full attention as the sky grew darker and the stars came out over Raven Hall. Markus' songs were like stories, and I closed my eyes, picturing Rocky Raccoon falling back in his room, and strawberry fields stretching on and on for ever . . .

Nina shook me gently awake. 'Come on, Beth, it's time for bed. Busy day tomorrow.'

After breakfast the following morning, Nina led me back up to my bedroom and cast her eyes over my still-unpacked bags.

'Have you got a swimming costume?'

'Yeah, somewhere.' I tugged clothes from the bags until I found it: my old black school costume. 'Will this do?'

Nina smiled. 'It's perfect. Put it on. I'll meet you downstairs in two minutes.'

When she was gone, I surveyed the tangle of clothes on the floor, and turned to the chest of drawers next to my bed. The entire contents of both my bags would fit into just one of those deep drawers. There was a huge dark-wood wardrobe in the corner too, and I swung open its doors and peered into the faintly lemon-smelling interior. Just one dress hung there, and strangely it looked to be about my size. I lifted it down on its hanger cautiously. An old-fashioned design, high-necked and long, in blue gingham checks with white embroidery on the front. I replaced it on the rail and closed the doors on it.

'Beth!' Nina was back. 'Aren't you ready yet?'

I began to scoop my clothes into the bottom drawer. 'Give me a chance. Why are you in such a hurry?'

'Jonas is coming.' She wrapped her arms around herself, as if her impatience with me was threatening to burst out of her.

'We're gonna swim in the drain on the other side of the lake, it's a good spot.'

'In a *drain*?' I pushed the drawer shut and stared at her. 'No thanks.'

But she merely grinned. 'Wait and see. Just – hurry up, will you?'

As soon as I stepped outside the front door, I could tell it was building up to being even hotter than the day before. The sky was a vibrant blue, and the sun turned the grey-white gravel into a dazzling sea of light. Nina and I shielded our eyes with our hands as we wandered over to the stable block that sat at right angles to the house. It was made of the same grey stone, and it had a low wall in front of it, which we perched on to wait for Jonas. I was mildly disappointed to see no evidence of real, live horses; the family seemed to use the building for nothing more than storage. Two bikes were propped against one of the stable doors, and I felt a pang of gratitude to Markus for keeping his promise and getting them ready for us.

'So, why *aren't* you allowed into the village?' I asked Nina.

She squinted down the driveway and sighed.

'Trust me, I've tried arguing about it hundreds of times. But Mum just hates me going there. She drives me mad sometimes. Bloody mothers!' She shot me a horrified look. 'Oh, Beth, I'm so sorry . . .'

I shook my head. 'It's okay.' I'd learnt how easy it was to complain about the people you loved when you still had the luxury of seeing them every day. I scratched my nails against the wall we were sitting on, up and down. 'So Jonas has to come out here to see you?'

'Oh, him.' Nina grinned. 'He comes for the swimming, really. And skating in the winter, if it's cold enough. That's why he came here the first time – his mum told him Avermere was the best place to skate, so even though all his mates were going down the other end of the village, he trekked up here by himself – he was only eight, then.'

'And your mum didn't mind?'

'Oh, well.' Nina wrinkled her nose. 'She wasn't massively keen, but he kept coming back, and – well, Mum knows his mum from when they were young, and says she can be trusted, so … Yeah. Jonas kept on coming back.'

I straightened, peering towards the road. 'Is that him now?'

A figure on a bike turned into the drive and drew nearer, and Nina and I got to our feet. I'd been picturing Jonas as around Nina's height and younger than me, but as he came closer, I saw he was taller and older – maybe even sixteen, I thought. He sprang down and dropped his bike on the grass by the stable block and squinted at us.

'Hi,' he said. He looked from me to Nina and back. 'Are you Beth, then?'

I nodded. 'Hi.' I was struggling not to stare. Soft reddish-brown hair, light hazel eyes, the longest eyelashes I'd ever seen …

He took a step backwards. 'So … are we going swimming, then?'

'Course we are.' Nina moved forwards, and the two of them fell into step as they made their way down the grass and joined a track that curved around the lake shore. I hurried along behind them. From this angle I could see the straps of Nina's swimming costume emerging from the neckline of her T-shirt: pale gold fabric that looked delicate and sophisticated against her brown skin. I adjusted my no-nonsense school-regulation straps with a twinge of embarrassment.

The path grew fainter as it ran along the side of the lake, and within minutes we had to hold our arms in front of our faces as we barged our way through a patch of weeds higher than our heads. The bitter-green smell of sap clung to my hair even once we'd emerged on the other side, and I swatted at clouds of tiny flies around my face, while my legs prickled from the brush of nettles. Nina pointed out a broad tree stump between us and the lake, barely visible under a coating of pale brown fungi.

'No one can see you from the house, once you're past the stump,' she said. 'Just an interesting fact that Jonas and I once calculated.'

Jonas laughed. 'We were pretty bored that summer, weren't we? It took us ages to check from every window.'

'Hey!' She punched his arm. 'It was fun. Anyway, it would have been quicker if you hadn't come off your bike on the second day.'

Jonas dropped back slightly, and it took me a moment to realise he was pointing out a scar to me, on the back of his arm.

'Twelve stitches,' he said, rather proudly. 'The doctor gave me the gravel he picked out of it in a little pot.'

I nodded, wide-eyed, but Nina rolled her eyes.

'Urgh, can we not talk about such disgusting things? So, what are we gonna do *this* summer? We need a new project . . .'

But Jonas squinted sideways at me. 'Are you going to join the high school in September, then?'

'Oh, I . . . ' I glanced at Nina. 'I don't know yet.'

Nina shrugged. 'Who cares? That's ages away. Let's not think about it now.'

We fell into single file by a low hedgerow, and yet again I was left to contemplate my uncertain future. I blinked sweat from my eyes and kept my gaze mainly on the uneven ground in front of me, glancing up only occasionally to examine Jonas' broad shoulders and the whorl of hair at the base of his neck, the scar on the back of his arm. Our conversation dropped to just an occasional comment.

We followed the curve of the lake until we'd travelled almost halfway around it. When I looked back, I could just see the chimneys of Raven Hall over the tops of the scrubby trees on the central island. Here, we turned away from the lake and walked along the edge of a field dense with glossy, broad-leafed plants, which Nina told me were sugar beet. Finally, we scrambled up a steep bank at the back of the field, and I found myself gazing down into a broad channel of slow-flowing water, bordered by lush grass and bright yellow flowers, glinting invitingly under the high sun.

'*This* is the drain?' I said.

Nina grinned. 'Yep. Milner's Drain. It takes the rainfall from the fields all the way along – it's lovely fresh water, not swampy like the lake.'

Jonas was already stripping off to his swimming trunks, and I half-turned away, heat flaring in my cheeks.

'Where does the water go to?' I asked, gazing as far up the channel as I could see.

'To the sea, of course,' Nina said.

Jonas sounded mildly annoyed. 'Don't say *of course*. How's she supposed to know?' He gave me a serious look. 'It's all reclaimed land, the Fens – it used to be mostly under the sea. The water's drawn out by big pumps now, and the coastal walls stop it flooding back in again.'

'Oh my God,' Nina said, 'I've just remembered why I hated school.'

'Very funny.' Jonas turned away, preparing to dive into the water. I watched his muscles tense. 'You hated school because you can't stand being told what to do.'

He dived in cleanly, creating the smallest of splashes. I held my breath as I watched him glide under the silvery-green surface.

'We're eight feet below sea level here, did you know?' Nina said brightly. 'If those sea walls gave way ...'

She didn't wait for me to respond, but stepped to the edge of the bank and dived in too. My heart rattled, and I scanned the horizon. How fast would the water come rushing inland? How quickly could we run back to Raven Hall? Did the family keep a store of food upstairs, in case of this eventuality?

'Beth!' Nina called from the water. 'Come in, it's wonderful!'

I checked that Jonas was still swimming away from us, not watching us, and I took a flying leap and plunged in feet first. My head went right under, and the shock of the cold took my breath away, even once I'd surfaced. Nina swam closer.

'You okay?'

I gasped in great lungfuls of air and then I laughed.

'Yeah, you were right. It's freezing. But I love it.'

The three of us swam for a while, and then we floated, chatting lazily, as the sun blazed down on us. Nina showed me a newt, peeking out from the long grass on the bank, and the newt and I stared at each other for several seconds before it pottered away. It was the first one I'd ever seen. Jonas pointed out a buzzard circling overhead, silhouetted against the blue dome of a sky, and I heard its *kee-yah* call. I learnt that the cheerful chirruping coming from somewhere nearby was a reed warbler.

Eventually, we hauled ourselves out of the water and sat drying on the bank with dragonflies flitting around us. I was much paler than the other two, and I draped my T-shirt across my shoulders, not wanting my sunburn to get any worse. If I wasn't allowed to cycle into the village to buy suncream, how would I get hold of any? Would Leonora let me add it to her shopping list? I'd ask Nina later, I decided, when we were alone.

'There's a party tonight,' Jonas said casually, after a spell of companionable silence. I assumed he was directing this at Nina rather than me, although he kept his gaze fixed on the blade of grass in his hand. 'A load of kids in the village. You could come, if you wanted to sneak out?'

Nina rolled her neck, considering. 'We can't. Not tonight. My parents are kind of twitchy at the moment; I think they'd be on the lookout.'

Her use of the word *we* – her assumption he was inviting both of us – gave me a glow of reassurance. I didn't miss the implication that she'd snuck out on previous occasions.

'Okay.' Jonas tossed his blade of grass aside and looked directly at me. 'Maybe next time.'

My pulse jumped and I looked away, turning to Nina.

'Why are your parents twitchy?' I said. 'Not because of me, I hope.'

When she didn't immediately reply, Jonas gave her a speculative look.

'Did you know,' he said, 'that Markus' dad is flying over from the States? He's booked himself a room at our place at the weekend. Is he coming to see you?'

'Markus' dad?' I said. 'As in,' I looked at Nina expectantly, 'your grandad?'

Nina's voice was surprisingly harsh. 'Yeah, great, he's finally decided to visit after all these years. He left the country before I was born, never even sends me a birthday card ... – I mean, it's nothing to do with wanting presents, but he's never acted like a grandad at all, even though he's the only grandparent I've got.' She made a noise of disgust. 'And suddenly he wants to come and meet me.'

Jonas and I exchanged looks. He seemed just as unsettled by this outburst as I was.

'That's weird,' I said. 'Do he and your dad not get on? Did they have an argument or something, and now he wants to patch things up?'

'I don't *know*, Beth.' Nina jumped to her feet. 'And I don't

42

want to talk about it. I'm going back to the house. Are you coming with me or not?'

I glanced again at Jonas, who showed no sign of moving. I kept my expression light and got to my feet.

'Of course I'll come with you,' I said.

Jonas said nothing further, and Nina and I left him lying there in the long grass, his golden arm shielding his face from the sun. We headed back along the edge of the field, talking of other things, and gradually her good mood returned. But I was careful not to mention Markus' father again and, privately, I added him to my growing list of prickly subjects where Nina was concerned. We retraced our route all the way to Raven Hall, and the cool air of the entrance hall felt like a welcome-home caress on my skin.

Sadie

JANUARY 2019

The silver Mercedes S-Class arrives precisely on time, gliding between the hatchbacks parked along Sadie's narrow street like a swan parting a flock of scruffy mallards. Sadie isn't quite ready. She dashes to the bathroom to touch up her lipstick, then makes a last-minute change back into her own shoes – hers are more comfortable than the pair the company sent. The rejected ones she slips back inside the suitcase. Then she makes one final check of her reflection in the hall mirror. The ivory silk dress is perfect; she's never worn anything so glamorous.

The doorbell rings, and she flashes herself a quick grin in the mirror before hurrying to open the door. The chauffeur helps her with her luxurious coat, and he carries her case for her as he escorts her out to the car. *I could get used to this*, Sadie thinks.

The night is bitterly cold, and once they've left the main roads, there's nothing to see through the windows but the occasional lit-up farm buildings in the darkness. They could be heading anywhere in the black night. Sadie forces herself to relax against the leather seat; this isn't an audition – she already has the part. No need to feel jittery. Drinks, dinner and a game. It's going to be fun.

She runs through her character details in her head automatically: Miss Lamb, newly arrived in the area, seeking employment at Raven Hall ... She locks eyes with her reflection in the blank window by her side, and she gives a wry grimace. Here in the real world, Miss Sadie Langton is twenty-eight, she can barely pay her own rent, and she's never had a relationship or a job that lasted longer than twelve months. She summons her mother's voice in her head: *You don't need money or a man to make you happy, Sadie. But you do need to think before you act. You're too impetuous.*

Her mother was fond of dishing out advice like that; statements that always seemed carefully rehearsed – her mother wasn't one for spontaneous heart-to-hearts. Growing up, Sadie had learnt that excessive displays of emotion on her part sent her mother into retreat, as if feelings were things that should be kept private and not shared, even between daughter and mother. When Sadie came home from school in tears, aged eleven, because she'd been given a detention for something that wasn't her fault, her mother ate nothing that evening and drifted upstairs to bed before it had even grown dark. When Sadie's first boyfriend rang her at home to tell her he was dumping her, her mother remembered an urgent appointment and went out for the rest of the day, leaving Sadie to sob on her bed all alone.

The car slows as they approach the sparse lights of another

village, and Sadie lets her reflection blur for a moment, focusing instead on the little she can see of the houses they pass. She never doubted her mother loved her when she was growing up; she just wished they could have been more open with each other.

Around the time Sadie left home, when she was eighteen, her relationship with her mother grew spikier, no doubt fuelled by what her mother described as Sadie's 'irresponsible attitude to employment'. Sadie was drawn towards acting, thrilled to be signed by Wendy at the drama agency, starry-eyed at the prospect of earning a living by pretending to be something she wasn't . . . but it quickly became clear that she needed a back-up income. So she lurched from one part-time job to another, keen to keep some of her time free in case, one day, Wendy was to ring with a truly exciting opportunity . . .

'You're too optimistic,' her mother had told her, only a few months ago.

Sadie had laughed, but the comment had stung. 'Why does that have to be a bad thing, Mum?'

'You need to stick with one job for a while. Your CV must look terrible. How many times have you been sacked now?'

'It doesn't—'

'Four, isn't it?' Her mother knew full well it was four.

'In ten *years*, Mum. And it was never—'

'And how many other jobs have you just walked out on?' Her mother's sigh filled the stuffy sitting room with her disappointment. 'Please, just *try* to think things through a bit more calmly, will you? Before making snap decisions.'

'You mean, *grow up, Sadie*,' Sadie had replied. 'Don't you? You can just say it. I know that's what you're thinking.'

Her mum had sounded weary. 'I just want you to be happy . . .'

The car hits a bump in the road, and Sadie's focus is jolted back to her reflection in the glass. She asks her mirror image, silently: *Are you happy?* Scraping money together from one month to the next, auditioning for sometimes quite dubious jobs, eating beans on toast every night . . . Her reflection's serious expression softens into a smile. *Happy enough*, is the soundless reply. *And this job tonight will make me a whole lot happier, when I get paid.*

A brightly lit B&B sign marks the end of the village, and they're quickly plunged back into the darkness of yet another country lane.

'We've made good time, Miss,' the chauffeur says from the front – the first time he's spoken since they set off. 'We're almost there now.'

A minute or two later, they swing off the road, and Sadie spots the grand house – lit-up in the distance, familiar from the images she's seen online. It reminds her of an ocean liner, all lights blazing in a sea of black. She peers around the chauffeur's hat, her pulse quickening. The tower is still there, she sees. But the ivy has been cleared away – that's promising.

They pull up by a flight of steps, and the chauffeur leaps out and strides around to open her door. She takes his gloved hand and steps lightly on to the gravel, one high heel after the other. A stunningly beautiful woman in a long emerald evening dress

47

comes down the steps towards her, all black hair and dark eyes and heavy mascara, her arms opened wide in greeting.

'Welcome to Raven Hall,' the woman says grandly. 'I'm Lady Nightingale, your hostess. And you must be Miss Lamb. Please – do come in out of the cold.'

She waits, hidden behind the scratchy leaves in the garden border, watching.

Eventually, there's movement by the back door. The fluffy dog lifts its head. A hand appears, gripping the door frame. Someone is stepping out cautiously on to the veranda, taking their time about it.

Is this the new owner of Raven Hall?

It's a woman in her forties. A loose summer dress billows over her bloated frame, and her pale hair is scraped back into a ponytail, creating the impression that her head is too small for her body. She shuffles across the veranda and collapses on to a swing seat with a groan that rolls out across the lawn. The fluffy dog springs up beside her and nestles into the folds of her dress, and she rests one puffy hand on its little head.

Almost immediately, a second, much younger, woman appears in the doorway. In stark contrast to the figure on the swing seat, this one is dressed to show off her slim frame: bright orange crop top, tiny denim shorts, enormous hoop earrings. She hovers briefly on the veranda without saying anything, then swivels and disappears back inside the house with a swish of her waist-length hair. The swing seat rocks and creaks, and the older woman tips her head back and closes her eyes.

So these are the new owners of Raven Hall. A slow-moving woman and her spoilt brat of a daughter.

She watches the woman on the swing seat for a while longer,

but her resentment is an ache under her ribcage, and her powerlessness makes her restless. She creeps back around the border of the garden and escapes over the curved branch, into the farmer's field. Insects buzz all around her, and she stands perfectly still for a minute, thinking, weighing up her options. She needs to get back to the village; she's got a long journey ahead of her, to return to her lodgings. But before that, she has a decision to make.

She lifts her chin and retraces her steps around the boundary wall, until she reaches the point where she'll have to veer out into the open – where she might be seen. Before she leaves, she places her palms against the warm stone wall again, and she tells Raven Hall: 'Don't forget me. I'll come back.'

Beth

Each evening, when Markus arrived back at Raven Hall after work, he asked me how my day had been, and how I was settling in. By Thursday, I was able to give him a genuinely unforced answer.

'It's been a brilliant day, thanks. I really love it here.'

He beamed, before hurrying away as usual, to check on his other projects. There was always a ditch that needed clearing out or a broken piece of guttering that needed mending, or on this occasion some old gazebos that needed to be retrieved from the stable block before Leonora followed through with her threat to hire a grand new one for their upcoming party.

Leonora grew more tense as the week wore on. She carried around guest lists and food lists, and several times I heard her chasing up the caterers on the phone. Nina and I spent our days outside, exploring routes around the lake, swimming with Jonas or rowing halfway across to the island, shelving the oars and stretching out in the sunshine with a good book each and a picnic for when our stomachs began to rumble. But that Thursday evening, after Markus had gone off to look for the gazebos, Leonora told Nina to go and tidy her bedroom, and then she asked me whether I'd mind doing her a favour.

'Of course,' I said. 'What is it?'

'There's a dress in your wardrobe. I wondered if you'd try it on for me. I want to see if it fits you.'

I hesitated. The dress had looked rather restrictive and uncomfortable, and I was perfectly content in my shorts and T-shirt; I didn't enjoy dressing up. On the other hand, Leonora had been nothing but kind to me, and my new life at Raven Hall had so far been one carefree day after another. I didn't want to seem ungrateful.

'Okay,' I said.

'Come down and show me when you've got it on.'

I hurried upstairs and lifted the blue checked dress down from its hanging rail. My prediction was right – when I pulled it on, it felt tight and scratchy – I didn't feel like *me* at all. There was a big cheval mirror in the corner of the room, and I examined my reflection morosely. It wouldn't be easy to scramble into and out of the rowing boat wearing something like this; I felt sorry for the olden-day girls who had to wear such things all the time. But I did as Leonora had requested, and I went down to the drawing room to show her.

'Ah, Beth.' She set aside her party list as if she'd forgotten she was waiting for me, but I wasn't fooled – her bright eyes scrutinised me intensely and there was a twitchiness in her movements. She walked in a circle around me, tweaking at the fabric, and then she lifted a lock of my hair, which was tangled from swimming in the lake that afternoon.

'Here,' she said. 'Come and sit down. Let me brush your hair.'

Warily, I sank on to a chair in front of the black marble fireplace. A fine mist coated my cheek as she sprayed something over my head. But as soon as she began to pull the brush through the tangles, I felt my muscles relaxing, and the smoother the brushstrokes became, the more soothed I felt. I closed my eyes and inhaled her rose-scented perfume, and the pleasant chemical fragrance of the spray, and the background lavender and polish smell of Raven Hall.

The sensation on my scalp took me back to a time when my mother used to brush my hair each morning before school. Sometimes she'd braid it into two long pigtails, and I'd skip all the way to my primary school, enjoying their thump-thump on my shoulders as I bounced. My brother, Ricky, used to walk tall in his high school uniform beside me, and he'd laugh at my enthusiasm and call me Skippy. I could have sat there and let Leonora brush my hair for ever; I didn't want her to stop.

'Now,' Leonora said finally. 'Let's see. Shall we plait it?' I nodded, my eyes suddenly stinging.

Deftly, she divided my hair into two sides, and wove a pair of plaits, producing blue ribbons from her pocket to tie at the ends. When she was finished, she stepped back, and it was only then that I noticed Markus hovering in the doorway. Leonora's voice was rather sharp.

'What do you think?'

She was looking at him, not at me. I kept quiet as Markus took a couple of steps into the room.

'Yes,' he said. 'That'll do.'

Then he spun on his heel and was gone.

Leonora turned away from me and picked up her party list. 'That's fine, Beth. You can change back into your own clothes now.'

I felt I'd missed something. I was strangely bereft, as if a spotlight of maternal attention had been trained on me for the last ten minutes, then abruptly turned off again. I watched her for another couple of seconds, but she didn't lift her gaze from her list.

'Okay then.' I hurried back upstairs and dragged the stiff dress over my head, sliding back into my own comfortable clothes before I glanced in the mirror again. The plaits looked all wrong. My reflection gave me a shiver of unease. I tugged off the ribbons and unravelled Leonora's careful weaving until I had a loose blonde mane again. I flung the dress into the bottom of the wardrobe and went off to find Nina.

There was no mention of the dress the next morning, but when I returned to my bedroom after swimming in the afternoon, something made me want another look at it. I creaked the wardrobe doors open and saw that the dress was no longer in a crumpled heap at the bottom: it was back on the hanger in the same place it had been when I first saw it. I banged the doors shut and held my hands against them for a moment.

Then I rubbed the goosebumps from my skin, and I went off to look for Nina.

Up in Nina's turret bedroom, we peered at the activity on the back lawn. A team of men in white tunics was assembling a huge gazebo – Leonora had got her own way, after all. Others were arranging garden furniture into companionable circles on the lawn. Leonora and Markus strolled hand in hand, observing the workers, and I studied the dress Leonora wore – a pretty, knee-length, pale green summer dress. Nothing like the thing she'd made me try on last night. She looked elegant and relaxed.

I sighed and turned away from the window. 'Do you have parties here a lot?'

'Nah.' Nina was restless, and I sensed she wouldn't be happy to stay up here for much longer. She too turned her back on the window. 'Apparently, my grandparents used to throw parties here all the time. But my parents only do it once every couple of years, when Dad thinks he needs to butter up his clients. He says it brings the work in.'

'Oh.' I chewed my lip. I wanted to ask more, but I didn't know which grandparents she meant, and since her grandfather was clearly a touchy subject, it seemed best not to mention any of them.

'They sent out invites for this one ages ago,' Nina continued, 'but I think Mum regretted it afterwards.'

'She does seem a bit stressed.' I frowned. 'Wait, are we supposed to dress up for this?' I was thinking of Leonora's intense gaze as she tweaked at the sleeves of the blue checked dress and straightened my plaits. Maybe she didn't approve of the clothes I'd brought with me, or perhaps it was my wild hair she didn't like – it was months since I'd had a haircut or been bought anything new to wear. I glanced at Nina. Her T-shirt was an expensive brand, her shorts less faded than mine, but the differences weren't *that* great, surely? I opened my mouth to ask her why her mum had wanted me to try on the blue dress, but again I hesitated.

'Nah, don't worry about it,' Nina said. 'We're not invited – we'll have to stay out the way, anyway.' She picked up a book and put it down again. 'God, I'm so bored, and there's no time to swim again and get dry before dinner. Let's go downstairs.'

We clattered down the spiral staircase and then down the next flight to the wood-panelled hall. From there we could see into the kitchen, and through the open French doors to the workers on the lawn. Leonora and Markus were now sitting at one of the garden tables, pouring themselves a drink.

'I know,' Nina said. 'I'll show you my dad's study. He's got some amazing collections.'

She pushed open a door I hadn't yet seen behind, and took me into a large, square room, screened from the bright sunlight outside by a slatted blind. A green-topped desk, as long as a bed, stood over by the window. It held a neat stack of paperwork, a pot of pencils, and one large, spread-out diagram of a garden.

'Why doesn't your mum work in here?' I asked, thinking of the cluttered laundry room that Leonora used.

Nina shrugged. 'She's never liked this room.'

'Are you sure we're allowed in?'

'Of course.' But she spoke softly, and she pushed the door gently closed behind us.

The wall opposite the door was made up entirely of bookshelves, from floor to ceiling. But only half the shelves held books; the rest were stuffed with all sorts of treasures: enormous, glossy shells and bulbous pieces of pottery; a stuffed bird on a branch, and a brightly painted globe; a wooden bowl on three legs and a log carved into the shape of a drum. Two of the other walls were lined with mismatched cupboards and cabinets, and these too boasted collections of objects. The room felt more like a museum than an office.

'Here,' Nina said, 'I'll show you ...' She strolled in a loop around the room. 'These are shells from the Philippines. And coral Dad collected when he was diving. These are pearls.'

'They're amazing.'

'There's a cello in there.' She patted a black instrument case leaning against one of the cabinets. 'And these are fossils – that's an ammonite, and a trilobite, I think. What do you like best?'

I was tempted to say the cello, but I forced my gaze to move on around the room.

'Those orange, spiky shells,' I said. 'They remind me of hedgehogs.'

Nina's grin was delighted. 'They're my favourite too.' With great care, she picked one up. It filled her cupped palms, and she showed me how its top and bottom halves were hinged at the back.

I moved my head to examine it from different angles, keeping my hands clasped behind my back. 'I love it.'

A sudden noise outside the door made us both jump – footsteps were passing, accompanied by the chinking of glasses.

Nina hurried to set the shell back down again. 'The caterers are here.' And just like that, the tour of the room was over. 'Come on. Let's see if there are goodies in the fridge. We can sample them to make sure they're okay for the party tomorrow.'

Sadie

JANUARY 2019

Raven Hall's entrance hall is warm and welcoming after the icy wind outside, and Sadie gazes in awe at the portraits and the huge bronze vases of hothouse flowers and the gorgeous foliage weaving up the banisters of the central staircase. She barely registers the chauffeur setting her suitcase down and leaving.

'What a beautiful house,' she says.

'Bloody hell.' Lady Nightingale lunges towards the floor, trying to catch the cards and papers she's just dropped.

'Oops,' Sadie says. 'Here, let me help.'

Together, they gather it all up. The cards are for the game, Sadie sees; they're numbered, and they're now in the wrong order. There are little envelopes too, with other animal names on, and sheets of paper similarly mixed up.

Lady Nightingale gives her a rueful smile. 'I'm Nazleen,' she says, dropping the cut-glass accent. 'You're one of the other actors, aren't you? I'm so glad I didn't do that in front of a real guest, I've got so many things to remember, I can't—' She glances around at the multiple doors leading off the hall. 'Do you think there might be a desk or something, down here, where I can sort these out?'

A young man in black tie hovers by Sadie's suitcase. 'Shall I show you up to your room, Miss?'

'Do you know if there's a desk we can use somewhere . . . ?' Sadie asks him, but the young man merely looks anxious.

'We're not allowed in the other rooms.'

'Right, okay.' Sadie indicates her suitcase. 'Well, if you don't mind taking my case up now, I'll go up and find it in a minute.' She turns back to Nazleen. 'Come on, I'll give you a hand.'

The two doors that stand already open reveal beautifully furnished interiors – one a drawing room with bright flames crackling in a black marble fireplace, the other a grand dining room with silver cutlery and crystal glasses sparkling on a snow-white tablecloth. They ignore these rooms and work their way down the hall. The first door they try is locked, the next opens into a dimly lit cloakroom filled with racks of coats. Then Sadie finds a door with the key still in it, and she unlocks it.

'In here,' she says. 'It looks like it used to be someone's study.'

Nazleen darts in after her and closes the door behind them.

'The next guests could be here any moment,' Nazleen says. 'But it won't take long.'

She takes the paperwork over to a dusty green-topped desk and spreads it out. Sadie stands in the centre of the room and turns in a slow circle, gazing at the many curious objects lining the walls. Shells and corals, mysterious bits of pottery, a heavy-looking cello case. Cobwebs trail from every surface, and Sadie could believe no one's been in here for thirty years.

'Okay,' Nazleen says, 'I'm done. I'd better get back out there.' She consults one of her sheets of paper as they return to the brightly lit hall. 'So, Miss Lamb's room . . . ah. Top of the stairs, turn left, you're in the second room on the left. You're supposed to be taken up there to freshen up, and then come back down for drinks at seven.'

'Got it.' Sadie watches Nazleen draw herself up in an effort to regain her former composure. 'You sure you're okay?'

'Yeah, I'm fine.' Nazleen's smile holds a trace of embarrassment. 'I just really want this job, you know? I'm hoping it'll turn into a long-term contract. So I can't afford to mess it up.'

Sadie hadn't considered the hostess job might not be a one-off, and she wonders fleetingly whether she should try for it herself. Nazleen is a few years older than her, and might have more relevant experience, but Sadie rather likes the idea of taking on the hostess role. She peers up the broad staircase. Perhaps she'll see how this weekend goes first, and then she'll ask Wendy to make some enquiries.

When she reaches the landing, she looks right, towards the room that appeared to show soot around its window in the photo she saw online. The whole corridor seems to have been recently wallpapered, its skirting and coving freshly painted – she can still catch a trace of the paint smell in the air. There's no evidence of any fire damage. She turns left, and makes for her allocated bedroom, and her heart lifts when she opens the door. The room is warm and beautifully furnished, with a high bed, a solid oak wardrobe and drawers, and soft

Turkish rugs laid over the carpet. A cheval mirror of darker wood stands in one corner, and a vase of pink roses sits on the bedside table. Her case has been laid out on a trunk near the window.

She strolls to the window and slides her hands down the thick embroidered curtains before parting them to peer out into the night. A pair of headlights is approaching from the direction of the road, and she glances at her watch – it's almost six-thirty. As the car draws closer, she catches a reflection from water to the side of the driveway and she remembers the lake from the photo, now swallowed by darkness. Another set of headlights appears in the distance, and she wonders how many guests have been invited to play this game.

It doesn't take her long to freshen up. She's eager to get the evening started, and she listens impatiently to the other arrivals being shown up to their rooms. She almost sticks her head out of the door to say hello and size them up, but she's mindful that she's being paid rather a lot for this and she probably ought to behave as instructed. At ten to seven, she can wait no longer. She checks her appearance in the cheval mirror, straightens her pearls, and descends to the drawing room.

Nazleen rises gracefully from a sofa near the fire as Sadie enters. The young man who earlier took Sadie's case up to her bedroom now offers her a glass of champagne from a silver tray. Sadie tries not to grin as she takes one; she must remember her part – newly arrived, looking for employment . . .

She joins Nazleen by the black marble fireplace, and they perch side by side on the sofa and sip their drinks simultaneously.

'Thanks for helping me out earlier,' Nazleen murmurs.

'No problem.'

Sadie's gaze roams around the room. Crystal wall lights and table lamps lend the air a shimmering quality, and there are more vibrant flowers in here, and abstract sculptures on the polished wood side tables. She runs her free hand over the velvet of the sofa. So much in here looks brand new. Such a contrast to that dusty study.

'How many guests are coming?' she asks.

'Seven.' Nazleen touches her necklace, as if checking it's still there. 'Well, six of you, plus me. I know I'm the hostess, but I don't know the answer to the mystery either. It's my husband who gets murdered.'

Sadie flinches, then feels silly. 'In the game,' she says. 'Of course.'

'Yes.' Nazleen laughs softly, her gaze on the door. Male voices are drifting closer; it sounds as though at least two guests are making their way down the stairs. 'In the game. I'm the lady of the house, and my husband has . . . well, I'm not supposed to tell you that yet. But you have to work out who's responsible, and how it happened.'

'Excellent.' Sadie, too, turns an expectant face to the door. 'It's going to be fun.'

Nazleen rises just as gracefully as she did before, and her upper-class accent has returned in full force.

'Welcome, gentlemen,' she says, as she crosses the room on her narrow heels.

Sadie sips her champagne like a new-to-the-area young lady hoping to land a job, and she thanks her lucky stars for whatever made the company pick her for this outrageously civilised role.

Then she, too, rises to greet the new arrivals.

Beth

JULY 1988

On the Saturday – the day of Leonora and Markus' party – Nina sent me upstairs after lunch to grab some blankets and cushions from her bedroom.

'Why?' I said.

'It's a surprise. I've got to persuade Mum first.' Nina grinned at me. 'But I always get my own way in the end.'

By the time I returned with an armful of blankets, Nina was cheerfully packing a selection of party food into a big wicker basket, and she added bottles of coke and a torch, and a game of Scrabble.

'Where are we *taking* all this?' I asked, but she merely laughed.

'It's a surprise, I told you. Just wait and see.'

Leonora hurried across the kitchen from her office. 'I'm going to get changed now.' She hesitated at the door, looking back at us. 'Nina, I'm really not sure about this. You'll get cold and bored, and you know you can't come down halfway through . . .'

'It'll be *fine*, Mum,' Nina said, rolling her eyes, and she grabbed the basket and headed out into the garden. 'Come on,' she called back to me, her dark eyes sparkling. 'Trust me, Beth. You're gonna love it.'

I followed her across the lawn, straight to the back of the garden, but I hesitated as she deliberately stepped into the flower bed and squeezed her way between two dense bushes further back in the border. It was only when I spotted the ladder, partially hidden among the foliage, that I realised what she'd brought me to.

'Oh, you've got a treehouse!' I peered up at the wooden planks amongst the branches. 'This is so cool. It reminds me of—' I'd been about to say *The Famous Five*, but I tried to think of something more grown-up. '*Swiss Family Robinson*.' I felt a twinge of embarrassment at the random comparison, but one of the great things about Nina was that she never tried to make me feel small.

'I know, it's amazing, isn't it?' She set the basket down and scrambled up the ladder. 'You'll have to pass everything up to me. Careful, don't shake the coke.'

We arranged our blankets and cushions with care, and then we sprawled out in our little hideaway and peered through the gaps between the planks and surveyed the garden.

'It's brilliant,' I said. 'We'll be able to see everything from up here. This is a genius idea.'

'I know.' Nina grinned. 'I can't believe Mum thinks we'll get bored – there'll be way too much interesting stuff to watch. I can't wait to see them all arrive, and the ladies' dresses, and their shoes, and their hair, and their jewellery . . .'

'Do you think anyone'll see us up here?'

'Nah, they'll all be drinking too much, won't they? And they'll be too busy gossiping and eyeing each other up to notice us.'

I liked this way of joining in the party – as a hidden observer. It felt thrilling, almost illicit, even though Markus and Leonora knew we were up here. Perhaps this is what it was like to be a spy, I thought, and I scanned the garden, assessing the current situation. I wondered how much longer we had till the first guests arrived.

Tables and chairs sat in clusters on the lawn and under the giant white gazebo. Strings of fairy lights hung in romantic loops from tree branches and all along the veranda railings, already glowing softly even though we still had hours of daylight left. At one end of the veranda, a bar had been set up, and a red-cheeked man in a white shirt and black bowtie was bustling around it. Nina and I had examined it surreptitiously on our way past: bottles in every different colour; glasses in every size and shape you could imagine; dishes of lemon and lime segments; mint leaves; glacé cherries; cubes of pineapple speared on to cocktail sticks . . .

'I wish I could try one of those cocktails,' I said. I'd only ever tasted cider and an occasional sip of illicit lager from older kids at the children's home. The thought of alcohol made me wonder what Jonas had drunk the other night, at the party in the village. I blurted out my question to Nina before I could think better of it.

'Why won't your mum let you mix with other people – is she afraid of germs or something?'

'Yeah,' Nina said without meeting my eye. 'Something like that. It's just one of those things.'

'Were you ill when you were little?'

She shrugged. 'I don't remember.'

'Have you ever been in hospital?'

'Yeah, once, when I got an ear infection.'

'Huh.' I shifted on my blanket and thought about the hundreds of hospital appointments I'd attended over the years with my brother. Sometimes Mum would find someone to babysit me, but mostly I'd had to trail along too, and they were *so* boring. 'I guess you're lucky, then,' I said. And then, more quietly, 'I guess we both are.'

A dramatic *pop* made us peer out again. The first guests were emerging from the French doors on to the veranda, and they gathered by the bar, chatting and laughing, while the red-cheeked man poured champagne into tall, elegant glasses. As we watched, Leonora and Markus joined the group, bringing a couple more people with them from the house. Leonora wore an emerald-green dress that went right down to her shoes, and her hair was pinned up; she had a string of pearls around her neck. Markus wore a suit so dark green it looked almost black, and underneath that was a white shirt, open at the collar, with no tie. I turned back to Nina.

'When's your . . . ' I hesitated, but my curiosity over-rode my instincts. 'When's Markus' dad coming to see you, then?'

'Tomorrow afternoon.' Her voice was low.

'How long for? Has he got other grandchildren? What are you going to say to him?'

'Oh, Beth, give it a rest.' She rolled away on her blanket and crossed her arms over her face. 'Can we just drop the subject of *me*? Please.'

Chastened, I asked no more questions, but watched in silence as the lawn filled with people. Music started up, and the chatter of the guests grew louder. Eventually, Nina suggested we eat our picnic, and then we wrapped our blankets tightly around ourselves and continued to watch the party as darkness gradually fell. Leonora had been right all along: we grew cold and bored. In the end, we both dozed off.

We were woken by Markus, poking his head above the top of the ladder and laughing at us in the beam of light from his torch. The garden was completely dark, and we blinked at him, disorientated.

'Come on, sleepyheads,' he said cheerfully. 'Party's over, everyone's gone home. Mum's making you hot chocolate indoors to warm you up. Come back inside.'

The following morning, Nina was sick.

'I should never have let you stay up in the treehouse for so long.' Leonora fussed around Nina's bed, feeling her forehead and straightening her blankets.

Nina's face was a ghastly colour against her pillow, almost green. She waved at me feebly, indicating I should step back.

'No point you catching it too.' She gave me a pained smile, then clutched at her stomach again.

I hurried back to my own bedroom and curled up on my bed, guilt gnawing at me. I shouldn't have asked Nina all those questions about germs and illness last night – what if this was my fault? What if somehow – despite my protestation to Nina that I didn't believe in such things – my questions had tempted Fate?

I closed my eyes, unable to push away memories of the worst night of my life. I'd asked a lot of questions that day, too: why did Ricky always have to fall ill just before we went on holiday? Would we still go, even if his cough got worse? Why couldn't he stay behind, with Mrs Jackson from next door?

I'd bought new sunglasses that morning from C&A: thick black frames, glamorous reflective lenses. I knew they'd transform me from a round-faced twelve-year-old into a cool teenager as soon as we arrived at the beach. But while I was still lying awake in bed that evening, Ricky's cough *did* get worse, and I heard other worrying noises too. Mum yelling that they didn't have time to wait for an ambulance. Dad running next door to get Mrs Jackson to babysit me. The squeal of tyres as the car roared away. Mum, Dad, Ricky ... I never saw them again.

I wore my sunglasses to the funeral, and I barely took them off for the rest of that summer. I wore them while Caroline explained why I could only stay with her in her apartment for just a few nights. I wore them while the staff at the children's home went off to find me a music stand for my alien new bedroom. Those sunglasses masked my emotions; they made me feel less vulnerable, less naked. And by the time they eventually broke, I didn't need them any more – I'd learnt to present a calm face to the world, no matter what I was feeling inside.

I sat up on my bed and frowned at my reflection in the cheval mirror across the room. Of course Nina's illness wasn't my fault, just like my family's accident wasn't my fault. Nina had caught a bug, that's all. With all those strangers passing through the house before the party – caterers and waiters and gazebo people – it was hardly surprising.

A soft tap at the door made me jump. I smoothed away my frown as the door was pushed open. Leonora poked her head in, as if not sure what she might find.

'Ah, there you are.' She hesitated. 'Are you okay?'

I nodded quickly. 'I'm fine.'

'Good.' She came in and closed the door gently behind her. 'I need to ask you a favour, Beth.'

My heart lifted a little. Leonora and Markus had been so kind to me. I'd happily do anything to show them how grateful I was.

'Of course,' I said. 'What is it?'

She walked across to my wardrobe, pulled open the doors, and gazed at the blue checked dress for a long moment. If she thought it strange that I hadn't hung any of my own clothes in there yet, she didn't comment. She gave herself a little shake and lifted the dress down from the rail.

'The thing is,' she said, turning to face me, 'we're in a bit of a pickle. Markus' father is coming to see us today. He moved to the States before Nina was born, and he always said he'd never come back, because this place holds a lot of . . . ' Her gaze drifted up to the ceiling. 'Bad memories. His wife died here . . . ' When she dropped her gaze again, her expression was clouded,

71

and she looked at me as though not really seeing me. 'But for some reason . . .'

'He's changed his mind.'

She blinked and gave me a tight smile. 'Exactly. And the thing is . . .' She came towards me with the dress clutched against her chest, and she perched on the bed as if about to confide a great secret. 'Obviously Nina's in no fit state to meet him this afternoon. So, we're very much hoping you'll help us, Beth.' She gave me an earnest, pleading look. 'We'd like you to put on this dress, and plait your hair, and pretend to be Nina, just for a little while.'

I stared at her. 'But – he'll know I'm not Nina.'

'He won't. He's never met her. He never asked for photos, and we never sent them.'

Sympathy for Nina blossomed in my chest – her only living grandparent, and he'd never even asked for a photo of her.

'Can't you just explain to him that she's ill?' I asked.

'The thing about Markus' father is . . .' Leonora closed her eyes and grimaced, as if she was remembering some previous, traumatic encounter with him. 'He likes to get his own way. He's flown thousands of miles to meet his granddaughter today, and . . .' She opened her eyes again and looked sorrowfully at the dress in her hands. Then she thrust it towards me. 'Just . . . trust me. All our lives will be much easier if we give him what he wants.'

I wasn't convinced, but I took the dress from her anyway. Leonora and Markus had done so much for me; of course I'd do what they asked, even though it sounded bizarre.

'Okay,' I said. 'I'll try my best.'

'You're an angel.' Leonora placed her hand over mine. 'Thank you. And don't look so worried. Just think of it as – a little game.'

Sadie

And so the game begins.

Nazleen leads the two men across the drawing room towards Sadie. They look like father and son, Sadie thinks; they have the same wiry, angular frame. The elder must be over seventy, but his gaze is sharp, his expression suggesting a lively enjoyment of the situation they find themselves in. The younger man looks to be in his late thirties, and he has softer facial features, and collar-length, dark hair.

'Professor Owl,' Nazleen says to the older man, 'allow me to introduce Miss Lamb.'

Before Sadie can shake Professor Owl's hand, he grabs hold of hers and bows over it to kiss it. He doesn't mime, either; the kiss is decidedly enthusiastic. Champagne whizzes through Sadie's arteries and she feels fleetingly unsettled by their character names – lamb, nightingale, owl ... As quickly as politeness allows, she withdraws her hand from the old man's talons, and then she laughs inwardly at her silliness.

'Enchanted, mademoiselle,' Professor Owl says. 'Please, call me Everett. Everyone else does.'

She suspects they're not supposed to be using their real names, but she smiles anyway. 'Sadie. It's nice to meet you.'

He turns back to Nazleen. 'My word, if all the guests are as pretty as you two, we're in for a marvellous evening.'

Nazleen's professionalism doesn't falter, but Sadie's smile evaporates, and she turns away to greet the younger man as Everett and Nazleen fall into conversation. In contrast to Everett's dinner jacket and deep maroon waistcoat, this man is in black jeans and a casual shirt. He gives Sadie an apologetic smile.

'I'm Zach,' he says. 'Sorry about the old man.'

'Sadie.' She gestures at his clothes. 'You didn't fancy dressing up, then?'

'Nah.' He pulls a face. 'I wasn't going to come at all, actually, but Dad talked me into it, last minute. He's been going on about how we should support local businesses and all that. I think he was just flattered they asked for his endorsement, really, you know.'

'You live locally, then?' she says.

He drains his glass of champagne as if he's parched. 'Yep. Born and bred just down the road.'

The young waiter steps forward and refills Zach's glass. A photographer moves around the room at a discreet distance, taking pictures, and Sadie tries to ignore her. She declines a top-up of her own glass, and her gaze settles on an amateurish but rather charming painting of Raven Hall hanging over a polished bureau in the corner.

'Well, it's a stunning house,' she says. 'Do you know the owner?'

'No.' Zach peers around at the luxurious furnishings. 'It's been empty as far back as I can remember. This is high-end stuff, though, isn't it? I hope the food matches up.'

They both turn as the next guest enters the room: a dark-haired, high-cheekboned young woman in a striking crimson dress. She dips her head slightly as Nazleen leads her across the drawing room towards the others. She must be in her early twenties, Sadie thinks. Everett can't take his eyes off her.

'Everyone,' Nazleen says, her accent slipping slightly, 'this is Miss Mouse.'

Miss Mouse nods a meek hello around the group and sidles over to stand next to Sadie.

'So, er, have you come far?' Sadie asks her, for lack of a more inspired question.

But before Miss Mouse can answer, Everett butts in.

'Owl and Mouse – we'd fit rather well together, wouldn't you say?' He looms closer to the young woman, and she blinks back at him, a flash of stunned repulsion in her eyes. Sadie gives Everett a steely look.

'Step back a bit, would you?' she says to him firmly. 'It's too warm in here to huddle together.'

Thankfully, Everett's attention is diverted by the arrival of another new guest – a man in his forties, who hovers in the doorway.

'Colonel Otter,' Nazleen says loudly, 'welcome. Do come in.'

By Sadie's side, Zach makes a pleased sound. 'Ah, I didn't know Joe was coming.'

Colonel Otter – Joe – is a good-looking man, a few years older than Zach and more athletically built. But he hesitates in the doorway for a moment longer, as if he thinks he's in the wrong place. The reddish tint in his brown hair clashes rather unfortunately with the bright yellow waistcoat he's wearing. Someone had a field day choosing all these outfits, Sadie thinks. She smiles to think that, according to her alibi card, she and this reluctant-looking man supposedly took a stroll around the garden together earlier.

'Well, well.' Everett strides towards the man, barging ahead of Nazleen. 'Joe, old chap, how've you been?'

Joe's gaze jumps around the room as he shakes Everett's hand.

'I'm fine, thanks,' he says. 'I didn't know you two would be here.'

Zach goes to join them. 'Good to see you, mate.'

Joe must be another local, Sadie guesses, drafted in alongside the hired actors for this trial event. As the men talk, Sadie turns to the young woman next to her and sees that she's ducking away from the photographer's lens.

'Are you okay?' Sadie asks her quietly, feeling an unexpected surge of protectiveness towards her. 'I'm Sadie, by the way.'

'Genevieve.' The young woman widens her eyes. 'Yeah, I only got offered this job a couple of days ago. I just . . . I didn't realise everyone would be so . . .'

'What?' Sadie says. 'Old?' She laughs. 'They're taking photos for their website, they've got to appeal to the right demographic – people who can afford a murder mystery weekend . . . '

The young woman pulls a face. 'I'd hoped they might be *nicer*.'

'Ah.' Sadie shoots a dark look at Everett. 'Well, some of us are nice, honestly.' She gives Genevieve what she hopes is a reassuring smile. 'Shall we stick together?'

But Genevieve merely looks at her sideways, as if trying to puzzle her out.

Zach re-joins them by the fire, and Sadie sighs with relief; he seems the easiest person here to chat to.

'So, what's the history of this house, then?' Sadie asks him. 'Why did the previous owners abandon it, do you know?'

Zach's expression is vague. 'Oh, someone died, I think. I was just a kid; I don't really know what happened. It's been empty as far back as I can remember. Dad said the owner went off to live abroad.'

'It seems criminal,' Genevieve says, 'to leave a beautiful house like this empty for so long. The owner should be ashamed of himself.'

Zach wags a finger at her. 'Or herself. How do you know the owner isn't a woman?'

Genevieve smiles graciously. 'Fair point.'

Sadie glances at the door; she's waiting for the final guest to join them. There are six of them so far: three men and three women, and she wonders who the seventh will be. Will it have to be another woman, to balance out Nazleen's – or rather, Lady Nightingale's – mysteriously missing husband in the game?

Again, the waiter comes to refill their glasses, and this time,

Sadie accepts a top-up. Zach must be on his third glass, at least. The photographer has disappeared, and Sadie's stomach gives a low rumble. If the last guest doesn't make an appearance soon, their dinner will be late.

Finally, there's movement by the door, and a formidable-looking, silver-haired woman in a rich blue evening gown glides into the room.

'Mrs Shrew,' Nazleen cries. 'How kind of you to join us.'

Mrs Shrew's gaze sweeps over them all, and her expression slides from distaste into something more like horror. Sadie hopes she's another actor, merely playing her part – because if not, the poor woman looks like she'd rather be anywhere but here.

She decides to take the long route back to the village: around the lake, across Milner's Drain, and up through the fields to the main road. She wants to distract herself from that scene on the veranda – those two women, the new owners of Raven Hall, the interlopers who stole her house. Also, she has a decision to make before she reaches the village. So yes, she'll take the long route back, and she'll hand the rest of her day over to Fate.

Walking around Avermere has always soothed her, even in the terrible days after her mother died, when Daddy locked himself away in his study and Raven Hall itself seemed to creak with misery. Today, she can feel her spirits lifting already. She passes the old tree stump and slows her pace, rolling up her sleeves in the gentle sunshine.

Flag irises nod at her from amongst the long grass as if they recognise her as an old friend. Memories drift through her mind as she strolls along.

Here is the tiny stone beach, only a dozen feet wide, where her mother taught her to swim, and where they brought their picnics each summer. It reminds her of her first experience of the pain of sunburn, and her mother taking her out to the kitchen garden and showing her how to turn strawberry leaves into a soothing lotion for her sun-scorched skin.

And here are more of her mother's much-loved medicine plants – cheerful button-headed tansy flowers, with their familiar

80

camphor-like odour. As she dips her head to inhale the scent, a grey heron flaps up out of the vegetation by the lake shore. It curves its flight path towards her, as if wanting to get a good look at her before it lifts away. She raises a hand in a silent greeting.

For a few golden minutes, she almost forgets that none of this is hers any longer – her beloved Raven Hall, her beautiful Avermere. But, inevitably, her mind drifts on to the last days of her mother's illness. She remembers arranging daffodils in a jug by her mother's bedside, and seeing their vivid yellow reflected in the whites of her mother's eyes. She remembers her mother beckoning her forward . . .

'Promise me, lovely girl, you'll never leave Raven Hall. You'll bring up your own children and grandchildren here, and you'll teach them to love it as much as we do . . .'

Suddenly she's picturing those two dreadful women again, and resentment swoops back into her chest like a kestrel dropping on to its prey.

How can this have happened? The slow-moving woman on the swing seat, the long-haired daughter in her orange crop top . . . For a moment, she tries to imagine herself wearing such an outfit, and despite the lump in her throat, she almost smiles. Daddy would have been scandalised. He'd have said she was encouraging the boys. As if boys ever came within a mile's radius of Raven Hall anyway. She sighs, poor Daddy. He had no idea it wasn't the local boys he should be worried about.

She thinks fleetingly of the young doctor. That's what Daddy always called him, as if it was his official name – The Young Doctor – even though she happened to know his name was Roy, and he was nearly thirty.

She hasn't seen the young doctor since the day Daddy died – not since they walked into Daddy's study together and found Daddy collapsed over the green-topped desk. For days afterwards, she didn't think of anything or anyone much at all. But when the shock had begun to subside – when reality came creeping back in – she'd dared to hope that the young doctor might reappear. She'd even watched for him from the windows of Raven Hall, while the lawyers argued in low voices behind her.

But he didn't reappear. Not when the lawyers told her the estate was bankrupt and Raven Hall would have to be sold. Not when a distant relation of her mother's begrudgingly offered to take her in as a lodger, eighty miles away. Not when they dragged her, sobbing, down the stone steps and into a taxi on the final day . . .

She frowns and picks up her pace. She needs to decide – should she knock on the young doctor's door when she gets back to the village? He's the only person who ever showed an interest in her. And now, living at her distant relative's house, she has no one to talk to at all. But what might he say if she knocks on his door this afternoon? 'I've missed you' or 'I'm not interested' – which is more likely? She's not an idiot – she knows he must have kissed other girls and told them they were special too, but . . . She plucks a daisy from the path and pinches its petals off as she marches along. He loves me, he loves me not . . .

'Hallo.'

She almost dies of fright.

A very tall young man emerges from the low hedgerow – he must have been crouching down – is he going to attack her? But he holds up his hands, and his smile is apologetic.

'I was just taking pictures of some toadstools.' He taps the camera hanging around his neck. 'I didn't mean to startle you, sorry.'

'Who are you?' She's alert for any sudden movement, ready to run if he looks like he means her harm. But his expression is earnest, and he's careful not to come any closer.

'Sorry, I'm not trespassing, am I?' he says. 'I'm just visiting for the weekend, for a housewarming party.' He indicates the direction she's come from. 'Raven Hall – do you know it?'

She's horrified to feel tears welling up, and she swallows hard. 'Not really. A bit.'

'Ah, well.' He looks away, towards the lake. 'I thought this was all theirs, but – anyway, I should be getting back. My girlfriend will wonder where I've got to . . .'

His gaze slides back to her, and she feels it like an electric charge on her skin. Of course, she thinks. The girl in the orange crop top. Of course she's his girlfriend.

She should say goodbye and walk on. But he hasn't moved to pass her yet. They stand there, holding each other's gaze, and she finds she can't walk on.

'Are you a photographer, then?' she says. 'I mean, of wildlife, or something?'

His smile makes her heart skip. 'Actually, I'm a student. In London. I'm studying horticulture. But I love it out here.' He gestures at the stunted hedgerow on one side of them, the bank of nettles leading down to the lake shore on the other. 'I'd love to live somewhere like this when I graduate. How about you?'

'Oh, I'm . . .' She wipes her palms on her skirt. 'I'm just visiting someone here too. In the village.' She wrinkles her nose. 'Or at least, I was thinking about it. I haven't decided yet.'

'Oh, okay.' He tilts his head. 'Well, you've got a long walk ahead, but I guess you know that. Do you want to come back with me? I could drive you down there, if you like . . .'

'No,' she says. 'I'm fine.' She narrows her eyes. 'I'm not lost, if that's what you're thinking. I used to live around here. I know the way.'

'Oh, right. Great.' He studies her with a puzzled smile. 'Well, I'll probably be back this way some weekends, from now on. Maybe we'll bump into each other again.'

She gives this suggestion some consideration. 'Maybe.'

'I'll try not to startle you so much next time.'

'You'd better not.'

His laugh is gentle, like the breeze in the reeds. 'It was nice to meet you, Girl-who-isn't-lost.'

She stares at him for a moment longer, drinking in his features, memorising them to pore over later. Then she turns away and hurries on, without looking back.

Beth

JULY 1988

I tugged at the neckline of the blue dress and frowned down at my salad. Leonora and Markus had barely eaten any of their own lunch either; they were too busy exchanging uncharacteristically snappy words across the dining table. I wished with all my might that Nina would skip down the stairs and interrupt the meal by announcing she was fully recovered and ready to meet her grandfather. But instead, I had to listen to her parents bicker while my skin itched and sweated under the uncomfortable fabric. I longed for the afternoon's visit to be over.

'We should sit outside, actually,' Markus said. 'Dad always liked the garden here ...'

'We are – *sitting* – in the drawing room.' Leonora enunciated each word with painstaking clarity. 'And your father hated the garden, I remember you saying. And Beth can't exactly play her violin outside, can she?'

'Can't she?' Markus sounded genuinely nonplussed. I jabbed my fork into a slice of cucumber and kept my gaze lowered.

'Of course she can't,' Leonora said. 'Stop trying to change everything at the last minute. We stick to the plan.'

Markus' cutlery clattered on to his plate and he held up his hands. 'Okay, okay.'

'Unless you're having second thoughts?' Leonora's tone was icy.

'Of course not.' Markus' prompt reply seemed to mollify her slightly.

She turned her attention to me.

'So, *Nina*, let's run through it again, shall we? What do you like doing in your spare time?'

I straightened in my seat. 'I like reading. Drawing. Anything to do with animals.'

'And?'

'Oh, and playing my violin.' I kept forgetting this part, since it wasn't true of the real Nina, but when I'd queried it with Leonora, she'd dismissed the question with a quick frown and a shake of her head.

Leonora scrutinised me now. 'You will sound a bit more convincing when he's here, won't you?'

I met her gaze sheepishly. 'Yes, I'll try.'

They rose to clear the table then, and I peeked at my watch. Markus' father was due at three; I still had an hour and a half stuck in these silly plaits and this horrible dress, and all to trick a grumpy old man. I'd go along with it for Leonora and Markus' sake, but it seemed a daft sort of game to me.

The Rolls-Royce was late. Only by a few minutes, but Leonora and I had been peering through the drawing-room window for quarter of an hour by then, and her tension was contagious. It made me wonder exactly what she was afraid Markus' father would do if he found out his planned meeting with his granddaughter had been thwarted – by a sickness bug, of all things. He must be a desperately unreasonable person, I thought. I had no memories of my own grandparents, but in the photos of them taken with me as a baby, they looked to be kind, caring people. I hoped this so-called little game with Nina's grandfather wasn't going to turn into an ordeal.

All the more reason to play my part properly, I decided.

'Here he comes,' Leonora said, and Markus sprang from the armchair he'd been pretending to relax in and marched out to the hall. A moment later I heard the front door open. By the time the car came to a halt on the gravel, Markus was waiting on the bottom step, and he held up a hand to the chauffeur and went forward to swing his father's door open himself.

I'd been expecting someone older, but Markus' father didn't even look sixty. He was just as tall as his son, and he had a thick thatch of white-blond hair that added at least another inch to his height. He unfolded himself from the car, and his expression when he turned to the house was severe. Leonora snatched me back from the window, out of sight.

'We'd better go and greet him,' she whispered, and when I saw the way her trembling fingers fluttered to her throat, I felt a wave of sympathy for her. She was *frightened* of this man – it shocked me to discover an adult could feel this way. What on earth could he have done to her, to make her fear him this much, and yet agree to let him visit?

In the hall, we came face to face with Markus and his father. The man's gaze locked on to mine, and his stare was so piercing, I was convinced he could see right through my eyeballs and into my brain. Heat flared to my cheeks. Could he read what I was thinking? I hadn't said a word to him yet, but what if he already sensed I was an imposter? I glanced at Markus and then at Leonora, but neither of them met my eye.

The visitor's gaze left mine and jumped to Leonora, and I let out a shaky breath. *I'm Nina*, I reminded myself. *He's never met me before. Of course he'll believe it.*

'Ms Averell.' His voice was silky smooth but not friendly. 'You look remarkably well.'

Leonora stuttered something unintelligible, and I frowned, not understanding why his phrase had sounded like an insult rather than a compliment.

'And you . . .' Again, he stared right into me. 'You are . . . ?'

I steeled myself. 'I'm Nina, Sir.'

He raised his bushy eyebrows high, as if waiting for more, but then he turned to Markus and indicated the door to the drawing room. 'Shall we?'

Leonora caught hold of my wrist as Markus and his father went into the room.

'We'll make some tea,' she said, a little too loudly.

I followed her down the hall to the kitchen, my heart still jumping uncomfortably. Had I done enough? Leonora pushed the kitchen door firmly shut behind us.

'You were perfect,' she said. 'We'll let them talk for a while, then we'll take in the tea and cakes.'

When we eventually joined the men in the drawing room, they broke off their conversation, and the visitor gestured for me to approach him. Markus flashed me an encouraging smile.

'So,' the older man said, 'tell me, Nina, do you know who I am?'

I cleared my throat. 'You're my grandfather.'

'Hm.' He studied me intently. 'I hear you're quite the musician, is that right?'

This was a question I'd normally be delighted to answer, but I felt a prickle of unease.

'Yes.' I said. 'I suppose so.'

'Would you play for me now?' he asked.

Leonora was already carrying my violin case towards me.

'Okay,' I said. 'If you like.'

I lifted out my violin and bow, and I took them across to the piano and struck an A, aware that all three adults were watching me intently. Usually, the act of tuning my instrument slid me into a calm, focused state, and I was desperate to recreate that reassuring feeling now. I adjusted my bow slowly, waiting for the familiar scent of the resin to transport me back to my carefree childhood days, the way it normally did. But my heart continued to race, and I couldn't shake the sensation of Markus' father staring at me with those glittering eyes. I marched across to the black marble fireplace, and I positioned myself with my shoulder turned against him, so I didn't have to see his expression while I played.

I began too fast, and I hurried through the piece, feeling increasingly resentful as my bewilderment about the situation swelled. It wasn't a terrible performance, but it was nowhere near the best I could do, and by the time I reached the end, I was close to tears. I lowered my instrument and bow.

I don't know what I expected – polite applause, perhaps. A condescending comment from the man I was trying so hard to fool. But when I reluctantly turned to face him again, I was horrified to see he was crying. Fat tears slid down his pale cheeks, and he gestured for me to sit next to him on the sofa. I desperately wanted to run from the room.

But Leonora spoke sharply. 'Nina.'

It jolted me into action, and I forced myself to join him on the sofa. He placed one of his gnarly hands over mine and took a moment to compose himself.

'That was beautiful, my child.' He gave me a surprisingly gentle smile. 'You remind me so much of your grandmother, Anneliese. She played the cello every day of her life up until she—' His face contorted briefly. 'Well, up until she grew too weak to hold it upright any more. I'll tell you something else. She'd have been very proud of you.'

I pictured the old cello case leaning in the corner of Markus' study, and I nodded mutely. But Nina's grandfather seemed to be waiting for a proper reply, and when I glanced at Leonora and Markus, they too were watching me with expectant expressions.

'Thank you,' I managed to say.

At that, Markus' father tightened his grip on my hand. 'Tell me, Nina, how would you like to come and live in America with me?'

Leonora made a choking sound, and Markus caught hold of her arm. His father's gaze was fixed on me, and either he didn't notice Leonora's reaction or he chose to ignore it.

'There's an excellent music school in my city,' he continued, 'and lots of wonderful opportunities for a bright girl like you. You could live in a big, airy apartment, go out to fancy restaurants, see a different show every night of the week. How does that grab you?'

I stared at him, thinking of the real Nina, upstairs, ill, in her bed. *What would Nina say to this?* Nina, who swam in the lake and the water channels around here every single day in the summer; who could row across to the island faster than Jonas could swim it; who loved her turret bedroom and her treehouse and the acres of Fenland she'd grown up in.

'Thank you,' I said, 'but I love living at Raven Hall too much. I think, if I ever had to leave, I might die of a broken heart.'

First, his white eyebrows shot up. Then they hunched down, and he pulled my arm closer to him, bringing his face right up to mine. I tried to wriggle away, but he wouldn't let me go.

'I see,' he said, and his voice had become a growl. 'I see exactly what's going on here. You've been brainwashed by your mother, haven't you? I should have guessed.'

I scrambled to my feet, desperately trying to tug my hand free of his.

'Let go of me!'

'Dad,' Markus said sharply.

Finally, his father dropped my hand with a look of disgust.

He got to his feet in one smooth, furious motion, and he glared at Markus, his body quivering.

'I've seen enough,' he snapped. 'I'll think about what you said, but I'm very disappointed in you, Markus. You're my only son—' He cut himself off and stalked to the door. 'I'll see myself out.'

Sadie

JANUARY 2019

Sadie deliberately hangs back as the guests set down their champagne glasses and leave the drawing room.

Nazleen leads the way, with an eager Everett hurrying to accompany her, for all the world as if he really is an owl, sizing up his prey. Mrs Shrew has regained her composure, but her expression is now severe. When Joe offers her his arm, she grants him the briefest of smiles, and she allows him to guide her from the room. Zach and Genevieve follow, arguing mildly about some aspect of the architecture of the house. Sadie brings up the rear, wondering which of them she'll be seated next to at dinner.

The dining room is a striking mix of old grandeur and modern luxury. Dark wood panelling gives way to a lustrous raspberry-coloured wallpaper above; dozens of flickering candles set the crystal glasses twinkling and the silver cutlery gleaming. The table is set for eight, and as the guests seek out their place cards, they see it's the head of the table that remains empty. An enormous portrait looms over it: a stern-looking gentleman with bushy eyebrows and a thatch of blond-white hair.

Nazleen, their hostess, hovers at the foot of the table while the others circle and find their places. Before they take their seats, she gestures theatrically at the portrait and glances around to make sure they're all paying attention.

'Ladies and gentlemen, this is my husband, Lord Nightingale.'

On Sadie's right, Zach murmurs, 'A bit old for her, isn't he?'

Sadie shushes him.

Nazleen continues. 'I regret to inform you that this afternoon, Lord Nightingale was found murdered in his study. He was killed by a toxic powder that was delivered to him inside a sealed envelope. When Lord Nightingale opened the envelope, he inhaled the powder and it killed him instantly.' She looks at each of the guests in turn. 'He died at three o'clock this afternoon, precisely.'

Sadie thinks of her alibi card. She visited Lord Nightingale in his study between two and three ... Her pulse quickens, questions already flitting through her mind.

'Now,' Nazleen continues, 'the envelope was addressed to my husband, and there was no stamp on it, so we know it didn't arrive in the post. Therefore, one of you must have delivered it to his study today. One of you, perhaps, slipped it under his study door, or left it discreetly on his desk, at some point this afternoon.' She draws herself up theatrically. 'As far as I'm concerned, one of you killed him.' Her eyebrows lift meaningfully. 'But you, of course, may suspect me.'

Sadie glances at the other guests. They're all watching

Nazleen with varying degrees of fascination – even sour-faced Mrs Shrew.

Nazleen eases her shoulders down ever so slightly, and when she speaks again, her tone is calmer. *She's good*, Sadie thinks. *I can see why they hired her, she's really good.*

'Now,' Nazleen says again, switching effortlessly from wronged wife to dinner party hostess, 'each of you should have read your preliminary alibi card, so you know certain things to be true about your own activities here today. You may refer to your cards as needed. Your task, ladies and gentlemen, is to question one another – and me, of course – on your movements leading up to three o'clock this afternoon.'

Genevieve claps her hands. 'How exciting!'

But Mrs Shrew's voice injects a mood-destroying contrast. 'Are you going to give us permission to sit down in a minute, Lady Nightingale?'

'Oh, er, yes, of course,' Nazleen says. 'Please, go ahead.'

They all pull out their heavy, high-backed chairs and settle into position before Nazleen resumes her instructions.

'Right, and, um, a new piece of information will be provided with each course – a new clue, if you like. Please remember, everyone, you must be truthful in your answers, but you don't have to share anything that you're not directly asked about.' She holds a pose while the photographer's camera clicks, and then, finally, she reaches the end of her speech. 'The last clue will be given at breakfast tomorrow morning, and then you will be asked to submit your theories and name your prime suspect.'

Sadie beams at Nazleen, and Nazleen shoots her a grateful smile in response.

'Well,' Everett booms, 'this is all very jolly.'

The young waiter appears in the doorway with a loaded catering trolley, and the photographer helps him to wheel it in, while the guests shake out their pleasingly heavy napkins and gaze wide-eyed around the room. Sadie is seated directly opposite Joe, and she watches him watching the others for a few seconds, until suddenly their eyes meet. She finds it amusing and smiles, but he seems rather disconcerted, and he turns to Mrs Shrew and murmurs to her, asking if she needs anything. Mrs Shrew shakes her head. Sadie wants to begin questioning everyone, but she can't decide which guest to start with, and she's distracted by the plate of food being set in front of her.

The first course is sea bass, served whole, with a light lemon-dressed salad. Sadie blinks down at the entire fish on her plate and its blank pupil stares back up at her. Her appetite shrivels, and she glances enviously at Genevieve's vegetarian alternative. On her left, Everett is already devouring his fish, while the waiter moves around the table pouring wine.

On the other side of her, Zach nudges her elbow. 'Free food. Don't knock it.'

'The chef has an impressive CV . . . ' Nazleen says, poking her fork into her own fish with an uncertain expression.

Everett strikes up a loud conversation about local fishing sites with Joe, and Sadie is tempted to interrupt him and steer him back to the game they're supposed to be playing. But she's curious about the white-haired man in the portrait, so she takes the opportunity to ask a quiet question of Zach.

'Is he the real owner, do you think?' She lifts a tiny portion of sea bass to her mouth and is pleasantly surprised by how tasty it is. 'Lord Nightingale, or whatever his name is.'

'I'm sure the name's made up, and I've never heard of a lord around here,' Zach says. 'But yeah, I guess the portrait looks real enough. Dad'll probably know – ask him.'

But Sadie's reluctant to interrupt Everett's rambling anecdote. She catches Genevieve's eye and they exchange a brief, raised-eyebrow grimace as Everett cracks another bad-taste joke. Sadie sips her wine, and before she can stop him, Zach grabs the bottle and tops her up again.

'Shouldn't we be asking each other questions?' she says to Zach. And then, 'So, what were you doing, leading up to three o'clock today?'

He grins. 'I was still in bed with a hangover.' But he takes pity on her and raises his voice. 'Okay, I was in the library with Miss Mouse all afternoon. I heard raised voices in Lord Nightingale's study at half past two.'

The other guests rapidly switch their attention to Zach, except for Everett, who concentrates once more on clearing his plate.

'Is that right, Miss Mouse?' Sadie asks Genevieve.

Genevieve pats around her crimson lips with her napkin, and Sadie guesses she's buying time while she recalls the details on her alibi card.

'Yes,' Genevieve says, 'except, I went to use the bathroom just

97

after two. I was only gone five minutes, but ...' She widens her eyes at Zach in mock-horror. 'It would have given you time to ...'

Zach thumps the table enthusiastically. 'I didn't deliver any envelope. I deny everything. I'm innocent, I tell you.'

Sadie leans forward and tries to catch Joe's eye. 'And where were you, leading up to three o'clock, Colonel Otter?'

But Joe is already shoving back his chair, and he looks only at Nazleen, with an apologetic expression. 'Please excuse me a moment. I need to use your phone.'

The room sits silent in his wake, like a deflated balloon. Everett, the only one of them who seems oblivious, spears something on to his fork and lifts it halfway to his lips before gazing around.

'Fish eyes,' he says. 'Very good for you. Omega threes, you know.' He pops the morsel into his mouth, and Sadie's not the only guest to turn her head away.

Sadie takes a large swallow of her wine, and once again Zach tops up her glass immediately; it's irritating. The only person who hasn't said a word since they took their seats is Mrs Shrew, and Sadie studies her, still unsure whether she's playing a role or is genuinely unhappy about being here.

'So, Mrs Shrew,' Sadie says brightly, 'do you live locally too?'

The woman's lips pucker as if Sadie's insulted her, and for several seconds Sadie thinks she's not going to answer. But eventually she gives a sharp shake of her head.

'No, I travelled a long way for this.' Her gaze rests on the pearls around Sadie's neck, and her expression tightens even further. 'Believe me, I'm beginning to wish I hadn't bothered.'

Zach snorts into his wine glass, and Sadie's mood dips. She feels out of place suddenly – the way Mrs Shrew looks at her … Can the woman tell that Sadie's never been inside such a huge mansion before, never eaten such a lavish meal, or worn such beautiful clothes and jewellery? But as soon as she recognises her reaction as embarrassment, she shakes it off. Sadie's just as good as anyone here, and she won't let them make her feel inferior.

The waiter clears their plates deftly, and as he leaves the room, Joe comes back in.

'The phone line's dead.' Joe's voice is tight with annoyance.

'Oh, I'm so sorry,' Nazleen says. 'They were supposed to reconnect it last week. I'll chase it up on Monday morning.'

Genevieve half-stands in alarm. 'But I haven't got a mobile signal either.'

'That's something you have to expect,' Everett says complacently, 'out here in the Fens.' He grins wolfishly at Genevieve, as she sinks back on to her seat. 'Don't worry, my dear, I'll look after you.'

Sadie smooths the tablecloth in front of her. She's tempted to blurt out – *Did you cut the telephone wire, Colonel Otter?*' – but she senses the feeble joke would worsen Joe's mood, and she's keen to get the game back on track so they can all start enjoying themselves. The waiter returns with the freshly restocked trolley, and Sadie excuses herself from the table and walks to the window. She parts the thick curtains and peers out at the faintly lit gravel. The chauffeur-driven cars have all gone, unsurprisingly, but two ordinary-looking cars sit over in the shadows by the stable block.

We can drive to the village for help, if we need to, she thinks, and then she smiles at herself for letting Joe's discovery unsettle her. Of course they won't need to go for help – she's being ridiculous. It must be the fish eyes that have made her jumpy. She lets the curtains fall back and returns to the table.

Their second course looks more appetising: pan-fried partridge breasts with celeriac chips. Nazleen makes a show of pulling out the next game card, and again, she pauses for the photographer to take some pictures. Then she lifts her chin and waits for her six dinner party guests to give her their full attention.

'Ladies and gentlemen,' Nazleen says, 'I, myself, heard footsteps approaching and leaving my husband's study on two separate occasions this afternoon. Either one of them might have been the person who delivered the envelope to Lord Nightingale.'

'If we're to believe you,' Zach says, but he's smiling, waiting for Nazleen to tell them more.

'One set of footsteps belonged to a woman,' Nazleen continues. 'Clearly high heels. The other must have been a man's – they were heavy, like boots . . .'

Genevieve rolls her eyes as if she's struggling not to protest at the wording. Sadie shoots Nazleen an encouraging smile. Yes, the company could do with a more politically correct writer, but it's good to gain new clues, and Sadie would dearly love to be the guest who solves this mystery – why shouldn't it be her who wins? Besides, what if Nazleen is secretly assessing Sadie and Genevieve's performances tonight? Sadie doesn't want to damage her chances of being re-employed by this company, and she certainly doesn't want to put tomorrow's pay cheque in jeopardy.

'What else can you tell us?' Sadie asks.

Nazleen gestures around the table. 'It's up to all of you, now. You need to ask each other more questions . . .'

Sadie turns immediately to Zach. 'Were you wearing men's shoes when you left the library?'

Too late, she realises this wasn't the right question, and she flinches as a ripple of laughter passes through the other guests. Even Mrs Shrew's lips twitch, and Nazleen gives Sadie a surprisingly grateful look. For the first time, there's a real feeling of camaraderie in the room, and Sadie feels mildly astonished that she was the one to create it.

'I'm afraid not,' Zach says. 'I was wearing pink stilettos.'

'I was so surprised when I saw him,' Joe says, 'I almost dropped the envelope I was carrying.' They all laugh again. 'Joke!' Joe adds. 'It wasn't me who poisoned him . . .'

'Do you call it poison,' Zach says, 'if you inhale it? Because I thought—'

But he's interrupted by a shout of annoyance from Everett, who scrapes his chair back noisily as he lurches to his feet.

'What's the matter?' Joe says.

'Damn lead shot in the partridge.' Everett leans forward and spits out a tiny metal pellet, which pings on to his plate surprisingly loudly. 'Nearly broke my bloody tooth on it.'

'I'm afraid,' Genevieve's tone drips with gleeful malice, 'that's something you have to expect, out here in the Fens.'

Everett coughs and glares at her, and Sadie turns her face the other way to hide her own smile. Mrs Shrew positively beams down the table at Genevieve, and even Zach is grinning. Nazleen tries to smooth things over. She calls back the waiter and asks him to let the chef know about the shot, and she apologises to Everett until even he has to concede it's no one's fault.

'Please,' Nazleen says to the rest of them, 'do carry on.'

Sadie's not sure whether Nazleen wants them to carry on eating, or to continue questioning one another, but she sets her cutlery down neatly on her plate and resolves to do neither until her head has cleared a little.

Beth

We sat in silence in the drawing room after Markus' father stormed out. First came the slam of the front door, then his angry footsteps across the gravel, then the double slam as he and the chauffeur got back in the car. The engine started. The sound of it faded. Finally, just when I thought my tears were going to spill over, Leonora rose and came to me, and she wrapped her arms around me.

'You were wonderful, Beth.'

I inhaled her rose scent and felt myself relaxing.

'Yes, very well done,' Markus said. 'You played it beautifully.'

But they both spoke cautiously, as if they weren't sure exactly what had just happened. And it was soon clear they no longer required my company.

'Don't wake Nina, will you?' Leonora said to me, as she and Markus headed out to the terrace with a bottle of wine. 'Leave her to rest, okay?'

But I was too unsettled to know what else to do with myself. So I crept up the spiral staircase and tapped cautiously on Nina's door.

'Come in.'

She still looked pale, but her eyes were brighter than earlier. She patted the bed next to her, and I decided I'd rather have her company and risk catching her bug, than sit in my own room alone with my churning thoughts.

'What on earth are you wearing?' she asked, and she reached out and tweaked the end of one of my plaits. 'And your hair. You look funny.'

'Your grandfather came,' I said.

'Oh.' She glanced at her alarm clock. 'I forgot. Is he still here?'

'He—' I didn't know where to start.

'Beth? What's the matter?'

I wondered, suddenly, whether Nina already knew about the game. I wasn't sure if that would make it better or worse. Perhaps this was the sort of thing her parents did all the time? Maybe she'd laugh. Maybe I was worrying about nothing.

'He – I – They made me dress up and I had to pretend to be you, Nina. Your grandfather believed I was you.' I gazed earnestly at her. 'Your mum said if I didn't, he'd be angry you were ill, and he . . . ' I didn't know what he'd have done, but I knew it must be something truly awful.

But Nina was shaking her head. 'You're making this up, right? This is a joke.'

'No. I swear, that's why I'm wearing this dress. And your mum plaited my hair, and—'

'You're saying you took my place?'

I stared at her, hesitating. 'Yeah. They asked me to.'

'You mean you actually called yourself Nina? And pretended my parents were your mum and dad?'

I nodded miserably. 'I was only trying to help.'

She sank back into her pillows, staring at me, and then she turned her face sharply away, and neither of us spoke for a minute. Then,

'Can you go, please?' she said. 'I'd like to be alone now.'

For the next couple of weeks, Nina wore her resentment like an outer layer of clothing. She was sulky around her parents, and short-tempered with me. I tried to talk to her about it, but she refused to discuss it, glaring at me fiercely when I made further stuttering attempts to apologise.

'This is *my* home,' was all she'd say. 'And *my* family. Just remember that.'

How could I possibly forget it? I was acutely aware of my position as a guest at Raven Hall. I had no family of my own to return to, and my once-happy childhood home was now inhabited by oblivious strangers. I was entirely dependent on the goodwill of Nina and her parents.

I spent hours alone, keeping out of Nina's way, mostly playing my violin – it was the only way I knew to numb my fears and soothe my loneliness. One evening, a few days after Markus' father's visit, I was approaching the top of the stairs when I heard Markus answer the phone in the hall and say, 'Ah, thanks for ringing me back, Caroline.' I scurried back to my bedroom and shut myself in, my heart pounding. He might have a client called Caroline, I told myself – but deep down I was convinced they'd decided I was no longer a suitable companion for Nina, and they were demanding my aunt come and collect me. And she would take me straight back to the children's home, I was sure of it.

I cried myself to sleep that night. After everything I'd been through in the last couple of years – losing my parents and brother; being treated as a nuisance by my aunt – Raven Hall had felt like a haven; a second chance at having a happy life, of feeling safe. I couldn't bear the thought of being sent away.

For days after that, I felt as though I was holding my breath, even though Caroline never did turn up to collect me. Leonora and Markus continued to behave quite normally towards me, but I knew the real decision lay with Nina, and she remained distant and uncommunicative.

In the end, it was Jonas who mended our friendship.

It was a particularly warm morning in early August, and Nina and I were finishing breakfast – without conversation – in the dining room, when we glimpsed a blur of movement through the window: Jonas arriving on his bike.

'I'm desperate for a swim,' he said, when we went out to meet him on the gravel. 'Are you two friends again, now?' He'd joined us swimming a couple of days earlier, but Nina's constant sniping at me had driven him to go home early.

I dropped my gaze and waited to hear Nina's answer.

'I expect Beth would rather stay in the house,' Nina said. She gave me a pointed look. 'In *my* house, that is.' She turned back to Jonas. 'But I'll come.'

I stepped back, ready to leave them to it, my mind already drifting to my violin and the music I would play to distract myself from the world around me. But Jonas' irritation was clear.

'Fine. Well, Beth, in that case – would you write down your new address for me?'

'What?' Nina said. 'She's not going anywhere.'

Jonas pulled a face. 'Well, I doubt she'll be happy to stay here much longer, if you keep treating her like this.'

My heart jumped erratically. How was Nina going to react?

She turned slowly and stared at me. It was probably the first time she'd looked me directly in the eye since I told her I'd pretended to be her for her grandfather's visit.

'I honestly don't want to take your place,' I said meekly. 'I never meant to—'

She gulped, and then she flung her arms around me.

'I know,' she sobbed. 'And I don't want you to leave. I've been really horrible, I was jealous of you getting to meet my grandfather, but I know it wasn't your fault. It wasn't anyone's fault. I'm sorry, Beth. I'm sorry.'

Jonas sighed loudly. 'Girls.' He raised his eyebrows. 'Are we going swimming, then, or what?'

Nina and I wiped away our tears, and we ran upstairs to change into our swimming costumes. She was extra nice to me for the rest of the day, but I was conscious that our reconciliation was down to Jonas, and I watched him more closely than usual as the three of us messed around in the shallows. When Nina floated out into deeper water, I seized my chance and thanked him privately.

'Well, I had to do something,' he said, holding my gaze. 'I'd hate to see you go. I like you, Beth.'

In that brief moment, I forgot about all my worries.

'I like you too,' I said.

'Do you think maybe, one day . . . ?' he began. But Nina was splashing towards us again, shouting that she'd seen a giant pike, that it had nibbled at her toes. Our moment of intimacy was over, but I smiled to myself each time I thought about his words. *I like you, Beth.* Things weren't so bad at Raven Hall, after all.

Sadie

JANUARY 2019

Sadie is surprised to see another savoury course wheeled in on the waiter's trolley. Thick lamb chops, a medley of green vegetables, and something round, stodgy and golden brown. She prods it with her fork; it's larger than the palm of her hand, and it's clearly been fried, but she can't work out what it is.

'Puffball mushroom,' Nazleen says, with more than a trace of unease.

'Ah, yes, lovely,' Everett says, and he tucks in with gusto, giving Sadie the confidence to nibble a tiny piece of hers. Not bad. She slices into her lamb, and a thin, blood-stained liquid oozes instantly across her plate. *It's just as well there are so many courses*, she thinks, *because at this rate I won't finish any of them*. She takes another sip of her wine.

The guests continue to ask each other questions while they pick at their food, and Sadie tries to keep track of the replies in her head, wishing she could jot down some notes. She's confident she's drawing closer to identifying the guilty party, but she keeps changing her mind, and the alcohol isn't helping . . .

Which guest swore they came downstairs empty-handed? Which clue has she overlooked? As people begin to set down their cutlery, Nazleen appears to remember something.

'Oh.'

She reaches for the game cards, but she takes a sip of water before she begins her next speech, and Sadie realises with a jolt of surprise that Nazleen hasn't been drinking wine like everyone else. Perhaps it's Nazleen's choice, or perhaps it's a condition of the hostess role; the rest of them have been plied with drinks all evening, but maybe the company felt one person should remain sober and in charge.

'It was Nazleen,' Zach whispers at Sadie's side. 'Don't you think? I'm pretty sure Lady Nightingale murdered her own husband . . .'

Nazleen raises her voice. 'Ladies and gentlemen, I have a card here for each of you that will provide you with details of the last conversation *you* had with Lord Nightingale. This will be new information for you, and something you will now want to question each other about.'

Mrs Shrew closes her eyes as if she's in pain, but Genevieve gives Nazleen a bright smile and helps her to hand around the small envelopes.

'Please keep your own cards private,' Nazleen says. 'And remember, you must answer all questions truthfully.'

Sadie tears open her envelope and pulls out a square card. *Miss Lamb*, it reads, *in your last conversation with Lord Nightingale, he told you he used to be a friend of your mother's.* Sadie blinks and reads on. *He said you must have been a great*

110

disappointment to your mother, unable to hold down a job, turning up at grand houses in the hope of employment.

Sadie's pulse races. She knows this is about her character, but it feels disturbingly close to home – to her recent sacking from the shop, and to her belief that she was a disappointment to her own mother. It's unnerving. She glances at the serious expressions of the other guests as they each read their private cards. Everett rips his into quarters and posts them into the empty gravy boat in front of him with a snort of disgust.

Sadie drops her gaze back to her own card and reads the second paragraph. *Lord Nightingale told you there would never be a place for you at Raven Hall. 'Over his dead body' was the phrase he used. He felt the same way as your mother – he knew you'd never amount to anything.*

Sadie's vision blurs. This is just a game, so why does it feel so personal – so *nasty*? At her side, Zach folds his card carefully in half and slides it into his jeans pocket.

'Is yours . . . ?' Sadie's not sure what she wants to ask him. 'Is yours what you expected? Does it, you know, does it make sense for your character?'

Zach frowns, hesitating, as if he's suspicious she might be cheating. 'I think I'm close to working it out. Is there a prize, do you know, if we get the right answer?'

His oblique reply only disconcerts her more. Across the table, Joe too seems to have disposed of his card entirely. Genevieve has rolled hers into a tube, and she looks mildly bored. Mrs Shrew's envelope sits unopened next to her plate, and an uncomfortable silence hangs heavily in the room. Nazleen looks like she wants to say something, but she can't seem to find the words needed to re-ignite their enthusiasm for the game.

Sadie slides her card back into its envelope feeling distinctly uneasy, the word *disappointment* rolling around in her mind like a marble in a jar. She's never had a problem keeping a character's story separate from her own life before, but this has touched a nerve.

'Oh, for goodness' sake!' Sadie draws herself up as everyone stares at her. She's determined to regain her former good spirits, to stop being so over-sensitive and to move the game along now. 'Come on, then, who's going to go first? The answer must be here somewhere.' She catches Joe's eye. 'Right, Colonel Otter, now tell me . . .'

The group fires questions and answers across the table for a few minutes. Sadie suspects Genevieve at first, and then Everett. Zach acts as though he suspects her. Joe accuses Nazleen, who in turn accuses Zach. Apart from Mrs Shrew, they're all smiling, all making an effort . . . But somehow it still isn't enough, and eventually the questions tail off again. Sadie's gaze rises to the portrait hanging at the head of the table, and she has the uncomfortable sensation that the stern man is glaring back down at her, rigid with disapproval.

'It's all red herrings, anyway,' Everett grumbles, leaning back in his chair. 'They won't give us all the information until tomorrow morning, will they? They can't have the game solved before breakfast, that would never do.'

'Oh,' Sadie says, strangely comforted by this thought. 'I suppose that's true.'

On her other side, Zach gives a heavy sigh. 'I'm sure I've almost got it. If I could just work out who ...'

While the waiter clears their plates, Sadie drains her water glass and refills it, vowing not to drink any more wine. She has an odd, hollow feeling in her head, and a prickling sensation that the unseen clue-writer knows too much about her. If that were true and they thought poorly of her, why would they have hired her? They wouldn't. She's being ridiculous. The waiter bustles out of the room, but he quickly returns with the dessert trolley, and all eyes swivel to the elegant glass dishes.

'Tropical fruit pavlova,' Nazleen murmurs.

Sadie wishes it was something simpler – what's wrong with plain English strawberries and cream? The waiter sets down her bowl in front of her, and her throat closes; a peeled lychee, resembling nothing more than a ghostly eyeball, stares back at her from its bed of meringue. Her stomach churns, and she can't tell whether it's nausea or panic, but in that brief, clammy moment she's seized by the overwhelming conviction that someone *has* been watching her ...

She shoves her chair back, desperate to get away from the table, away from these strangers. She thinks she might faint if she stands up, but she lurches to her feet anyway.

'Are you okay?' Nazleen half-stands, but Sadie composes herself and gestures for Nazleen to sit down again.

'Yeah, I'm just ...' Sadie tries to keep her body language calm as she heads towards the door; she's a little unwell, that's all, and she can't bear any fuss. 'I just need some fresh air. Just give me a few minutes.'

It's much cooler in the hall.

She stands in front of a huge gilt-framed mirror, resting her fingertips on the polished wood of the table beneath it, and slowly her heart rate settles and the panic-inducing flashes of heat and cold on her skin ease. Perhaps it was something she ate. Perhaps it was just too warm in the dining room. She studies her reflection and gives herself a rueful grin: fancy seeing eyeballs in her pudding, how embarrassing. She feels well enough to go back and join the group now, but she's struck with the idea of sending Wendy a quick text about this – it'll make her laugh.

A clattering of pans somewhere at the back of the house jolts her into action – she's supposed to be a sophisticated dinner guest, she doesn't want to be caught lurking out here, pulling faces in the mirror. She hurries up the stairs, relieved to have a clear head again, but when she reaches her bedroom, she discovers that, just like Genevieve's phone, hers has no reception.

Oh, well. The humorous text to Wendy will have to wait.

Back out on the corridor, Sadie eyes up the other bedroom doors. She's curious about her fellow guests. She's learnt all sorts of details about their game characters, but next to nothing about them as real people, and the chances are, she'll never see them again after this weekend. She'll probably never stay in such a grand house again, either. In a couple of days' time, she'll be slumped on the sofa in her flat, browsing uninspiring job adverts and waiting for that big-break phone call from Wendy that never comes. But tonight, she has a chance to explore this mansion, and to peek into the lives of the strangers she's sharing it with.

It's not spying. It's just harmless curiosity. A quick look into their bedrooms, that's all, and then she'll re-join the dinner party downstairs.

The first room is clearly Nazleen's. Two long green dresses are draped over the bed, and the dressing table is scattered with creams and make-up. A small, framed wedding photo sits rather endearingly on the bedside table, and Sadie smiles to see a younger-looking Nazleen arm in arm with her red-haired wife. She closes the door again gently.

The room on the other side of Sadie's own is blatantly Mrs Shrew's. Deep blue items are still folded neatly in the open suitcase, and a feather brooch lies discarded on the bedside table. No photographs in this room; nothing particularly personal at all. A faint floral scent hangs in the air, and Sadie closes the door softly and moves on to the next room.

This one's owner is harder to identify. The suitcase is closed, so Sadie tiptoes across the layered rugs and lifts the lid. An array of sickly yellow items brings a faint smile to her face – poor Joe. He'd have suited a darker colour better – racing green perhaps, or a navy blue. A pair of trainers and a running kit are tucked in at one end of the case, and she smiles at his optimism – presumably planning a run before breakfast tomorrow, despite the freezing weather and the excesses of tonight.

After Joe's room comes a large, old-fashioned and fully tiled bathroom, and beyond that is a door set into the end wall of the corridor. Sadie pulls this open and peers up a rising spiral staircase. This must be inside the tower. She glances at her watch and hesitates; it's tempting. But if she doesn't return to the others soon, one of them is bound to come up looking for her, and she'd rather not be caught prying. The door falls shut with a clunk.

She moves more quickly as she works her way back down the corridor. The first bedroom is less luxuriously furnished than the others. Thinner curtains, a single bed, a slinky red dress puddled on the floor. Poor Genevieve has been given a lower grade of room, it seems. Perhaps because she was a last-minute hire.

Another, rather chilly, bathroom, and then a room with no vintage suitcase in sight, just a sports bag dumped by the bed. Sadie frowns and then her brow clears; this may well be Zach's room – he of the 'nearly didn't come', couldn't-be-bothered-to-dress-up attitude. She closes the door softly and moves along to the last room on this side of the staircase.

And yes, her hunch about Zach's bedroom was right, because this one clearly belongs to Everett. Purple fabric bulges from the open suitcase, and she spots an invitation card poking out from among the clothes. She can't resist; she tiptoes across the room and draws the card out to read the personal message in its loopy blue handwriting. *Hendrik will appreciate your support.* She pulls a face and slides the card back under a soft mauve sweater. Perhaps Hendrik is the owner of the murder mystery company. She can see how such a message would have appealed to Everett's sense of self-importance.

Out on the landing again, a faint thud makes her glance beyond the staircase to the opposite end of the corridor – the fire-damaged end, as she thinks of it. Did someone follow her up here? Suddenly, she feels acutely aware of the house around her. So many rooms. So many nooks and corners and potential hiding places ... The hairs on her arms rise, and before she can tear her gaze from the double row of identical doors, an odd yelping sound comes from behind one them, like a laugh morphing into a cry.

She races for the stairs, hurtling down them, almost slipping in her heels before she reaches the bottom, only just saving herself in time.

As before, the hall is deserted. She stands at its centre, trying to catch her breath, and when she stares, wide-eyed, back up the staircase, there's nothing to be seen. No ghost, no sinister shadowy figure ... *What on earth was I thinking?* A rumble of conversation drifts from the dining room, dishes clank in the kitchen, and she presses her hand against her chest and waits for her heart rate to settle.

It was probably an animal, that's all. A fox, maybe, or a bird, that found a route into the once-abandoned house and still returns to scavenge now. She draws herself up, trying to summon her former confidence, her sense of amused appreciation at finding herself in this privileged situation. But as she reaches for the dining-room door handle, she glances over her shoulder at the door of the dusty study that she and Nazleen discovered earlier. She's as sure as she can be that it was shut when she went upstairs. And now it's ajar.

Beth

Jonas may have given me a new reason to feel happy at Raven Hall, but I never saw him alone – Nina and I did almost everything together. As the summer holidays drew to an end, Jonas asked me again whether I'd be joining him at the high school in September, and I felt embarrassed that I couldn't give him a definite answer. The prospect of being at the same school appealed to me, although I'd be in the year below him, so I probably wouldn't see him all that much. I asked Nina if she knew what the plan was, but she merely shrugged and suggested we ask her parents that evening.

It seemed Leonora and Markus hadn't given any thought to my ongoing education either, but they quickly came up with a suggestion.

'Not the local high school, no,' Leonora said, 'but let's go and look at this other place.' She glanced at Nina. 'Perhaps you both might like to try it there.'

Nina was surprisingly agreeable, and three weeks later we were both enrolled at a small and very welcoming private school. The other girls there were friendly, and I hit it off with my new violin tutor straight away. The only downside was the school was miles from Raven Hall. We left in a taxi early in the morning and got home late, but Nina was cheerful about it, so I was determined to be happy too.

At first, I fretted every time money was mentioned at school – why were Leonora and Markus insisting on paying for my education, and what would happen if they stopped? I still felt I had to be careful not to antagonise Nina. Not that she ever referred to the 'game' again or said anything pointed, but I knew that if she asked her parents to send me away, they would – they'd always put her first, and quite rightly, too. So, I stayed alert for any sign that the family might be preparing to send me back to the children's home. But as the months passed, and my school life grew more absorbing, I began to relax.

Caroline paid me a short visit in the October, staying for barely an hour, during which time we made polite conversation in the drawing room and I ate a lot of biscuits to fill the awkward silences. She said she'd see me again before Christmas, but in the end, she sent a parcel and her apologies – she'd been assigned work in South America for six weeks. Eventually, at the end of January, she made a second visit to check on my welfare.

'You seem very settled,' she said.

She'd hardly been in the house two minutes. Leonora, Markus and Nina had retreated promptly, leaving us to chat privately by the fire that crackled in the black marble fireplace, a tea tray placed on the coffee table between us. I scrutinised her expression, sensing that she was, more than anything, relieved that I was no longer her problem. I was tempted to make a snide retort. *Yes, how convenient for you, Aunt Caroline.* But as ever, I masked my resentment of her.

'They're nice people,' I said. 'It does feel like home now, I have to admit.'

'Hm.' She looked as though she might say something disparaging, but thought better of it. 'Well, that's good. It all worked out for the best, then.'

She reached forward for her teacup, and there was something about her profile – the line of her jaw, the lowering of her eyelashes – that reminded me suddenly, quite overwhelmingly, of my mother, her sister. Raven Hall had gradually softened my grief, like a layer of new life growing over a raw tree stump. Caroline's unwelcome presence ripped that protective layer away and reminded me forcefully of the life I'd lost. In that moment, I hated her for it. I'd rather have been left completely alone in the world, I thought, than have *her* as my aunt.

I grabbed my own teacup and made an effort to bring my emotions under control. Caroline was grieving too, I reminded myself. Although she'd never been particularly interested in my brother and me, I'd seen photos of her and my mum growing up together – they must have been close at some point.

'You've spilt tea on your skirt.' She eyed me sternly. 'I do hope you're behaving yourself here, Beth. The last thing I need is to hear they don't want you anymore.'

Heat rose to my cheeks, but I met her gaze without flinching.

'They seem to like me well enough. They say I'm part of the family now.'

It was Caroline who looked away, then, although whether her conscience pricked her or she was merely growing bored, I couldn't tell. I waved her off soon afterwards, but the weight of her words added to the usual pressure I'd grown used to: I was still an outsider. I had to be on my best behaviour, all the time.

I'd been living at Raven Hall for nine months when something happened that changed my perception of my position there. It came about because Nina got a part in the school play, and her rehearsals went on well into the evening as the performance night drew closer. Leonora and Markus took pity on me and offered to send two taxis for us, just for those few dates. So I was back at Raven Hall by late afternoon, without Nina, when Jonas knocked on the door.

We strolled around the lake, talking about everything and nothing. I glanced sideways at him frequently, wondering what was going through his mind; wondering whether he might tell me again that he liked me; wondering whether I should tell him that I liked him. A short way past the old tree stump, he came to a sudden halt by a little stone beach, and I carried on for a couple of steps before swinging around to face him.

'What?'

'Let's swim.'

I laughed. 'No way, Jonas. It's April. It'll be freezing.'

He gestured at his short-sleeved T-shirt. 'It's fine. Practically summer.'

'You're crazy.' But I followed him down to the water's edge, and I watched him undress, my pulse jumping.

'Come on, scaredy-cat,' he said, and he plunged into the green-black water, splashing wildly, yelling at the shock of it. My heart raced. Could I bear it? But could I bear not to join him? Quickly, I tugged off my school skirt and jumper, and I took a running leap.

I was swallowed into a different world. I hung there, staring sightlessly into the water, unable to move. No air in my lungs, no gentle spring sunshine on my skin, no background chirrup and rustle of life. I waited for something to happen as the tightness in my chest grew.

'Beth!' Jonas was shaking me, and suddenly the sky had returned, and I could breathe again. 'Bloody hell, are you okay?'

I made a supreme effort to move my fingers, my arms, my legs, and I felt my blood start moving again.

'I hate you,' I said to him. And then I laughed. 'I *told* you it was too cold.' I kicked away from him and felt warmth flood back into my body as I swam clumsily further away from the shore and then back again.

We clambered out, teeth chattering, and Jonas' face was unusually serious. He insisted on me replacing my own soaked blouse with his dry T-shirt, turning away as I made the switch. Then he wrapped his arms around me.

'I admit,' he said, 'that was maybe a bit stupid of me.'

And then we were kissing, just like that. As if it was the most natural ending to our first swim of the season. As if it was the most natural thing in the world.

Later that evening, when Nina came home, she tapped on my bedroom door. I was already in my pyjamas, sitting in my bed. She came in full of gossip about the rehearsal, her costume, the make-up she was planning to wear. It took her several minutes to ask me how my afternoon alone had been.

I hesitated, and it was in that fraction of a second that I realised – I *wasn't* dependent on Nina for my happiness; I didn't *need* her approval on everything I did. I was fifteen now, and the adult world was within touching distance. Suddenly, I knew I had a future ahead of me, with or without the support of the family at Raven Hall.

'Oh, Jonas called round,' I said, 'so we just went for a walk around the lake.'

Nina stilled. 'And?'

I pulled a face. 'And nothing.'

She went off to her own bedroom soon after that – to her round Rapunzel room in her fairy-tale tower. But as she passed my empty laundry basket on her way out, she glanced into it – so fleetingly, it wouldn't have registered if I hadn't had a guilty conscience.

I waited until the next morning – until the last minute, as our taxi was turning on to the driveway and heading towards us – to scurry back up to my room, claiming I'd forgotten my maths homework. I snatched my damp clothes from under my mattress and dropped them into the laundry basket, hoping the daily cleaner wouldn't comment on their state. I'd already washed Jonas' T-shirt by hand in the bathroom next door and dried it on my bedroom radiator. I sat in the taxi and plotted how soon I could return his T-shirt and see him again.

I did feel guilty about keeping a secret from Nina, when up until now we'd shared everything, but I also felt ... powerful. Independent. Strong. For the first time in my life.

Unfortunately, that feeling didn't last. Events at Raven Hall had no regard for my blossoming love life. It was only a few weeks later, on a Saturday, when I was skipping into the house after a brief, secret rendezvous with Jonas, that Leonora called me into the drawing room.

'Oh, Beth,' she said. 'There you are. I'm afraid I need to ask you a favour.'

I hovered in the doorway, my heart sinking. 'Yes?'

Her gaze ran over my hair and down to my new sandals, and I stiffened – had I failed to straighten my clothes after kissing Jonas so passionately just now? How much did Leonora know? But I discovered her mind was on another subject entirely.

'Markus' father has announced a surprise visit, Beth. He'll be here in a few hours. And poor old Nina's feeling unwell again, and – well, now that he's met you it would be so hard to explain, anyway, and ... Beth, we need you to play the game again.'

Sadie

Sadie is ridiculously relieved to find the other guests still sitting around the dining table as if nothing has happened. Nothing *has* happened, she reminds herself sternly. It's an old, creaky house; you have to expect odd noises now and then. She returns to her seat, and Nazleen breaks off mid-sentence to ask her if she's feeling better. Sadie nods briskly, and as she picks up her spoon, Zach leans closer.

'You missed the speech about the evening's clues being at an end,' he murmurs.

'Uh-huh.' Sadie pushes her lychee aside and scoops up a spoonful of mango and cream.

'And now we're getting the legend of Raven Hall,' he says. 'It's very rich, isn't it?'

It takes Sadie a moment to realise his second statement refers to her pudding. She nods and sets her spoon back down again.

'Ah, perfect timing,' Nazleen says. 'Here comes the coffee.'

The trolley clatters and clanks as the waiter wheels it into the room, and the rich aroma lifts Sadie's mood instantly. She sits up straighter, admiring the tall coffee jugs and the dainty china cups and saucers. The waiter turns and nods stiffly at the photographer, like a prearranged signal, and the photographer approaches Nazleen discreetly and dips her head. She murmurs something about the roads icing over, and Nazleen waves a gracious hand.

'Of course,' Nazleen says to her. 'I'll take it from here.'

As the two staff members hurry away, Nazleen stands and pours coffee for all of them. Sadie declines cream, but she drops a granular brown sugar cube into her cup; she doesn't normally take sugar, but this evening, she feels a need for it.

'So,' Nazleen says, taking her seat again. 'Yes. The legend of Raven Hall. Let me begin by asking you, ladies and gentlemen – have you ever felt desperately, horribly, painfully *lonely*?'

The gentle noises of the room – clinks of spoons against china, soft coughs, slurps of coffee and murmurs of appreciation – all fade to silence. Sadie focuses on the dainty handle of the espresso cup in front of her, sensing that the others, too, are avoiding eye contact. She curls her fingers around the cup, using the heat from the china to drive away the ache she feels from missing her mother. When Nazleen speaks again, her voice is lower, as if she knows for certain she has their full attention.

'Well, pity the poor spirit in my tale, then. It's just a shadow now, a faint shimmer in the corner of your eye, a haze of memories and longing and loneliness . . . but it's real.'

Sadie lifts her gaze to Nazleen. Their hostess has a printed sheet of text in front of her, but she doesn't appear to be reading directly from it; she must have rehearsed this thoroughly. Sadie tries to focus on the professionalism of the delivery, rather than the pathos of the story. But despite her determination to remember this is all just part of a game, she leans forwards over the table, willing Nazleen to continue, wanting to know more about this supposed ghost.

'This poor spirit is all that's left,' Nazleen says softly, 'of a once-happy family that lived here at Raven Hall a long time ago. But betrayal struck at the very heart of the family, and it was torn apart, ripped apart . . .'

Sadie holds her breath. How much truth is behind this tale? Does it relate to the reason the house was abandoned in the late 1980s?

Nazleen gestures towards the curtained windows. 'If you take a stroll around the lake here, around Avermere, you might just glimpse this spirit. But only ever at dusk, in those eerie few minutes when the sun is slipping behind the horizon and the world is shifting into darkness. That's when it appears.' Her voice grows louder. 'It rises out of the lake, out of Avermere. And it drifts up to Raven Hall, slowly, slowly. And it presses itself against the windows, like a breath of mist against the cold glass, peering in with its hollow eyes, peering . . . peering . . . desperate for one last glimpse of its lost, destroyed family . . .'

Sadie's heart races. And then what happens? Is the ghost inside the house now? Roaming around upstairs, watching guests explore where they shouldn't?

'But,' Nazleen says sharply, 'here it meets the ultimate

betrayal. Raven Hall refuses our poor spirit entry. No matter how desperately it scratches at the windows, rattles the letter box, moans down the chimneys ... Raven Hall is heartless; it won't let our spirit in. And so it continues, night after night, rising at dusk, roaming around the stone walls, searching, searching for a crack or a gap it can enter through – listen!'

Sadie strains her ears, certain that the other guests must be doing the same, but the noise that erupts isn't outside the window; it's across the table. Mrs Shrew is stifling a cough – or could it be a sob? – with her napkin.

Joe shoves his chair backwards sharply. 'Okay, that's enough!' He makes a visible effort to compose himself. 'I think we've heard enough for one night, thank you. Shall we take our coffees through to the drawing room, and—' He glances at Nazleen, and his expression slides from apology to concern. 'Are you okay?'

Nazleen doesn't look okay; if anything, she looks more distressed than Mrs Shrew. For a moment, Sadie wonders if Joe's interruption has offended her, but then Nazleen moans quietly and curls forward over the table, until strands of her dark hair rest in her almost-empty dessert bowl. Joe starts towards her, and Sadie and Everett both rise to join him, but Nazleen straightens again and waves them away.

'I'm so sorry.' Nazleen sounds embarrassed. 'I actually don't feel very well at all. I think I'll go up to my room, if you don't mind.' She stands without help, but she looks a little hunched as she walks to the door, as if she's in pain. Before she leaves the room, she turns back to them with a strained smile. 'Please, do take your coffees through and sit by the fire. Breakfast at eight, don't forget. I'll see you in the morning.'

The six guests gaze wide-eyed at one another as Nazleen's footsteps fade up the stairs. Then Sadie grabs her coffee cup and indicates the door.

'Shall we?'

Zach accompanies her across the hall and into the drawing room. Everett shuffles close behind, and Sadie doesn't begrudge him grabbing the armchair nearest the fire. He's certainly the oldest in the group, and he's looking pretty tired. Mrs Shrew comes in soon afterwards, and she heads to the far corner of the room where she perches on a chaise longue as if she doesn't plan on staying for very long.

'It was probably the pudding,' Zach says to Sadie in a low tone. 'Don't you think? Nazleen ate all of hers. It was very rich, I didn't eat all mine . . . '

Sadie pulls a non-committal face; she's watching the door, straining her ears for the other two guests. Where have Joe and Genevieve got to? She feels unsettled without Nazleen's presence, as if the whole evening might unravel now that their hostess has been taken ill.

A minute later, Joe makes his entrance. He carries a glass of water, and he takes it straight to Mrs Shrew. Zach spots a deck of cards on one of the many occasional tables, and he asks Sadie if she wants a game, but she shakes her head.

'I might just sit for a bit,' she says, her hand drifting to her abdomen. 'And let my food settle.' Her stomach feels delicate again, and she's growing increasingly convinced that something she's eaten tonight has disagreed with her. Each time the nausea stirs, she thinks uneasily of the storyline of the game – the toxic substance that supposedly killed their host. She sinks on to a velvet armchair and wonders how soon she can head up to bed.

Finally, Genevieve appears in the doorway, but she looks upset – her face is pale, her dark eyes enormous. She clutches a long fur coat against her chest, and she doesn't come any further into the room. Sadie glances at Joe – did he say something to her out there to distress her? But Joe looks just as surprised and concerned as the rest of them. Genevieve clutches the fur coat tighter against herself, and she rushes to give her own explanation.

'I don't feel very well either, I'm afraid. I'm, er, I might go outside and get some fresh air.'

Zach sounds triumphant. 'I *told* you it was the pudding. She ate a lot of hers too.' The others ignore him.

'Do you want me to come with you?' Sadie asks, but she's relieved when Genevieve shakes her head.

'No, no.' Genevieve forces a smile. 'I'll be fine. It's freezing out there, you stay indoors.'

They listen as her heels clack away down the hall and the front door slams.

'And then there were five . . .' Zach says.

'Shut up, Zach.' Sadie hurries to the window and pulls back the curtain, and she watches Genevieve, now wearing the coat, march away – across the little pool of light on the gravel and into the darkness. Her further progress is indicated only by a thin beam of white light from the torch on her phone. Behind Sadie, Joe clears his throat, and he joins her at the window, peering over her shoulder just as Genevieve's phone light flicks off and a tiny orange glow appears.

'She's on the dock,' he says. 'A quick cigarette and she'll be straight back in, don't worry. It's bitter out there.'

Sadie lets the curtain fall back. 'I'm not worried. Who says I was worried?'

Joe makes a placatory gesture. 'I just meant . . . '

Sadie turns away, and she sees that Zach is shaking Everett's arm.

'Dad? Dad!'

Everett blinks awake and mumbles a denial.

'Everyone's feeling ill, Dad,' Zach says, and he adds in a smaller voice, 'Even me.'

Everett sits forward and glares at Sadie and Joe, as if it might be their fault. Sadie's tempted to suggest Zach's symptoms might be alcohol-related, but she bites her tongue.

'Well,' Everett says. 'Not vomiting? No? Milk of Magnesia, then, and sleep it off.' He eases back in his chair and pats his stomach through his purple waistcoat. 'Too much of the fine stuff.' He chuckles. 'It was worth it, though.'

Mrs Shrew rises without even glancing in Everett's direction.

'I shall retire to bed myself,' she says. 'And hope we all feel better in the morning.'

She waves away Joe's offer of help and leaves the room. Sadie looks at her remaining three companions, and a sudden thought makes her return to the window.

'Both the cars are gone,' she says.

'What?' snaps Everett. 'Has that young filly driven off and left us?'

'Not Genevieve,' Sadie says. 'They were already gone when she went out.'

Joe's tone is tense. 'They must have been the staff's cars. The chef and the waiter and the photographer – they all went home a while ago, didn't they?'

Sadie fails to suppress a swell of panic. The seven of them arrived in chauffeur-driven luxury. Now they're stuck out here, in the middle of nowhere, with no phone signal, no transport, and they're all feeling unwell ... And then her heart lurches with a greater shock and she leans closer to the glass, searching for, and failing to find, either a white light or an orange glow.

'Where's Genevieve?'

Beth

Leonora gave me a different dress to put on for Markus' father's second visit – it was still blue, but in a more adult style, so it was a little more comfortable to wear. I'd grown taller since I'd moved to Raven Hall, and I was slimmer and fitter from all the outdoor exercise I'd had. I studied my reflection in the big cheval mirror in my bedroom, and my mind churned with questions.

The details didn't make sense; I must be missing something. I didn't mind helping Leonora and Markus out – I didn't even mind too much if Nina's grandfather shouted at me again – I just couldn't understand the way it had all happened.

Surely Nina falling ill *again*, just before her grandfather's visit, was a remarkable coincidence? But I couldn't believe she was faking it – certainly not last time, when she'd looked so washed-out and weak. Was it psychological – was she so terrified of meeting her grandfather, it brought on physical symptoms? But, despite her mother's apparent fear of germs, Nina was one of the toughest, bravest people I knew.

Besides which, since Markus' father now believed *I* was Nina, of course it made sense for me to play her again for this second visit. There was no alternative – Nina could hardly go skipping in and claim to be the same child he first met ten months ago. So, perhaps Nina's current illness really was just a coincidence. I frowned at my reflection. I just didn't know. But something didn't feel right.

'I think … yes, I think we'll plait your hair again,' Leonora said, eyeing me critically in the drawing room. 'I'm sure he won't stay long, Beth. It'll all be over soon.'

I closed my eyes as she tugged the brush through my hair, and this time I thought not about my parents, but about Jonas.

Jonas was in favour of us breaking the news to Nina that we were an item, but I'd asked him to wait. I worried that Nina would be hurt, and I felt guilty that my friendship with her had loosened in the last few weeks, while I was sneaking around meeting Jonas in private. What if Nina was angry? What if she asked her parents to send me away from Raven Hall?

A little voice whispered in my head: *They can't very well send me away now – what if Nina's grandfather came back for another visit?* But Leonora's heavy brushstrokes reminded me of how determined she was; she'd find a way around any obstacle, I knew it. I couldn't trust in my own importance. I had to keep Nina – and Leonora – happy.

'There,' Leonora said, standing back. 'Perfect.'

I felt detached from my surroundings as I sat in the drawing room with Leonora and Markus, waiting for Markus' father to arrive. My thoughts meandered up two flights of stairs to the turret room, where Nina lay. I should have rushed up to see her when Leonora told me she was ill, but instead I'd spent too long staring at my own reflection in that stupid mirror, puzzling over another odd aspect of this game. *Why the plaits?* Nina never wore plaits. I considered asking the question aloud, but thought better of it.

'He's here,' Leonora said tightly, from her position at the window. I smoothed down my skirt. I would do this calmly and properly, for Leonora and Markus' sake, and for Nina's.

This time, when Leonora tried to hold me back in the hall, Markus' father snapped at her: 'Let the girl come in with us.'

I followed him into the drawing room and took a seat next to Markus on the sofa. The two men ignored me for the first few minutes, and I didn't pay too much attention to their conversation. Markus' father grumbled about wanting Markus to help him run his business in the States, but I knew Markus would never do it – Leonora and Markus would never agree to leave Raven Hall. And I, as Nina, was ready to back up that sentiment.

Leonora brought in the tea tray more promptly than on the last visit, and once we'd finished our tea and cake, Markus' father turned to me.

'So, Nina, will you humour an old man and play for me again today?'

I'd never shared Nina's love of drama lessons at school, but I felt a strange calmness slide through my veins as I drew the role of Nina over myself this time, as if I was stepping inside her skin. I knew Nina inside-out – she was almost a sister to me now, and in that moment, I almost believed I *was* her.

'Of course,' I said, rising to take my violin from Leonora's trembling hands. 'I'd be happy to.'

I played for him – much better this time, thanks to the months of teaching that Markus and Leonora kindly paid for at my school. This time, I didn't turn my back on him, and he smiled at me through his tears. When I finished, I sat down next to him, and his expression seemed genuinely apologetic.

'I'm sorry I raised my voice at you last time.' He patted my hand awkwardly. 'Your playing brings back so many memories, I may have become a little . . .'

'Emotional?' I met his gaze straight on.

He blinked. 'Well, that's a strong word, but—'

I laughed then, and he gave me a puzzled smile in return. He wasn't scary at all, I realised. He just didn't know how to deal with his feelings. I felt suddenly, surprisingly, sorry for him, and for the trick we were playing on him.

'So,' he said, clearing his throat, 'have you thought any more about my offer?'

In my peripheral vision, I saw Leonora reach for Markus' hand; their faces were tense. I almost smiled at how easy it would be to say yes – *Yes, please, Grandfather, take me back to America with you.* Instead, I frowned gently.

'I appreciate the offer,' I said. 'I really do. But you know – my life is here, my friends are here, I have exams at school next year . . .'

He bowed his head. 'I understand. But,' when he looked up again his eyes were glittering fiercely, 'I won't stop asking you.'

I smiled. 'Okay. Till next time, then.'

After his chauffeur had driven him away, Leonora and Markus seemed unnerved, casting me odd, anxious looks.

'Did I do all right?' I asked, suddenly worried I'd messed it up.

Leonora said nothing, merely stared at me, but Markus pulled himself together and patted me on the back.

'You were great,' he said. 'You kept him happy; you clearly know how to handle him.' As he headed for the door, he gave Leonora a pointed look that I was unable to decipher. She turned away. I unravelled my plaits with my fingers and headed up to see Nina.

'You don't need to hide it,' Nina said.

I was pouring her a fresh glass of water from a jug on her bedside table, and the handle slipped, sloshing liquid on to the wooden surface. I hurried to dry it with a tissue, hoping my cheeks weren't growing as red as they felt. Was she talking about her grandfather's visit or about Jonas?

'Your dress,' she said sadly. 'And your hair's all wavy. Did Mum plait it again? What was he like?'

I sank back on to her bed. 'You know I couldn't say no, don't you? I mean, after doing it last time . . .' I sighed. 'He was here less than an hour. He's – he's grumpy, I suppose, but underneath that, he's quite nice, I think. He goes back to the States tomorrow.'

Her dark eyes were enormous. 'Did he like you?'

'Why do they do it, Nina?' I searched her gaze, desperate to find an answer. 'Why didn't they just tell him the first time that you were ill? It's just . . . I don't understand . . .'

A tear slipped down her cheek. 'I don't know. How am I ever going to meet him now, if he thinks you're me? My own grandfather . . . '

My heart squeezed with sympathy, and I leant forward and hugged her, despite the risk of germs.

'I'm sorry,' I said. 'I'm so sorry about everything.'

But she didn't reply to that. She merely asked me to leave, so she could go back to sleep.

Remembering the cautious air of celebration after Markus' father's last visit, I went back downstairs half-expecting to find Leonora and Markus drinking wine, but they were nowhere to be seen. I carried Nina's empty water jug into the kitchen and set it down next to a couple of mugs by the sink. I was already thinking of Jonas again, wondering whether I might ring him at his mum's B&B – I felt bad for thinking it, but Nina's illness was an ideal opportunity for Jonas and me to spend a whole evening alone together. I don't know what made me notice the mugs – perhaps the novelty of the faint chocolate aroma, when we hadn't drunk hot chocolate since the end of the winter. I almost moved away, and then I leant back over them.

One mug was the standard Raven Hall china, and the other was Nina's own – a custom-made, satisfyingly chunky mug with her name painted on. Both had the usual thick chocolate dregs at the bottom. But Nina's held an extra layer – a thin, oily layer that didn't look like anything I'd ever seen before. I picked up the mug tentatively and tilted it to the light, and my skin prickled. There was definitely something unusual in there. What on earth could it be?

Suddenly, it was as if the mug handle was burning my fingers. I set it down quickly and glanced behind me to the door. Had something been added to Nina's drink? Is this why she was sick? The idea was shocking, but the more I tried to come up with an alternative explanation, the faster my heart raced.

Poison.

I backed away from the sink and retreated up the stairs to my bedroom as quietly as I could. Who could I ask about this? Who could I go to for advice?

It would be appallingly disloyal to mention this to anyone outside of the family. And what might the repercussions be if I mentioned it to Leonora, or to Markus, or to Nina? What if I was wrong? They'd be hurt, offended – outraged, even. It didn't bear thinking about.

My only option was to keep it a secret.

I crawled into my bed and pulled the sheet and blanket over my head, and a single word rolled around and around in my mind.

Poison. Poison. Poison.

I thought back to earlier that morning when Raven Hall had felt like a safe place. Now, I wasn't so sure.

She spreads her meagre picnic around her on the grass and sighs. She spent all of last Saturday roaming around Avermere without managing to bump into the tall, kind-eyed horticulture student. It took her three hours to hitchhike to Raven Hall again this morning and, so far, her luck hasn't picked up.

Where is he?

There were several cars parked in front of the stable block again today, but she's never been good with car makes. She recognises the young doctor's Ford Capri – mink blue, he told her it was, once; his pride and joy – but other types are just a blur, and she couldn't begin to work out whether the student's car was here this morning. She imagines him at home in London instead – perhaps his long-haired girlfriend has gone to visit him there.

She's brought her sketchbook with her, and she tries to distract herself by drawing her view of the lake and its little island, but her heart's not in it. She closes the book with a snap. Then, just as she's packing away her uneaten food and preparing to leave, along he comes, striding down the trail with a long stick in his hand, like an overgrown schoolboy. She scrambles to her feet, heart booming.

'Aha!' he says. 'Hallo. I was hoping I might bump into you.' He eyes the flattened patch of grass and her crumpled clothes, and he narrows his eyes. 'You don't live out here, do you? In a little burrow by the lake, or something?'

She laughs, delighted. 'I wish I did.'

'I've got some tea, in a flask . . .' He pulls a face as he swings his rucksack from his shoulder. 'Sounds boring, I know, but . . .'

She shakes her head. 'It sounds lovely.'

They make themselves comfortable on the grass, and the student pulls out more than just a flask – he has a Tupperware container packed with perfectly ripe strawberries, and two generous slices of treacle tart wrapped in brown paper. She discovers she is hungry after all.

'They're from the garden,' he tells her as she bites into her first strawberry. 'At Raven Hall. They're good, aren't they?'

She closes her eyes and pretends to be savouring the taste while she squashes down memories of nurturing those strawberry plants with her mother, years before.

'They're gorgeous,' she manages to say at last. 'What's it like, then, studying horticulture in London?' What she really wants to ask him is: Doesn't your girlfriend mind you taking picnics out into the countryside to share with a girl you barely know? But she's worried what the answer might be – that he feels sorry for her, or that any old companion would do. If either of those are the case, then she'd rather not know.

He gives an exaggerated sigh, then grins at her. 'It's harder than people think, actually. I've just finished a load of exams, and there's never enough time to do what I want . . .'

'Isn't this what you want?'

'Well, yes, what I mean is – I feel guilty about doing nice things like this, when I should be . . .'

'Working?'

'Yeah . . .' He tosses a strawberry husk into the undergrowth.

'And my mum's not very well, so I feel like I should spend as much time with her as I can.'

'Oh,' she says. 'I'm sorry. My mum was ill too, for a long time.'

He squints at her, and then he sits up straight and gives her a concerned look. 'Do you mean . . .'

'She died, a few years ago. I—' She shakes her head, not sure what she wants to say. 'I miss her so much, every day.'

'Oh.' Tentatively, he reaches out and touches the back of her hand. 'I'm really sorry, if I'd known, I wouldn't have . . .'

'It's fine,' she says. 'It's just – I suppose, I might know a bit more how you feel. Than other people do, I mean. Luckier people.' She's thinking of the long-haired girlfriend in the orange crop top.

He nods slowly. 'We don't actually know what's wrong with my mum. The doctors can't work it out . . . She's a medical mystery.' He tries to smile. 'But they're trying different treatments. And, you know, we're lucky in other ways. Mustn't take stuff like this for granted.' He gestures at the tangled weeds behind them. 'When you think of what other people go through – did you know the poor family who lived at Raven Hall before? They had a daughter about your age—'

'No,' she says abruptly. 'I never knew them.'

They sit in silence for a minute, watching a swallowtail butterfly explore a patch of thistles.

'Well . . .' The student crumples his treacle tart paper into a ball and drops it back into his rucksack. 'You're right, we should talk about happier things before I have to get back. Did you meet up with your friend the other day?'

She stares at him, trying to get past the phrase 'before I have to get back'. Has he grown bored with her already? Is he missing his girlfriend? And what friend does he mean? Oh, of course – the young doctor.

'No, I didn't bother seeing him in the end,' she says. She drains her tea and hands the cup back to him. 'I need to get going myself, actually.'

They don't speak as they gather their belongings together and brush crumbs from their clothes, but once they're ready to go their separate ways, the man stretches out his hand.

'I'm Markus, by the way,' he says. 'It was nice talking to you, and thanks, you know, for understanding about my mum.'

She nods. 'I'm . . .' But the tip of her tongue hesitates on the roof of her mouth as his earlier words rattle through her head: the poor family who lived at Raven Hall before . . . She lifts her chin. 'Lara,' she says. 'I'm Lara. I'll look out for you again next weekend.'

Beth

My thoughts were haunted by that oily gleam in Nina's hot chocolate mug.

For days, I tried to find an innocent explanation. I scoured the pantry for vitamins or medicines that might account for it, with no success. When the others were occupied elsewhere in the house, I experimented furtively with marshmallows and other sweet ingredients, attempting to dissolve them in boiling water, then letting them cool. But I failed to recreate the strange-looking, shiny layer.

I kept replaying the night before Nina's grandfather's first visit: Markus popping his head into the treehouse and saying, *'Come on, sleepyheads . . . Mum's making you hot chocolate to warm you up . . .'*

Twice, Nina had fallen ill just before her grandfather's visits, and each time she'd drunk hot chocolate in the hours beforehand. Hot chocolate that, on the second occasion, looked to have had something unusual added to it. Hot chocolate that, on the first occasion at least, Leonora had made for her.

But why on earth would Leonora want to poison her own daughter?

I withdrew into myself, telling Jonas I needed space, telling Nina I needed to concentrate on my schoolwork. I sat in my bedroom for hours, flicking through prospectuses for residential apprenticeship schemes, wondering whether I should apply for one the following year, to give me an escape route from Raven Hall. When I wasn't worrying about poison, I was brooding on my lost family, wondering what my brother, Ricky, would be doing now if he was still alive. I longed to ask my parents for advice. I resented the fact that I didn't have Ricky here as a role model.

Meanwhile, Nina bounced back to full health, and the rest of my life rumbled along in its normal routine, and as the weeks passed, my anxiety about the possibility of poison eased, and my melancholy mood gradually lifted. I stayed alert for any recurrence of illness in Nina, or any sign of odd behaviour in Leonora, but nothing happened to raise my suspicions. Eventually, I decided I might have been mistaken. Perhaps I hadn't seen anything strange in the mug after all.

By the time Nina's birthday came around in June, I'd made a conscious decision to put the whole strange episode out of my mind. If anything, the memory of my initial reaction to it made me feel guilty – how could I have leapt to such a dreadful conclusion about Leonora, when she was never anything but kind to both me and Nina? As if to reinforce my guilt, Leonora and Markus took us to a West End show for Nina's birthday and showered both of us with all manner of treats and gifts.

Life seemed good again. The long summer holiday was fast approaching. And I felt secure enough in my position at Raven Hall to switch my focus back to trying to see more of Jonas.

But it was as difficult as ever to meet up with him alone during the holidays. Nina and I ate breakfast together, chose our daily activities together – we did almost everything together. Finally, at the dinner table one evening, Leonora reminded Nina that she had an optician's appointment the following day – miles away, over near Cambridge – and I sensed an opportunity. When I trudged down to the dining room for breakfast the following morning, I complained of a thumping headache.

'I think I might have to go back to bed,' I said. I kept my eyes narrowed, as if the bright sunlight streaming through the window was hurting my eyes. 'If that's all right with you? You don't need me to go with you today, do you?'

Leonora frowned and came over to feel my forehead. 'Have you been drinking enough water? Do you want some paracetamol?'

I told her I'd already taken some, and I plodded back upstairs with a guilty conscience. My head was fine, I'd taken nothing. I cracked open my bedroom window and got back into bed, waiting to hear them leave.

As soon as Leonora's car had disappeared down the driveway, I ran downstairs and phoned Jonas at the B&B. Then I strolled out to the kitchen garden and picked a bowlful of luscious strawberries, and I ate them out the front, sitting on the stone steps in the sunshine, revelling in having the whole house to myself while I waited for Jonas to arrive.

'Let's get away from this place,' Jonas said, before he'd even kissed me.

I pulled a face. 'I don't know. I'm supposed to be ill. I don't want them to come back and find me gone . . . '

'You can say you went for a walk to clear your head, can't you?' He hooked his fingers into mine and drew me closer, his smile widening. 'Come on, grab your bike and let's go into the village. I can introduce you to my mates, or we can go back to mine . . . '

'No.' Reluctantly, I pulled my hands from his. 'I can't. I'm not allowed . . . '

He sighed. 'Okay. So – what then? Are you going to invite me in? First time for everything.'

It took a moment for the significance of his words to sink in.

'You mean you've never been inside the house?'

He shrugged. 'Nope.'

'That's weird.'

'Well, yeah. But it's probably the least weird thing about this place, don't you think?' He searched my gaze. 'C'mon, Beth, what would *you* like to do? Don't you fancy getting away for a bit?'

'I . . . ' I shook my head. How could I tell him the truth? That I was scared to break the rules, frightened of what Leonora might say if she discovered I'd snuck off into the village as soon as her back was turned. 'Actually, I – my head doesn't feel that great . . . '

Jonas' gaze slid past me to the shadowy interior of the hall, and he took a step back. 'Okay. Well, it's up to you.'

'I'm sorry,' I said. 'I've wasted your time.'

'You know what I think?' His expression was tight. 'This isn't right. Not being allowed to go anywhere or see anyone. I think you should ring your Aunt Caroline and ask her to take you away from here, find somewhere more normal to live. That's what I think.'

'Wait.' I followed him down the steps and across the gravel to his bike. 'I know what you're saying, Jonas, but they're still nice people. I like it here. It's my home, now. So I have to follow their rules, you know? Does that make sense?'

He scowled. 'Yeah, I get it.'

'Look, why don't you come in? I'll make us a drink; we can sit in the garden . . .'

For a moment, I thought he might say yes. We leant towards each other, and we kissed with his bike jammed between us. But he'd already made up his mind.

'I'm just not sure I can keep doing this.' He frowned down at his handlebars. 'You won't tell Nina about us. You're not allowed to come round to my house. Every time I come up here, I've got to pretend we're just—' He bit back the rest of his sentence. 'It's not really working, is it?' He swung himself on to his saddle and put one foot on a pedal.

'But . . .' I said. 'You'll still come back, won't you? You'll come swimming with us?'

'I don't know, Beth.' He squinted at me. 'Just ring me, okay? If anything happens. If you need me. For anything.'

I returned slowly to the top step and watched him cycle away until he was out of sight. Then I went back inside to find some painkillers with a sense of wounded irony – I really did have a headache now. I couldn't see a way of keeping everyone happy. Leonora, Markus, Nina, Jonas. And as much as I liked Jonas, I *had* to keep Nina and Leonora happy, if I didn't want to jeopardise my position at Raven Hall.

So, Nina and I swam without Jonas that summer, and whenever she grumbled about his absence, I tried to look innocent and changed the subject. And, unsurprisingly, Nina invented new ways of entertaining us. She decided she would throw a party for me at the end of the holiday, to belatedly celebrate the anniversary of my arrival at Raven Hall.

To my surprise, Leonora agreed to the plan, and it kept Nina and me busy for a couple of weeks. We drew up a guest list of school friends for Leonora's approval, and we baked a huge cake and ordered sparklers, and we arranged for an up-and-coming band from London to come and play in the garden. On the evening of the party, Jonas joined us for a while, and he pecked me on the cheek in front of the other guests, which made me blush. But when I looked for him a while later, hoping to grab a few minutes alone with him, he'd already set off on his bike for home.

September, and the new school year, came around quickly, and my sadness about the situation with Jonas was replaced with worries about coursework and exams. In the middle of October, Markus went off to Malaysia on a six-week diving trip, and not long after this, Leonora called Nina and me into the drawing room one evening with a glint of excitement in her eyes.

'I was thinking,' she said, 'now you're both getting older, maybe I should take you on a shopping trip. We could go into London next Saturday, have a day of trying on clothes – what do you say?'

Nina and I were thrilled. Up until now, Leonora had ordered all our clothes for us from a catalogue, but my jeans were becoming too short again, and I fancied something a little more elegant, anyway. In the end, not only did we go on a huge and successful shopping spree, I also got my hair cut at a posh salon, and Nina persuaded Leonora to let her have her ears pierced. I knew we were being spoilt, but there was no point resisting it, and both Nina and I were very pleased with the outcome: we felt much more grown-up.

It was only days later that Jonas paid us a surprise visit at Raven Hall. He greeted both Nina and me with equal friendliness, and he asked us casually – out of earshot of Leonora – whether we fancied sneaking out that weekend, to go to a party in the village with him. I kept my expression neutral, and he didn't stay long – he said he'd leave us to talk it over.

'Oh, go on,' I begged Nina, after we'd gone up to her turret bedroom to discuss it in private. 'What harm can it do? Your mum'll be none the wiser, and we'll have a great time.' I was already imagining myself wrapped in Jonas' arms, swaying to dreamy music, with Nina conveniently distracted by some other good-looking village boy.

But Nina gnawed at her fingernail. 'I just don't think we can when my dad's not here. If Mum *did* realise we were missing, and she was here all by herself . . . '

I flexed my fingers, frustrated. 'How's that different from both of them finding us missing? And she'd guess what we were doing, wouldn't she? It's hardly the crime of the century, is it? It's just a party.'

But Nina shook her head. 'If Dad was here, he'd come into the village to look for us, but Mum by herself ... She'd be distraught. I can't risk it.'

'Oh, for God's sake.' I glared at her. 'This is ridiculous. I'll go by myself, then.'

'You won't.' Her eyes glittered. 'You wouldn't dare.'

I wanted to cry with frustration. But I couldn't risk disobeying Nina. I could feel all my old insecurities returning: sliding along my skin, slipping into my pores and creeping around my body. I stomped away down the spiral staircase and slammed my own bedroom door behind me. I loved Nina like a sister, but sometimes I hated her too. I couldn't sneak out without her, in case she told Leonora. Despite my sometimes ambiguous feelings about Raven Hall, I still didn't want to be sent away.

We didn't go to the party.

I was still in a bad mood with Nina when Markus returned from his trip abroad. Nina and I stood side by side on the top step as Leonora hugged him on the gravel, and Markus laughed as he swung his suitcases from the car boot.

'These are twice as heavy as when I left, I've stuffed them with so many presents for you.'

But as Nina trotted down the steps and launched herself into his arms, his gaze slid over her head and landed on me, and his taken-aback expression made me feel acutely self-conscious. Had he forgotten I lived with them now? Or perhaps he hated my new look? I tucked my hair behind my ear and waited for Nina to let him go, and by the time he came up to greet me, his face was friendly again.

'How's things, Beth?' he said. 'You've both been growing up again, I see.'

I trailed after them – Leonora hanging on to one of his arms, Nina on the other – and I knew they all noticed how quiet I was at the welcome-home dinner that Leonora had prepared for him. But I didn't know how to hide this painful loneliness that gnawed at me in spite of the warm chatter around me, and as soon as I could, I slipped away and went to play my violin in my bedroom. I missed my parents and Ricky as if it was three weeks they'd been gone, instead of three years.

It was a sign of how much of an outsider I was feeling, that I even began to look forward to Caroline's dutiful Christmas visit. She might be cold and selfish, but at least she was my real family.

Sadie

'*Where's Genevieve?*' Sadie says again, this time more loudly, as if she might somehow have missed a reply in the hush of the drawing room. But Zach merely shakes his head, one hand pressed against his abdomen, while Everett blinks at her, bleary-eyed, from his armchair by the fire.

'What?' the old man mutters. 'What's the silly girl playing at?'

Joe joins Sadie at the window and he too peers into the darkness.

'She was right there,' Sadie says. 'She hasn't come back in – we'd have heard her.'

'She might have her back to us,' Joe says. 'Shielding her cigarette . . . ' But he heads for the door, and Sadie hurries after him. 'Let's call her in.'

They grab a couple of coats from the cloakroom and head outside, down the stone steps and across the gravel. Joe switches on his phone torch as he calls out Genevieve's name, and Sadie curses her lack of pockets, which made her leave her own phone upstairs. It's freezing out here, and despite the lamps either side of the front door, they're plunged into darkness before they're even halfway across the parking area. But Joe seems confident about his bearings and, sure enough, after hurrying down a gentle slope of grass by the light of his phone, they reach a little dock, nestled in among the reeds. At its far end, the lake gleams oily black in the feeble torchlight, and a small rowing boat scrapes gently against a wooden post as if inviting them to climb in. There's no sign of a young woman in a fur coat.

'Genevieve!' Sadie calls. And again, more frantically, 'Genevie-e-eve!' She's shivering, and she can hear the note of panic in her voice.

The only reply is the soft lapping of the lake water and the rustle of reeds.

Joe casts his thin beam of light around until it picks out a pale object on the wooden planks. A half-smoked cigarette, with bright crimson lipstick marks still on it. He swivels the light in every direction, but it doesn't penetrate the darkness far enough to make out more than reeds and grass and the cold reflection of the water.

Sadie nudges the cigarette butt with her toe. 'What shall we do?'

'Maybe,' Joe says slowly, 'she did go back inside, and we just didn't hear her.'

'Let's go and check,' Sadie says. 'I think I know which room she was given.' She tries to push away the memory of that unearthly cry from the other end of the corridor.

154

They dash back into the warmth of the house and try calling Genevieve from the hallway, with no success. Zach hovers in the drawing-room doorway looking concerned, but he has no helpful suggestions.

'Okay, I'll check down here,' Joe says. 'She might have come in the back door, maybe. Are you happy to check her bedroom?'

'Sure,' Sadie says, although she's far from thrilled at the prospect of making her way up those stairs again by herself. 'And what if she's not there?'

Joe's face creases with doubt. 'Well, we'll have to disturb Nazleen, I suppose. She's the company's representative, isn't she? I still can't believe they didn't reconnect the phone line . . . '

Sadie tries to look more confident than she feels. 'We'll find her. Just – shout if you find her first, okay?'

Joe starts trying doors on one side of the hall, and Sadie heads upstairs. The corridor is empty, as before; all the doors on either side are closed, except for one halfway down the smoke-damaged end. Before she can change her mind, she marches down to it and peers inside. It's a junk room: boxes are stacked high on the floor, and on the dark wood furniture. The walls are painted a fresh cream, but Sadie's fairly sure this is the room that had the blackening around its window in the photo, and when she sniffs the air, she detects a faint scent of soot. For a second, she imagines someone breathing, ducked down behind the boxes, watching her. She shakes her head and hurries out, closing the door behind her with a bang.

At the other end of the corridor, Genevieve's room is unoccupied. The red dress still lies puddled on the rug, and the curtains are partly open. Sadie crosses to the window and peers down into Raven Hall's walled back garden, but there's little to be seen beyond the weak yellow light from the rear windows downstairs. Faintly, she hears Joe calling, 'Genevie-e-eve!'

Sadie doesn't need to guess at Nazleen's room; she taps sharply on the door.

'Nazleen? I'm sorry.' Slowly, she turns the handle. 'But it's important. I'm coming in.'

Nazleen is already swinging her legs out of bed, fumbling with her dressing gown, looking frightened.

'Listen,' Sadie says, 'Genevieve went out for a cigarette and she ... we can't find her. We've looked for her outside, and we're hoping she came back in again, but ... '

Nazleen stares at her, wide-eyed. 'Well, where is she?'

'That's what I'm saying. We don't know.'

'Shit.' Nazleen stumbles to the dressing table and jabs at buttons on her phone. 'Still no signal. This bloody house ... ' She turns to Sadie with a hopeful expression. 'Maybe she's with one of the others?'

'Zach and his dad are downstairs, and so is Joe. They've no idea. It's only Mrs Shrew we haven't asked ... ' Sadie swings around. 'Come on.'

Nazleen hangs back in the corridor as Sadie raps loudly on Mrs Shrew's door, and if Nazleen wonders how Sadie knows which room to try, she doesn't show it.

'It's me,' Sadie calls out, her knuckles still resting on the painted wood. 'Sadie. Or Miss Lamb, whatever. I need to talk to you.' She turns the door handle slowly. 'I'm coming in.'

'What on *earth* do you think you're doing?'

Mrs Shrew is still fully dressed. She stands in the centre of the room, and her expression is furious.

'Mrs – uh.' Sadie remembers it isn't the woman's real name, and she feels unbalanced. 'Um, the young woman in red – Miss Mouse, you know? – we can't find her. She went outside for a cigarette and . . .'

Mrs Shrew's shoulders relax a fraction. 'Oh, is that all. There's no need to panic. She told me she was thinking of walking into the village and spending the night there. I suppose that's what she's done.'

'But—' Sadie stares at her. 'When did she say that?'

'When we were leaving the dining room. We spoke in the hall for a moment.'

'But why would she? It's freezing out there. And she won't—' Just in time, Sadie stops herself from saying *she won't get paid.* Mrs Shrew would no doubt find that terribly vulgar.

'Who knows what goes on in the minds of young people these days?' Mrs Shrew says primly. 'Perhaps she wasn't enjoying the company. I can't say I blame her.'

Sadie frowns. 'Okay, well. I think we might just check around the place anyway, just in case . . .'

'Very wise, I'm sure.' Mrs Shrew turns away dismissively.

Back out on the corridor, Nazleen huddles deeper into her dressing gown, gazing at Sadie with wide brown eyes.

'Do you think that's what she did?' Nazleen whispers.

'Walked to the village?' Sadie considers it. 'I suppose it's possible. There's a B&B, isn't there?' She remembers the way Genevieve hovered at the entrance to the drawing room, clutching her coat against her chest. The young woman certainly had her phone and cigarettes with her by then, and she was the last guest to enter the drawing room by several minutes. What else might she have been hiding under that coat – a night bag, perhaps? A pair of trainers, for the walk into the village? Sadie sighs. 'Maybe she did get fed up with us. She felt a bit out of place, I think.'

Nazleen nods, as if trying to convince herself. 'Or maybe she just thought the house was too spooky . . .'

Sadie gives her a sharp look. 'Or she realised she had a lower-grade bedroom than the rest of us.'

Nazleen looks surprised. 'Does she? That's nothing to do with me.'

Footsteps thump up the stairs, and Zach appears. He looks hopefully at Sadie.

'Any sign?'

Sadie shakes her head. 'Mrs Shrew thinks she might have walked into the village.'

Zach raises his eyebrows. 'Seriously? That's a good half-hour walk.'

'Look, why don't you check the rooms up that end?' Sadie indicates the fire-damaged end of the corridor with a twinge of guilt. 'And, Nazleen, you check the rest of the rooms this end. I'll go and look in the, er . . . ' She frowns at the end door. 'In the tower. And then we'll meet downstairs in the hall, if we don't find anything.'

'Okay.' Zach's already turning away. Nazleen opens the door to Sadie's own room, calling Genevieve's name. Sadie hurries to the end of the corridor, and this time she heads straight up the spiral staircase before she can change her mind.

Beth

DECEMBER 1989

Caroline's Christmas visit fell early in December, because she was much too busy to fit me in later in the month. I'd bought her a silk scarf from my allowance, and she gave me some sheet music for my violin that she told me she enjoyed playing herself. I almost asked her if it was a joint Christmas and early birthday present, since she'd missed my birthday entirely the previous February, but I knew that would be rude and, in fact, the music was perfect – a genuinely welcome gift from one violinist to another. But when I went to give her a grateful hug, she flinched, as usual.

After fifteen minutes of stilted conversation in the drawing room, Markus suggested Caroline might like a little walk by the lake before she headed home. Caroline looked so relieved at the word *home*, she sprang up immediately, and Markus winked at the rest of us behind her back.

'Leonora might be best staying indoors, actually,' he said. 'She's brewing up a bit of a cold, I think.'

Leonora gave him a faint, relieved smile, and we left her behind, although I didn't really believe she was coming down with anything. Once we reached the lake shore, Markus told Nina and me to go ahead and take the boat out, if we were brave enough.

'The lake'll freeze soon, with a bit of luck,' he said, 'and then there won't be any rowing till it thaws.'

Relieved to have an excuse to escape Caroline's strained attempts at friendliness, I followed Nina on to the dock, and we leapt down into the boat. Nina grinned at me as she took the oars, and I was reminded forcefully of the fun we'd had in my first summer at Raven Hall. I smiled back at her, and suddenly the day seemed a whole lot brighter.

Nina waited until we were past the island before she set the oars down.

'So, what's going on between you and Jonas?'

'Nothing.' I knew I'd answered too quickly. 'I mean, why do you even ask? You know Jonas and I are just ...'

She tilted her head. 'Friends?'

I nodded, frowning. 'Friends. Exactly.'

'I wish ...'

'What?'

'I just wish you'd be honest with me, Beth. I wish you'd tell me what you're thinking. You go around all wrapped up in your own thoughts all the time, it's like sometimes you think ...' She hesitated, gazing at me earnestly. 'That I'm your enemy. Like you don't trust me. Or Mum and Dad either.'

'That's not true.' I tried to laugh. 'Of course I trust you.' But a series of memories pulsed in my mind: Leonora thrusting the blue checked dress into my hands; Markus' wary expression when he came back from his diving trip a few weeks ago; the oily film at the bottom of Nina's hot chocolate mug. I blinked them away. 'You know I'm very happy here.'

'Are you?' Nina said quietly. 'Are you really?'

I shifted uncomfortably. 'Ah, come on, can we stop this now? I just want us to be friends. All of us. Jonas, too.'

She scrambled forward and indicated for me to switch places. 'Fine. Your turn to row, then.'

I seized the oars, glad of the opportunity to use my muscles. I took us on a circuit around the island, and it was a while before I looked across to the dock and saw that Markus and Caroline had left us to it. By the time Nina and I returned to the house, Caroline had already set off for home.

Markus was right about two things. Leonora *was* sickening for something. She spent days locked away in her bedroom until she felt well enough to re-join us downstairs, and even then, she remained pale and withdrawn. And the lake *did* freeze over the following week.

Markus announced he was taking the rest of the month off as holiday. He checked the ice obsessively each morning, drilling bore holes, checking air and water temperatures, and goodness knows what else. His excitement radiated through the house.

'We've been getting fewer and fewer properly cold winters,' he told me. 'Last year was terrible, but this year . . . ' He beamed at me. 'With a bit of luck, we'll be out there on our skates before New Year's Eve. You'll love it, Beth. A proper Fenland tradition. And you're a proper Fens girl now, aren't you?'

I laughed, slightly unsettled by the intensity of his gaze. 'I suppose so.'

'You can come out with me tomorrow,' he said, 'if you like. I'll show you how I check the ice depth . . .'

'Oh, leave the poor child alone,' Leonora said from the doorway. 'Beth, Jonas is on the phone for you.'

I was relieved to escape to the hall, and I pressed the phone to my ear. 'Hello?'

'Beth? It's Jonas.'

I smiled. 'I know.'

'Have you got plans for Christmas Eve? Because my mum's having a little party here, and I wondered—'

'What does he want?' Nina's voice from the staircase was sharp. I turned to look at her. She held my gaze.

'Nina's here too,' I said into the mouthpiece.

'Well,' Jonas said, 'she's invited too, of course.'

I tilted the phone away slightly. 'Jonas' mum is having a little party on Christmas Eve; he wants to know if we'd like to go.'

'Mu-um!' Nina called.

A moment later, a cross-looking Leonora appeared in the hall. 'What, darling? There's no need to bellow for me, you should come and find me.'

'Jonas' mum is inviting us to a party at his place on Christmas Eve,' Nina said.

From the phone by my ear, I heard Jonas groan.

Leonora fixed me with a stern look. 'Tell him it's kind of him, but no, Beth. Anyway, we do our own thing here on Christmas Eve.' She took stock of my disappointed face and her tone softened slightly. 'It's nice of Stephanie to invite us, but we just can't make it. Do thank them, all the same.'

I waited for her to return to the drawing room, and then I said to Jonas, 'Did you get that?'

'Bloody Averells,' he said.

I glanced up to where Nina still hovered, watching me.

'Funny you should say that,' I said sweetly, 'I was thinking the same thing.'

When I hung up, Nina hurried down to the hall and caught both my hands in hers. 'I'm sorry. That was mean of me. I'm really sorry, Beth. If you want to go – or maybe we could both sneak out and go . . .'

But it was hardly the sort of party I wanted to go to anyway – a boring adult affair in the middle of the day in the village B&B. I wanted loud music and dim lights and sweet cider and Jonas' arms around me.

'It doesn't matter.' I gave her a weary look. 'Honestly. I'm sure we'll have a nice time here.'

She was very childish, Nina, sometimes. I pitied her. But underneath that, I felt a sort of protectiveness of her. She'd grown up in this strange, isolated bubble at Raven Hall and she didn't know any different – it wasn't her fault. Perhaps, when I eventually left, I'd persuade her to come with me.

On Christmas Eve, the family had a tradition of giving each other one small present after dinner, to kickstart the festive celebrations. I'd bought my offerings on our shopping trip with Leonora in November, and I'd wrapped them carefully:

rose-scented hand cream for Leonora, a bag of his favourite toffees for Markus, and a notebook with daisies on the cover for Nina. I was looking forward to seeing them opened.

Nina gave out her presents first, and then I did. We all cooed over our gifts and held them up for each other to admire. Then Leonora looked at Markus.

'Dad did the Christmas Eve shopping this year,' Leonora said, raising her eyebrows in mock alarm.

'Uh-oh,' Nina said, and she and I giggled.

'Just you wait,' Markus said, and with a flourish, he produced two identical wrapped boxes. He switched them between his hands with a show of consternation. 'Which one's which? How to tell?' He held one out to each of us. 'Luckily, they're both the same.'

We tore into the paper, eyeing each other's as much as our own, laughing in our competition to see which of us could reveal the contents first.

'Oh,' I said.

'Wow,' Nina said.

We both tilted our boxes towards Leonora to show her. Inside each was a delicate gold charm bracelet, twinkling with reflections from the dining-room lights.

We lifted them out and helped each other to fasten them around our wrists.

'They're beautiful,' I said.

'Thanks, Dad.' Nina ran around the table to give Markus a hug.

'The charms represent the wildlife around the lake.' Markus' voice was gruff with a sudden shyness. 'There's a flag iris, a greylag goose, a reed warbler . . . ' He cleared his throat. 'Anyway, I'm glad you like them. And for my beloved wife . . . ' He produced a third box, which turned out to hold a beautiful necklace, the same shade of gold as our bracelets.

'These aren't small presents.' Leonora said quietly.

Markus looked uncomfortable. 'I know, but,' He turned to Nina and me, 'I thought they'll always remind you of Raven Hall, when you're grown-up. And you know, maybe you'll want to pass them on to your own daughters, for their sixteenth birthdays, say. I just thought it was a nice idea . . . '

He turned back to Leonora and helped her fasten the necklace under her hair. She didn't look as happy with her gift as I thought she ought to, but that was Leonora for you. She wasn't like normal people. I knew that by now.

She's in love.

This is nothing like the childish feelings she had for the young doctor. What she feels for Markus is real love. Proper, soulmate, meeting-of-minds, forever-and-ever love.

It took her a while to hitch a lift to anywhere even vaguely close to Raven Hall today. She's now taking the field route around the village rather than risk being recognised walking down the high street. Not that she doesn't have every right to be here – it's a free country, isn't it? But she can't bear the thought of curious questions – or worse, pity – from the people she used to feel mildly sorry for because they all live so clustered together in the village instead of somewhere proud and magnificent like Raven Hall.

But she doesn't mind taking the long route; she's content to be alone with her thoughts. The sun is high, and her T-shirt sticks to her skin, but she smiles to herself as she strolls along. She's thinking of Markus.

On their third meeting by the lake, she told him an edited version of her life story – that her father had died last year; that she now lodges with a distant relative of her mother's, who barely speaks to her from one week to the next.

'I feel like my whole life was stolen from me,' she'd blurted out, in an unguarded moment, as they watched a hobby catching dragonflies above the lake. 'Mum, then Dad, then my home—' She bit the rest of the sentence back; this was dangerous territory.

What would Markus do if he discovered she was the 'poor girl' who'd been turfed out of Raven Hall when his girlfriend's parents bought the place? Would his sympathy be replaced by awkwardness? Would he feel obliged to tell his girlfriend's parents he'd found this strange, traumatised young woman roaming around their property? And what would they do then? Prosecute her for trespassing? Or worse – offer her pity and fake condolences?

Markus had tried to comfort her. 'I expect things will look brighter next year. If you do apply to art college . . . '

But he'd inadvertently touched on her greatest fear, and a tear slid down her cheek.

'What if things never look brighter, though? What if I can't ever move on? I'm just so angry at the man who did this to us.'

Markus looked surprised. 'Who?'

She wiped at her cheeks. 'The Backstabber. That's what my dad used to call him. He was supposed to be my dad's friend, but after Mum died, he accused my dad of making mistakes at work, of being drunk.' It was a relief to say it out loud, to feel listened to. 'He got my dad sacked, in the end. And he – he—'

'What, Lara? What did he do?'

'He kept trying to buy our house from us. That's what he was after, all along . . . ' She covered her face with her hands, forcing herself to stop talking before she blurted out anything more incriminating – that that's why she'd been here, the day she and Markus first met – she was spying on her beloved former home, to see whether it was the Backstabber who'd finally succeeded in buying it.

'Hey.' Markus shuffled closer to her, and even that single word managed to comfort her. He touched her lightly on her arm. 'You can always come and stay with me, you know. In London. If your mum's cousin, or whatever she is, doesn't mind . . .'

And so, the following weekend, she told her mother's relative she was going to meet up with an old friend, and she took the train to London. Markus cooked for her in his student flat, and he made her laugh, until she forgot about her sadness for the first time since her father died.

And a couple of weeks later, when she went back for a second visit, Markus had opened the door with a charmingly sheepish expression.

'What is it?' she'd said. (She can tell when his emotions are high, even when he tries to hide it. She knows this is a sign they're meant to be together.)

He waited until the door was shut and then he blurted it out.

'I've broken up with Kat.'

'Oh, that's . . . I'm so sorry.' She tried to look sympathetic, but her heart swelled with a joy that felt tainted – like relief mixed with triumph. The young woman in the orange crop top still had Raven Hall, but she'd lost Markus; perhaps there was some fairness in the world after all. 'Why?' she asked. 'What happened?'

'Ah.' Markus had scrunched up his face. 'We weren't that well suited, really. We wanted different things in life . . .' He hesitated, as though tempted to say more, and she leant closer to him.

'I think,' she said, 'we're well suited. You and me. Don't you think?'

'Lara.' There was an apology in his smile. 'I really like you, but

169

if we're going to do this, we have to take it slowly. I'm four years older than you, you've been through a tough few years, a lot of trauma. I don't want to—'

She tried to kiss him then, but he held her back gently.

'Seriously,' he said. 'I mean it. Slowly.'

'But I'm eighteen.'

'I just . . .' He searched her gaze. 'I feel like there are things you're not telling me.'

Her heart lurched. He knew. She didn't try to deny it. In fact, she almost blurted it all out, then and there: that her name wasn't really Lara; that the home she'd lost was Raven Hall.

'There is something I haven't told you . . .' she began.

But he drew her into his arms, as if she was some injured creature he'd found by the shore of the lake. 'It's okay. There's no rush. I won't ask you any more questions. Let's just get to know each other, until you're ready, okay?' He'd stroked her hair softly. 'I'm not going anywhere.'

While he cooked them dinner that evening, she pottered around his flat and cleared away all evidence of the former girlfriend. Hairbands, magazines, a silver earring, an alarming pair of black lacy knickers, and – worst of all – a photo of Markus and Kat together, sitting in the garden at Raven Hall. She collected it all into a carrier bag and, when Markus wasn't looking, stuffed the whole lot into the kitchen bin.

That was two months ago, and she's spent almost every weekend with Markus since. And he's been true to his word – he hasn't asked her any more questions. But as she cuts across the field now in the baking afternoon sun, she smiles to herself. She's going to tell him everything next weekend. She trusts him completely; she knows he'll understand why she lied.

She was planning to do it this weekend, but he rang her a couple of days ago, full of apologies. His mum's health is deteriorating, so he's gone to visit his parents instead. She doesn't mind, she completely understands, but the prospect of an empty weekend unsettled her, so she decided to pay one last visit to Raven Hall. Mostly, she wants to say a final goodbye to her beloved home. But it's true, she wouldn't mind catching a glimpse of the girl in the orange crop top looking just a little bit miserable.

She jumps across a ditch and pushes through a hedgerow, and she's back on the road, just beyond the village. It's still a fair old walk to Raven Hall from here, and she glances over her shoulder at the sprawling yellow-brick house at the tail end of the village. It's the local B&B, and she remembers that the owner used to spruce up old bicycles, ready for guests who want to explore the flat Fenland countryside, or just to cycle to the pub. She'd save herself a lot of time if she could borrow one, and she'd return it within a few hours – they'd never need to know.

She creeps up the B&B's drive, eyeing the collection of battered bikes in the open-fronted bike shed, and she spots one that looks ideal. But as she's easing it out from between its neighbours, she hears the creak of a door, and she swings around to see a young woman with a baby on her hip, standing at the side door of the house, clutching a basket, staring at her.

Her heart thumps as she searches her memory. This must be Stephanie Blake – she remembers her vaguely from school – a couple of years older, always seemed a kind, quiet sort.

Stephanie raises her eyebrows as if waiting for an explanation.

'Is it okay if I borrow it?' She tries to smile. 'I'll bring it straight back, I promise.'

Stephanie nods slowly, and then she tilts an ear to the open door.

From indoors, a man shouts, 'Steph? Bring some raspberries in too, will you?'

'Okay, Dad.' Stephanie gives her one last, assessing look, before hurrying away around the back of the house.

The bike squeaks a little, but it's a lot better than nothing, and Stephanie's kindness stays with her as she pedals away. Is it possible, she wonders, that for every bad person in the world, there's a good person? For every cruel, greedy man like the Backstabber, there's a thoughtful, generous woman like Stephanie? For every spoilt, careless girlfriend like Kat, there's a warm-hearted, patient man like Markus? Is there some kind of moral balance in the universe?

She pedals harder, the rubber handlebars clammy under her palms. She wants to be a good person, too. But frequently, she feels so furious about everything that's been taken from her: her mother, her father, the house that was meant to be her birthright. She knows a good person would accept this fate and walk away, yet here she is, sneaking back yet again to spy on her former home, wishing ill on its new owners, knowing she'd seize any chance to get her house back, no matter what the consequences.

She knows this makes her a bad person. But maybe when she confesses it all to Markus next weekend, he might help her to change, to improve, to become more like him.

Meanwhile, she just wants one last look at Raven Hall. It won't alter anything, but she's so close now, she can feel it calling to her. Just one last look, that's all she wants, and then she'll try her best to put it all behind her.

Beth

It was the day before New Year's Eve. Nina, Leonora and I were in the dining room, eating croissants and admiring the patterns of frost on the windows, when Markus came charging up from the lake, waving his arms and shouting.

'It's ready!' he declared, as he burst through the door. 'The ice is thick enough. Come on, sleepyheads.' He beamed at the three of us, still sitting there in our dressing gowns staring at him. 'Get your skates on!'

We scrambled upstairs to get dressed, and then Nina and I went out to the stable block to rummage through a huge box of skates. Most were of a similar design: leather, lace-up boots with a long metal blade underneath that jutted out front and back. As we pulled them out, searching for a good fit, I held up a pair that looked quite different: simple wooden base sections with straps and blades attached.

'Those are Fen runners,' Nina said. 'They belonged to my grandparents and great-grandparents. They used to have big skating parties here, when it froze like this – races with

174

prizes. And people came from – from miles around – not just the village – and they had big feasts in the evening. I wish . . . ' She gazed out towards the lake. 'I wish I could have seen it.'

'It sounds amazing.' I ducked my head as an unexpected sadness washed over me. Not about the bygone era of skating parties on Avermere, but about the sensitive subjects I wasn't supposed to ask Nina about – the mysteries and secrets at Raven Hall I'd learnt not to query. What I wanted to ask was: *Which grandparents – the Meyers or the Averells? Why are people from the village no longer invited to events here? Why aren't you allowed to show your face at the rare parties your parents do hold?* But instead, I frowned down into the box and pulled out another pair of skates.

The rumble of a car engine made us both scramble to our feet. Jonas had recently passed his driving test, and he was roaring down the driveway in his mum's old Volvo. I stayed where I was and watched Nina jog across the gravel to meet him, her breath rising in puffs of steam, her arms hugging her body against the cold. More and more, I felt pulled in two directions these days. Did I want Nina's friendship, and a stable family life at Raven Hall? Or did I want Jonas? I couldn't have both.

Oh, snap out of it, I told myself. *You're seeing problems where there are none, as usual.*

I started forward to join them. Nina held on to Jonas' arm, chattering excitedly about the first time he'd walked here by himself to skate on Avermere – did he remember? – and how many times they'd fallen over, and how fast they'd gone, and how much fun it all was. Jonas nodded as he listened, but his gaze slipped around her to me before his smile widened. Suddenly, I desperately wanted him to give Nina the full attention she deserved, so I turned away.

Markus and Leonora were striding down from the house, all wrapped up and bright-eyed.

'Have you ever skated before?' Markus asked me.

'Yeah, a bit.' I'd been to the indoor ice rink in Peterborough a few times when I was younger, and I'd considered myself a pretty decent skater back then. But now that I was contemplating stepping out on to the surface of a real lake, I saw it had a different look entirely, and I slowed my pace as we approached the edge.

Nina and Jonas glided out on to the frozen lake first, and Markus and Leonora quickly followed. I stepped on to it hesitantly. Under my skate blades, the ice was translucent, but when I gazed out across the expanse of frozen water it looked like a mottled mirror, reflecting the clouds and sky above. And I knew how deep the water was under that six-inch crust.

Nina and Jonas whooped as they shot across the ice, leaving swooping lines scored into the surface behind them. I stood still and watched. She went left, and he right, and then they looped around towards each other, and picked up speed, the ice crackling and snapping around them.

I held my breath. They were going to collide.

Nina barrelled into Jonas. He caught her, and they spun around and around, both laughing. I felt like a terrible person suddenly, inserting myself into Nina's family and interfering with this beautiful friendship she had with Jonas. I tore my gaze away from them and scraped my skate blades against the ice, my heart still jumping.

Seconds later, they were in front of me: Nina flushed and beaming, Jonas stretching a hand towards me.

'Hey,' Jonas said, 'come on, we'll help you.'

I allowed him to take my right hand, and Nina my left, and together, the three of us slid away from the reeds and out on to the milky expanse. I lifted my chin, not wanting to look at the ice directly beneath my feet.

'There,' Nina said. 'You see? You can do it.'

I found my balance, and we picked up a bit of speed. It felt surprisingly good, having the three of us linked together. Maybe everything would work out, after all. I lifted my face to the bright, pale sky and I laughed, and Nina and Jonas joined in with me.

'Okay,' Jonas said. 'Now, try by yourself.'

They let go of me, and I mimicked their body posture, leaning forward, clasping my hands behind my back. We peeled apart, heading in three different directions, and I realised with a surge of delight that I no longer felt afraid. The ice was hard under my blades, and the surface was pitted, but I picked up speed, curving to the right and then to the left. I felt weightless, as if I could carry on gliding for ever, leaving all my problems behind me. With a smile, I turned and swooped closer to the others, then away again, relishing the wind in my hair and the sudden warmth of the sun on my face. It was exhilarating.

'Okay,' Markus called out from the shore. 'Now the races begin.'

He and Leonora proceeded to roll two wooden barrels on to the ice, and they stood them upright a good distance apart. I joined Nina and Jonas by the first barrel, and our breaths mingled overhead in a cloud.

'Right,' Leonora said. 'One lap, Nina and Jonas first, start on my whistle.'

I hung back next to Markus, watching entranced, as Nina positioned herself on one side of the barrel, and Jonas on the other. They were both serious-faced, poised to set off. Leonora raised her hand, then dropped it sharply while making a noise like a whistle.

Nina set off faster, but as they raced towards the far barrel, Jonas overtook her on his side of the ice. He was first to spin around the second barrel, and first to return, flying past Leonora and Markus and me, his arms raised in jubilation. Nina came to a stop by grabbing the barrel at our end, and her eyes were shining. I felt a surge of excitement. I wanted a turn.

'Okay, winner against Beth,' Leonora said, laughing. 'No chance to get your breath back, Jonas.'

Jonas beat me, of course. Leonora almost beat Jonas. Leonora beat Markus, and Nina and Markus were neck and neck. When I raced against Markus, I won, but only because he let me.

It was intoxicating: the speed, the brilliant sunlight glinting on the ice, the good-natured teasing. When I wasn't breathless from racing, my chest filled with an unfamiliar sense of no-strings-attached joy. Nothing else mattered, that morning on the frozen lake. All my private worries about Nina's isolation, my secret relationship with Jonas, that oily residue I'd seen in Nina's mug – all were scorched away by the dazzling winter sun and the adrenalin in my blood.

I wanted the morning to go on for ever. But eventually, we staggered back up the slope to Raven Hall, our stomachs rumbling, our legs suddenly wobbly at having to lift our clumsy feet against gravity for every step. I wondered briefly whether Leonora and Markus might invite Jonas into the house for lunch, but Jonas glanced at his watch and said he'd promised to go home and eat with his mum.

I should have said goodbye to him then. I should have followed the others into the house. But Jonas had a certain expression – raised eyebrows, eyes sparkling – that I could never resist, and I hung back and waited for the front door to close before I went to him.

'Hey, you,' he said, pulling me even closer to him. 'Am I allowed to kiss you now?'

For the next few seconds, I was aware only of him – but as we pulled apart, I realised belatedly that the front door had re-opened. Nina stood on the top step, watching us.

'Oh,' I said. 'Nina, I—'

Her voice was flat. 'Maybe you should go and have lunch at Jonas' house, Beth.'

I stared at her. 'I can't—'

'Mum!' she bellowed back into the hall. 'Beth says she's going to eat at Jonas' house instead.'

I tensed, waiting for Leonora to come scurrying out, to tell me this wasn't allowed, to drag me back into Raven Hall. But instead, Leonora's voice floated calmly down the hall.

'Okay, that's fine. Come inside then, Nina, and close the door.'

It was like the sun scorching through winter cloud: the truth hung there, clear and shocking, in front of me. Why had I never realised it before? I could leave whenever I liked; I could go wherever I liked. It was Nina who was banned from the village, not me. Nina who was kept here in a little bubble. Not me.

'But I don't want to . . . ' I began.

Nina's voice was tight. 'A bit late for that, don't you think?' She retreated into the house, slamming the door behind her.

I turned to Jonas, my heart rattling.

'What do I do?'

He gave me a cautiously optimistic smile. 'Come home with me?'

I felt dazed as I walked to his car, not sure what I was committing to – not in regard to Jonas, but in terms of leaving Raven Hall, and walking away from Nina. Would the family – would Nina – definitely allow me to go back? I sat in silence on the short drive to the village, gazing sightlessly through the windscreen. Jonas cast me concerned glances, but he didn't speak again until he'd turned on to the B&B's driveway and parked by the bicycle shed.

'My mum'll be pleased to see you, you know,' he said. 'Delirious, actually. I mean, I'm downplaying it, if anything. You really don't need to worry.'

'It's not that,' I said.

He studied me. 'I'm worried about you, you know. That family. It's like, you hide your feelings all the time, in case they don't approve, but – it's not right. You shouldn't have to pretend to be something you're not . . . '

I gulped, thinking of the two occasions I'd tricked Nina's grandfather into believing I was Nina.

'I shouldn't have left,' I said. 'I need to get back. It feels disloyal . . . '

'Beth.' He took my icy fingers in his, and tried to rub some warmth back into my hands. 'Look, you're almost sixteen; you can leave Raven Hall if you want to. Talk to your Aunt Caroline, come and live here, with me. I mean, it doesn't have to be . . . Mum would happily put you up, as a friend of mine, I promise you. And then we'd be . . . ' He squeezed my fingers gently. 'You can be yourself, here. And we could see each other whenever we like.'

I shook my head slowly, feeling like the worst person in the world.

'But that's not what I want.'

Jonas blinked a few times. 'What isn't? Being with me . . . ?'

I pulled my fingers free of his, and I indicated the yellow-brick house in front of us. 'It's such a nice offer, but it's not—'

'Nice?' Now he sounded insulted.

I twisted in my seat to face him, trying to find the right words. 'It's just that . . . I'd still be so close to Raven Hall, and . . . I can't even think it all through. They'd stop paying my school fees, wouldn't they, if I left? And for me to move just down the road would seem so . . . rude, somehow. But you're so close to your mum, and the business, and this whole place – the village, everything. I can't expect you to leave that behind and—'

'What do you mean?' He searched my expression. 'Move somewhere else, together, you mean?'

I shook my head. 'You can't. You can't leave this place, you belong here. And I can't just leave Raven Hall but stay nearby. I'd need to make a proper break, a clean break.' I sat back in my seat then, and turned my head to the side window. 'Which I'm not ready to do. So,' I took a deep breath, 'I need to go back.'

'You're really not making sense,' he said.

I curled my fingers around the door handle, feeling dizzy, as though I was teetering on the edge of the dock back at Raven Hall, unsure whether to fall one way or the other. All I knew was I couldn't have it both ways: I couldn't have Jonas *and* my life at Raven Hall. I had to decide between them. And there was no point trying to explain that to Jonas, because there was nothing he could do about it. He'd be better off without me. I couldn't give him the happy, carefree, *normal* relationship that he was looking for, or that he deserved.

'I'm sorry,' I said. 'Look, I'll walk back. You go in. Your mum's waiting for you.'

The hurt in his voice was clear. 'Fine. Go running back to them, then. But things won't get any better, you know. Markus' dad's coming back again, and Mum says he's determined to sell the house this time, did you know that? He has an appointment with an estate agent while he's here. He's desperate to get Markus and Nina out to the States with him, with or without Leonora, and Mum reckons he won't accept any more stalling.'

My mouth fell open and I grabbed his sleeve. 'When? When's he coming? Why didn't you tell me before?'

Jonas looked taken aback. 'I didn't think of it. I only heard this morning. Mum said his secretary rang late last night, asking for a last-minute room. He's arriving tomorrow, just staying the one night, apparently . . .'

My breath scraped in my throat. What did it mean? Could this be good news for me? They'd *need* me back at Raven Hall now, to play the role of Nina, wouldn't they? But an image of the hot chocolate mug shimmered in my mind, and I felt paralysed.

'It's so little notice, for New Year's Eve,' Jonas grumbled. 'Mum could do without the hassle, really, but she doesn't like to turn people away. I don't know if he's trying to make it a surprise visit, but Mum'll ring and tell Leonora, like she did before – to give her a bit of time to prepare, you know . . .'

With a supreme effort, I found my voice again.

'Do you think your mum's already rung her?'

Jonas frowned. 'I've no idea. Mum went out first thing. And Leonora was skating with us all morning, wasn't she? Mum could be ringing her right now, for all I know.'

'Please, Jonas.' I gripped his fingers in mine, this time. 'Please, *please*, will you drive me back?'

'Why?' He stared at me with growing concern. 'Beth? What is it?'

'I can't—' I squeezed my eyes shut, thinking of that oily

residue in the hot chocolate mug, and Nina's sickness. The word was back, hissing in my ears, pulsing through my body: *poison, poison, poison.* 'I need to check on Nina. Please, Jonas. Take me back to Raven Hall.'

The B&B's bike makes her journey so much quicker. Raven Hall soon comes into view, and she keeps her gaze fixed on it as she pedals: the welcoming grey stone frontage, the familiar chimneys, the proud turret. She feels bolder today, and she cycles down the centre of the driveway with her back straight and her chin up – what's the worst that can happen?

Instead of cutting across to the garden wall as on previous visits, she leaves her bike on the verge and strolls closer to the front of the house, pulled like a magnet to the drawing-room window. Is this where the long-haired Kat will be sitting, weeping into her hands, comforted by her slow-moving mother? She can't resist – she walks right up to the glass and peers in. If anyone challenges her, she'll say she's collecting money for charity.

The drawing room is unoccupied. But the familiar contents make her heart squeeze painfully. The black marble fireplace is still there, of course, but she's surprised to see so much of her parents' furniture too, and her old piano. Was it all sold as one lot, together with the house? Nobody consulted her. Even her mother's painting of Raven Hall still hangs above the old, polished bureau. She grips the windowsill tighter and cranes her neck to see more.

'Oi! What do you think you're doing?'

She whirls around. A tall man is striding up the grass from the dock. She opens her mouth to begin her charity-collecting excuse, *but the words shrivel in her throat; she knows this man. Her stomach lurches, and she crashes back against the stone wall.*

It's the Backstabber. Daddy's so-called friend; the man who stole Daddy's job and got him sacked; the man she blames for Daddy's death. It's her father's murderer.

'Well?' the man snaps. 'What do you want? You're trespassing.'

She struggles to accept the evidence in front of her: can the Backstabber really be the new owner of Raven Hall? She didn't think he had a daughter, but she must be wrong. Can he really be the husband of the slow-moving woman she saw on the veranda; the father of Markus' ex-girlfriend, Kat?

'Are you just going to stand there?' he says. 'Come on, clear off, or I'll set the dog on you.'

It's his hollow bluster – an image of that fluffy white dog trying to chase her down the driveway – that jolts her out of her terror.

'You don't even recognise me, do you?' Her voice grows louder. 'You forced my dad out of his job. You made him drink himself to death. And you stole our house. You took everything from me. And you've got the gall to say I'm trespassing?'

The man's brow lowers. 'Who the hell are you?'

Her voice slides up in pitch. 'Isn't it obvious? How many men have you done that to? You must be so proud of yourself, tearing families apart—' A sob overtakes her.

'My God,' he says. 'You're Charles' daughter, aren't you? Look, you clearly don't have the right information, young lady – I tried to help your father, many, many times . . .'

'You destroyed him,' she snarls. 'You killed him.'

The man narrows his eyes. 'There's no point us having this conversation, if you're not going to listen to me. I can see you're just as obstinate as your father, but I'll tell you one thing for free. If your old man had agreed to let me buy this place when I first offered, he'd still be alive today.'

She gasps. *'No.'*

'I don't even like this bloody house. My wife took a shine to it, and I knew it would solve your father's financial problems, so I made him an offer. You could have moved somewhere smaller together, he could have got help with his drinking . . .'

'No,' she whispers.

'And he'd have cleared all his debts instantly, instead of descending into bankruptcy.' The man gives her a surprisingly sympathetic look. *'It was your father's obsession with keeping hold of this house that killed him. You must be able to see that. He should have put your welfare before his attachment to his bloody ancestral home – I told him that – but he wouldn't listen . . .'*

'That's not true,' she says. And again, louder. *'That's not true! You just wanted to get your hands on Raven Hall, you didn't care who you hurt. You never thought about me while you were taking away my home, my memories of my parents . . .'* She curls her fists and fights back a sob. *'You don't even remember my name, do you?'*

In her peripheral vision, she sees the front door swing open. A large figure in a billowing dress shuffles forward on to the top step.

'Hendrik?' the woman says. *'What's going on?'*

But neither of them glances up at her. They hold each other's gaze, and he scowls as though he's searching his memory, desperate to recall this trespasser's name and prove her wrong. And somehow, on top of all the very real harm he's done her, this feels like the ultimate insult.

'I'm Leonora Averell,' she says, 'and Raven Hall should be mine.' She steps forward, but before she can say any more, a single word punctures her fury.

'Lara?'

It's like ice-cold water sluicing over her skin.

She spins around on the gravel and – it's quite inexplicable. On the far side of the large, pale-faced woman, supporting her on his arm, is Markus. And Leonora looks from Markus' straw-coloured hair to the Backstabber's; from the Backstabber's tall, broad-shouldered frame back to Markus'. The facts stir and rearrange themselves like autumn leaves picked up by the breeze, and they settle with deceptive gentleness into a new explanation.

This never was the home of the girl in the orange crop top. Markus wasn't visiting his girlfriend, Kat, here. He and Kat came together to visit his parents here.

She can see it now. She can't believe how stupid she's been. Markus is the Backstabber's son.

She runs for her bicycle and flees.

Beth

DECEMBER 1989

I leapt out on to the gravel in front of Raven Hall, and I forced myself to dip my head to say something to Jonas before slamming the door on him.

'Thanks for bringing me back,' I said. 'But please, just go now. I'll explain everything later.'

'Well, when?' he said. 'Tonight? Will you ring me?'

The prospect of trying to explain any of this on the phone from Raven Hall, where I might be overheard, made me shake my head quickly. But I was afraid Jonas would refuse to leave if I didn't suggest an alternative, and I feared it would make everything worse if I burst back into Raven Hall with an inquisitive Jonas hard on my heels.

'Tomorrow,' I said. 'Wait for Markus' dad to get back to the B&B after he visits us, and then ...' I glanced at the frozen lake. 'Just park up on the road, so they don't know you're here, okay? Walk across the ice to the island, and I'll sneak out and meet you there.'

Jonas muttered a few words of annoyance, clearly thinking

189

my caution was over the top, but he put the car into gear and left me to it.

I was more than a little relieved to find the front door of Raven Hall wasn't locked against me. I hurried inside, straining my ears for any sound of the family's whereabouts. The drawing room and dining room were empty, but in the kitchen I found Nina, perched on a breakfast stool, finishing off a mince pie, with an empty mug beside her. Warm savoury aromas drifted from the oven – they hadn't eaten lunch yet.

'Back already?' she said, sounding more wounded than hostile. 'Didn't you like the food at Jonas'?' Then her tone sharpened. 'Hey, what are you doing?'

I grabbed her mug and tilted it towards the feeble light from the window, but there was nothing unusual to be seen. Just tea dregs. No oily residue. I eyed her plate, my pulse still jumping.

'How many mince pies have you had?'

She opened her mouth, but it took her several seconds to answer. 'What the hell's got into you?'

'Nina, seriously. How many have you had?'

'Two – I was starving, and lunch'll be another half an hour. Is that okay with you?'

'Are they—' I snatched the remnant from her fingers and examined it in the palm of my hand. 'Are these the ones your mum made? Who gave them to you?'

'Beth, you're scaring me.' She slipped off the stool, gazing at me, wide-eyed. 'Mum gave them to me, just a few minutes ago. She warmed some up for all three of us. Why are you being so dramatic about it?'

'I think—' But suddenly I didn't know what to say. What if the substance in the hot chocolate really was something innocuous? How could I blurt out the word *poison* without making my position here completely impossible? How could I expect Nina ever to forgive me if I wrongly accused her mother of deliberately making her ill?

I set the fragment of pastry back on the plate, thinking frantically.

'How are you feeling?' I asked her. 'Do you feel sick? Do you feel okay?'

Nina glanced over my shoulder towards the door, and I heard light footsteps come in behind me.

'Ah, Beth,' Leonora said. 'Back already?' She hesitated, glancing at Nina and back to me. 'Is something wrong?'

I shook my head stiffly.

Leonora smiled. 'Well, not to worry, you can eat with us, then, after all.' She gestured to the oven. 'Would you like me to warm you up a mince pie?'

I shook my head and circled around her, stumbling backwards towards the door. 'Thanks, no, I'm— Did Jonas' mum ring while I was out?'

Markus' voice behind me made me jump. 'Stephanie? Yeah, she did, but it wasn't about you. Why, did you and Jonas have an argument or something?'

All three of them watched me with frowns on their faces.

'No, I . . .' I raised a trembling hand to my cheek. 'Actually, I'm just very tired, I'm going to go and have a . . .' I made a vague gesture.

'Nap?' Leonora suggested, after a moment of silence. 'Don't you want any lunch?'

'No. Thanks.' I escaped from the room and none of them followed me, but even after I'd shut myself into my bedroom, my skin still prickled from their bemused stares, and I pressed my fingers to my burning cheeks. *What must they think of me?*

I forced myself to take several deep breaths.

Concentrate on the facts. Nina's grandfather *is* coming back to Raven Hall tomorrow, for a third time. Stephanie Blake *did* ring a little while ago, almost certainly to warn Leonora and Markus about the visit. In which case, Leonora *will* ask me to pretend to be Nina again. Of course she will. She has no choice.

I am the powerful one in this situation, I tried to insist to myself. But it didn't feel like it. I sank on to my bed and waited for Leonora to knock.

But when the knock eventually came, I knew straight away it wasn't Leonora. Nina slipped into my room and she hovered by my bed, her face painfully, distressingly pale.

'I don't feel very well,' she whispered. 'What's going on? You've got to tell me.'

All those months of worrying, yet I had no idea how I could possibly articulate what my fear was. In the end, I patted the bed and waited for her to sit down beside me, and my heart wouldn't stop drumming.

'First of all,' I said, my voice also barely above a whisper, 'I don't have any answers. And you're not going to like what I'm going to say. So you can change your mind right now, if you want to, and walk away. I wouldn't blame you.'

'You're scaring me, Beth.'

'I'm scared myself. That's the trouble.'

She thought for a moment. 'Okay. You have to tell me. Just say it.'

'You know I don't want to hurt you?'

She nodded. 'Just say it, whatever it is.'

'How many times have you felt sick like this, since I started living here?'

She barely paused. 'This is the third time.'

'And what happened the first and second time? Who came to visit?'

Her voice was quiet. 'My grandfather.'

I swallowed hard and nodded. 'Well, Jonas just told me your grandfather's flying back for a third visit. He's on his way right now. I'd guess he's likely to turn up here tomorrow afternoon, if what Jonas says is true.'

'That's what Stephanie was ringing Mum about?'

I jerked my shoulders stiffly. 'That's what I'm guessing. Jonas said she would.'

Nina frowned. 'But why did you . . . ? How did you know I was going to be . . . ? What were you looking for in my mug?'

I ground my teeth, hoping she'd work it out herself. But her frown only deepened.

'Tell me, Beth, for God's sake. What were you *looking* for in my mug and my mince pie?'

'Okay. The thing is, I saw something odd in your hot chocolate mug, after your grandfather's last visit. You must have drunk it just a few hours before he arrived, and it had a . . .

like an oily substance at the bottom. And you felt sick after drinking it.'

She gazed at me. 'And . . . ?'

'Well, I don't know, Nina.' I felt angry with her suddenly. 'You tell me. Why would you get sick every time, if it isn't just some weird, enormous coincidence?'

Her eyes were enormous. 'I don't know.'

'Well, maybe . . . maybe . . . ' I had to force the words out. 'Maybe someone put something in your drink. Or your food. To make you sick. That's all I'm saying.'

Nina shook her head slowly. 'No, that can't be it. Who would? And why would they? You're making this up. I don't believe you.'

'How are you feeling right now?'

She frowned down at her lap, and when she eventually replied, her voice was small.

'Sick. Nauseous. Like I want to throw up, but I can't.'

'Well, let's go and see a doctor. They'll know . . . '

'No!' She looked horrified. 'I'm not allowed. Mum would never . . . '

I leant forwards. 'Come on, Nina, you can do it if you want to. I'll ring Jonas. He'll pick us up, take us to the surgery in the village . . . '

'I'm not allowed,' she repeated, but this time her tone was blank, and I sensed she wasn't to be persuaded.

Slowly, I leant back against my headboard. My muscles were already aching from the morning's skating, and a wave of tiredness crashed over me.

'I told you I didn't have any answers,' I said.

She gave me one last, long look, and then she left, closing the door softly behind her. I curled into a ball on my bedspread and waited for another knock. Whether it came that afternoon or the next morning, I knew Leonora would seek me out and ask me to play the role of Nina again.

I was sure it wasn't my imagination. Leonora seemed much warier of me, as we waited for Markus' father to arrive this time, than she had done on the previous visits.

'Don't forget,' she said, 'you can be short with him. Make it clear there's no question of you ever wanting to join him in America.'

I nodded stiffly.

'Tell him again what you said the first time,' Leonora said, 'about never wanting to leave Raven Hall or it would break your heart.'

'Got it,' I said. 'I'll remember. Don't worry.'

I twisted my bracelet around my wrist, squeezing each charm in turn between finger and thumb. 'Flag iris,' I whispered. 'Greylag goose. Reed warbler.' As if the chanted words might somehow bring me luck. Leonora still watched me from the corner of her eye, and I wished she'd focus on the driveway like she had on the previous visits. Did she know what I'd said to Nina yesterday afternoon? An image of Leonora eavesdropping on that conversation sprang up in my mind, and my skin felt cold.

I had to concentrate on getting through this visit, and

making sure Nina recovered properly. What else could I do? If I told anyone outside the family that I was worried Nina had been poisoned, they'd never believe me. I wasn't sure I even believed it myself. The whole thing seemed so unlikely. I was beginning to think it more likely there was something wrong with *me*.

'Here he comes,' Leonora said, finally.

I fought back déjà vu and trudged after her to wait in the hall while Markus went out to meet the car. Earlier that morning, I'd dragged the cheval mirror out of my bedroom and left it in a room at the far end of the corridor. Now, I turned my back on the hall mirror for the same reason. I couldn't bear to see my reflection any longer – the juvenile plaits, the uncomfortable, high-necked dress. *Hurry up, old man*, I thought. *Let's get this stupid game over and done with.*

'Ms Averell,' he said, as he stalked into the hall.

'Hendrik.' Leonora nodded stiffly by my side.

The old man's expression softened as he turned to me. 'Well now, Nina. This is a flying visit, but I'm very interested to hear your views on a little proposal I have for you . . . '

He turned towards the drawing room, clearly expecting me to follow. Leonora reached out and pinched my arm as I moved away from her. A silent reminder of what I was supposed to tell him. She hurried away to the kitchen, then, to fetch the tea tray.

Markus' father settled on the sofa nearest the fire, and I perched next to him. Markus took a seat opposite me, and his smile was surprisingly relaxed.

'It's great to see you, Dad,' Markus said. 'Really good.'

I frowned at him. I doubted Leonora would be pleased to hear him sound so sincere about his father's visit, but she was still out in the kitchen.

'I'll cut to the chase,' my supposed grandfather said. 'I want you to come back with me, Markus. I've got a position all lined up for you, and in five years you'll take over the company. It'll be the best thing for Nina. And for you, too, of course. I won't hear any argument. This place is going on the market next week.'

Markus' mouth gaped like a startled fish.

His father turned to me. 'What do you say, Nina? You can take a few months off, switch schools, and pick up where you left off, no problem. Are you ready to make a fresh start?'

Teacups rattled in the doorway behind me, and I knew Leonora must be standing there, hastily grabbed tray in hand. I gazed into the older man's eyes, and I tried to communicate my real feelings to him, even as I opened my mouth to parrot Leonora's words.

'I couldn't bear to leave Raven Hall, Grandfather,' I said mechanically. 'Please don't make me go. It would break my heart.'

His blue eyes looked beyond mine into my skull, into my soul, and my skin tingled with the certainty that he knew I was acting – that he saw the real me underneath. And I *wanted* him to see me. I kept my gaze fixed firmly on his, and I pleaded silently with him, with all my might. *Help me. Get me out of here.*

'I understand,' he said slowly. He reached into his pocket and pulled out a handkerchief. And then, in one swift movement, he caught hold of my hand, as if to give it a conciliatory squeeze, and he slipped a small rectangle of card into my palm. 'I'm sure we can sort everything out,' he said, without breaking our eye contact. 'I'll do whatever it takes to make sure you're happy.'

The clink of china came nearer, and Leonora set the tray down on the coffee table.

'Tea?' she said brightly.

But Hendrik was already rising. 'No thank you.' He frowned at Markus. 'I meant what I said. I won't put up with this any longer. Let me know Nina's exam dates, and I'll take that into account. But this house has been a curse on our family, and it's going to be sold, whether you like it or not.'

He stalked from the room, and as Markus and Leonora hurried after him, I dropped my gaze to the small rectangle of card in my hand. It was a business card, with *Hendrik Meyer* printed across the centre, and several phone numbers. I now had the means to contact my supposed grandfather whenever I wanted.

I was still sitting there, feeling dazed, when I heard a new note of urgency in the voices from the hall.

'Is that smoke?' Hendrik said. 'What's going on?'

'My God!' Markus said, his voice rising to a shout. 'Something's on fire!'

I ran out to the hall. Thick grey smoke obscured the landing and billowed down the stairs. Markus was already disappearing into it, his arm held across his nose and mouth, and I couldn't see whether he turned left or right at the top. A sharp, acrid smell filled my nostrils, and a moment later I began to cough.

'For God's sake,' Hendrik bellowed at a frozen-looking Leonora, 'phone the fire brigade. We could lose the whole house!'

Hendrik started up the stairs after Markus, calling his name. Leonora turned to me, white-faced.

'Nina,' she whispered, and the sound of her own voice seemed to snap her into action. Ignoring Hendrik's instruction, she too ran up the stairs and was swallowed by the smoke.

The sound of crackling flames reached my ears, and I heard a choked shout from Markus, followed by a prolonged bout of coughing that could have come from any of them. My heart battered in my chest like a bird trapped in a chimney. Nina was up there, sick or asleep in her turret bedroom – and what if she couldn't get out? Before I could change my mind, I held my sleeve over my nose and mouth and I ran up after them.

She didn't know she had so many tears saved up inside her. She pedals furiously towards the village, feeling her heart shattering into thousands of tiny, jagged-edged pieces. The Backstabber is Raven Hall's new owner. And Markus is the Backstabber's son.

She's lost everything. Her parents, her home, and now Markus. All gone.

She swipes angrily at her eyes and swerves closer to the grass verge as a car approaches from behind. It slows, and she's horrified to see Markus' concerned face glide alongside her. The Backstabber himself is in the driver's seat – she remembers, now, that his name is Hendrik. That's what Daddy used to call him before Daddy started drinking, before everything went so horribly, terribly wrong.

'Lara, please,' Markus says, 'let us give you a lift somewhere, at least . . .'

'Go away!' she shouts. 'I don't need you! Leave me alone, or I'll—'

She looks around wildly, wondering if she should discard the bike and run into the fields, but a car is approaching from the other direction, and she feels a glimmer of triumph.

'I'll flag these people down,' she shouts, glaring through the open window at both of the men. 'I'll tell them you're trying to kidnap me.'

'Oh, this is ridiculous,' Hendrik says loudly, and a moment later he accelerates away.

The second car whizzes past, and she focuses on the road ahead and continues pedalling. But Hendrik must have swung his car around in the farm track further along; he and Markus are heading towards her again, this time on the other side of the road.

Markus leans across Hendrik and calls out, 'Please, Lara . . . Leonora . . . '

She doesn't even look at him. And a second later, they're gone, heading back to the house they stole from her.

She cycles on towards the village, knowing she's entirely alone now. There's no one left in the world who cares about her any more.

Her tears have run dry by the time the village finally comes into sight, and she hops off the bike in front of the B&B. As she slots it back into the bike shed, Stephanie appears at the side door again, frowning.

'Are you okay?' Stephanie asks.

She draws herself up, forces herself to smile. 'Yeah, I'm fine.' She nods at the baby on Stephanie's hip. 'Is he yours?'

Stephanie presses her lips into the child's chestnut hair. 'He sure is.'

'He's gorgeous. Thank you for the loan of the bike.' She turns away.

'Do you need help with anything else?' Stephanie calls out.

But a familiar car is drawing to a halt in front of the bungalow next door – a mink-blue Ford Capri – and her heart lifts.

'No, thanks.' She doesn't glance back.

It's Fate. It must be.

She hurries towards the car, a tentative smile forming as she sees the young doctor spring out from the driver's seat. He never misled her, she thinks. She always knew exactly who he was, and where he lived, and who his family were.

'Leonora?' *The man's startled gaze runs over her tear-stained face, her sweat-soaked T-shirt, and the rip in her skirt where she caught it on the roadside brambles.* 'What on earth are you doing here? Are you hurt?'

She shakes her head, her pulse jumping as she takes in his familiar sharp-jawed face, his wiry frame, the doctor's bag in his hand. She glances at the bungalow behind him.

'Are you on a visit?' *she says.*

'I am.' *He tilts his head.* 'How about you? I haven't seen you since . . .'

They blink at each other, remembering that awful scene in her father's study.

'Oh,' *she says,* 'I'm . . . I'm living with a kind of aunt now. But she doesn't care where I am. No one cares . . .'

He glances up the road behind her. 'Ah. Boyfriend jilted you, has he?'

Leonora's knees feel weak – he knows her. The young doctor knows her. He can read her emotions, just like she thought she could with Markus.

Stop thinking about Markus.

'Could I—' *She lifts her chin, tries to smooth her skirt.* 'Is there any chance you could drive me back to my aunt's place tonight? I hitchhiked here, but . . .' *She gestures down the road.* 'It's been an awful day, and I'm just so tired.'

The man studies her thoughtfully. 'I can't tonight,' *he says slowly.* 'But maybe in the morning. If your aunt won't worry . . .'

'Oh, thank you, Roy. Thank you.' She hurls herself into his arms, almost knocking the bag from his grip. He glances across the road to the B&B and pushes her gently away, but he's smiling.

'Wait in my car while I just get this visit done. We'll have a nice evening together then, okay? We fit rather well together, I think, you and me.'

Sadie

Sadie pauses at the top of the spiral staircase and listens outside the door for a moment.

'Genevieve?'

There's no reply. She can hear Nazleen and Zach's voices calling out the same name on the floor below, and it gives her a moderate amount of reassurance. Gently, she pushes open the door and feels around on the wall for a light switch; her fingers find it easily.

The room is circular – *of course it is* – and it must once have belonged to a child. There are children's books mixed in with classics on the bookcase, and collections of dusty feathers and pinecones and bead necklaces scattered over a long, curved dressing table. Cobwebs drape from the high ceiling, and the air smells musty, but when Sadie studies the bed, she thinks it looks recently slept in. The pillow has a dent at its centre, and the covers are thrown back, and there's a glass of clear water on the bedside table.

Slowly, Sadie turns, and she almost screams when she sees

a whole bank of glassy eyes staring back at her. Dusty carnivorous creatures wearing human clothing; their malevolent glares bore right through her skin. She presses her hand over her thudding heart.

'Genevieve?' she murmurs. 'Where are you?' But the room remains silent, and there's no obvious hiding place. Still feeling uneasy, she hurries back down the spiral staircase.

When she emerges on the corridor, she hears Zach and Nazleen talking on the floor below, so she goes down to join them in the hall. Joe is with them, swinging a heavy torch in one hand, and he gives Sadie a tight smile that holds no trace of amusement.

'You'll come out with me, won't you?' Joe says to Sadie. 'Make sure I'm not seeing things.'

Zach grumbles at him, 'I said I'd come, didn't I? I just don't feel very well . . .'

Nazleen tightens her dressing gown belt and waits for Sadie to answer.

'What have you found?' Sadie asks, but Joe merely indicates the front door. They leave Zach and Nazleen behind, and they make their way back out into the freezing darkness.

'Come on, what is it?' she says. They crunch across the gravel. Joe's torch gives a much broader, brighter beam, but for some reason it makes Sadie feel more anxious rather than less.

Joe shakes his head. 'You have a look first, see what you think.'

Her heart pounds as they approach the dock for a second time. The reeds are a ghostly silver, swaying and rustling, as if they're trying to escape the darkness behind them. The black surface of the lake rumples gently like oil. A sudden flurry to one side makes her cry out.

'Hey.' Joe touches her arm briefly. 'It's just a bird. We woke it up, that's all.' He swings the torch beam away from the dock to the frosty grass beside it, and he slides the light left and right. 'What do you make of these?'

At first, Sadie can't see anything but white-tinged grass. She peers closer. Actually, there *is* something – a faint trail of impressions – two different sizes of indentations in the frost – half of them round-cornered triangles and half of them small circles. She straightens slowly.

'You think they're Genevieve's footprints?'

Joe nods and swings the beam away in the direction of the driveway. 'High heels, don't you think? And they join the drive just over there. And there's no other tracks next to them.'

'Except yours.' Sadie blinks at him. 'Presumably? If you followed the trail . . .'

'Well, yes, I meant—'

Sadie turns towards the house and gazes at the yellow glow seeping around the drawing-room and dining-room curtains. She's not sure she can trust anybody here. But sometimes you have to trust somebody.

'Mrs Shrew thinks Genevieve was planning to walk to the village. To stay at the B&B instead.'

'Yeah, Zach told me.' Joe rubs his mouth. 'I suppose that must be what she did, then.'

Sadie peers at him in the gloom. 'Do you know her? Mrs Shrew.'

He takes his time replying. 'I used to, when I was young. I grew up round here.'

Sadie considers this. Mrs Shrew said she'd travelled a long way to get here this evening, but it doesn't surprise Sadie that she too used to be local – it fits, somehow, with her uptight behaviour and reactions tonight.

'Do you trust her?' Sadie asks. 'Only she seems a bit . . .'

He frowns, as though trying to weigh up the evidence to give Sadie a fair answer. 'I feel sorry for her, mainly. And I don't trust her, particularly, no. But equally – I can't see why she'd lie about this.'

Sadie hates feeling so powerless; they ought to be *doing* something. 'Well, we can't phone anyone, can we? And we don't have a car. Do you think one of us should walk to the B&B, to check Genevieve got there okay?' She suppresses a niggling worry that the company won't pay her if she ends up following Genevieve into the village and spending the night at the B&B. And all because the selfish young woman couldn't be bothered to let them know what she was planning to do.

But Joe doesn't need any more of a hint. 'I'll go. I know the route.'

'No!' Sadie grabs his sleeve. 'Actually, no, you're the only one here I can rely on. You can't leave me with that lot.' She jerks her head towards the house, picturing the four remaining guests – self-centred Everett, arrogant Mrs Shrew, cowardly Zach and indecisive Nazleen. *And how would they describe me?* she thinks, cringing inwardly. *A pathetic, desperate actor, who puts money before her own safety?*

Joe searches her expression in the torchlight, frowning, and she waits for him to reassure her, to tell her she's over-reacting. But instead he tilts his head as if he's more confused than ever.

'You know, it's been niggling at me all evening,' he says, 'you really do remind me of someone. Do you mind me asking – what's your mother's name?'

Beth

DECEMBER 1989

I hesitated at the top of the stairs, blinded by the thick grey smoke, coughing with every other breath.

'Where are you?' I shouted. 'Where is everyone?'

Someone crashed into me in the gloom. It was Leonora. And she pulled a frightened-looking Nina behind her.

'Get downstairs!' Leonora said. 'We need to get out.'

We stumbled down the stairs, and as Leonora yanked open the front door, Markus and Hendrik emerged from the smoke behind us. Markus' eyes were red-rimmed and streaming. Hendrik was bent double, coughing and wheezing, gripping Markus' arm for support.

Leonora tugged Nina and me across the threshold, and we all gasped in lungfuls of cold, fresh air.

'I've shut the door on the flames,' Markus shouted. The smoke in the hall was thinning, now that the front door was open. 'It'll buy us some time, the fire's contained. Did anyone ring 999?' When nobody answered, he peered around and reached for the phone. He dialled the number, then turned to Hendrik. 'Get outside, Dad. Go with Leonora. I'll follow in a second.'

I tried to move back into the hall, wanting to help Hendrik who was struggling to breathe and pressing his fingers and thumb against his streaming eyes. But Leonora's grip on my arm was strong, and she shoved Nina and me down the steps ahead of her, as if she couldn't get away from Hendrik fast enough.

'Leave him. He'll be fine.' Her voice was surprisingly bitter. 'He always is.'

'What happened?' I said. 'Where's the fire?'

Leonora's fierce stare made me shrink inside my skin. 'It's in your bedroom, Beth. Were you burning a candle in there?'

I shook my head, appalled. 'No, I—'

'Did you leave something switched on? Your hairdryer?'

'No!'

Leonora made a sound of disgust, but she cut it off sharply and checked over her shoulder. Hendrik still hadn't emerged from the house. Leonora glanced across to the stable block with a calculating expression on her face. It was dusk; in another few minutes, it would be completely dark.

'Go and sit on the wall,' she said, gesturing towards the shadowy end of the stable block. She dropped her voice to a hiss. 'Whatever happens, he mustn't see there are two of you.'

Wordlessly, Nina and I linked hands, and we stumbled away across the gravel together. My chest ached from the smoke I'd inhaled, but also from something else – this confirmation that the deception of Hendrik had never been a game at all. It was something far more serious.

Before Nina and I reached the stable block, a crash of shattering glass made us look up to see flames bursting out through my bedroom window. I staggered backwards, clutching at Nina, my heart racing. How had this happened? It wasn't really my fault – was it?

When I turned away from the bright flames, the surroundings seemed even darker in comparison. I could just about make out Hendrik sitting on the gravel beyond the steps, batting away his chauffeur's attempt to get him up on his feet, still with one hand shielding his eyes. Leonora and Markus stood side by side a little closer to us, their upturned faces bathed in the angry red light from the flames at my bedroom window.

A sudden thought stopped my breath. They were going to blame me for this, weren't they? It was my bedroom; of course they'd blame me. My throat tightened at the injustice of it, and I dropped Nina's arm and stepped away from her. It *wasn't* my fault. I was sure it wasn't my fault. But what difference would that make? I wasn't really part of their family; I'd only ever been a guest.

Nina was still transfixed by the fire, and I took the opportunity to turn away and scan the frozen lake in the gloom, desperately hoping to catch a glimpse of Jonas. Might he have come over early? Might he already be waiting for me on the island? The idea of moving in with him and his mum was suddenly vastly more appealing.

I tried to creep away across the gravel, but before I reached the lake shore, I heard Nina close behind me.

'What are you doing?' Her voice was heavy with bewildered hostility.

'I'm just ...' I peered again towards the island, but dusk was rapidly giving way to night, and it was impossible to see more than hazy shapes. There was no gleam from a torch, no sign of Jonas.

'Did you start the fire?' Nina said. Her face was a smudge in the gloom, her dark eyes glittering. 'Did you put something in my food to make my sick? Was it you?'

'No!' I stared at her, aghast. 'How can you even say that?'

'Well, you think it was my mum – how can *you* even say *that*?'

'I don't know, Nina. I don't know!' I stepped on to the ice in the brand-new pixie boots I'd been so pleased to unwrap on Christmas morning. 'Please. Just go back.'

Nina's tone changed as she followed me on to the slippery surface. 'I'm sorry. I don't know what to think. Don't leave me, Beth, please. I need you.'

I swung around, skidding a little. 'No, Nina. Go back to your parents.'

'I'm not supposed to show my face to my grandfather, remember?' She sounded close to tears. 'Where are you going? You can't leave me here.'

I shook my head and half walked, half slid away from her as fast as I could. A new thin layer of powdery snow covered the ice, and I swung my arms as I ploughed ahead, trying to generate some speed, to widen the gap between us. But it wasn't long before I realised she was still following me.

'Beth,' she sobbed. 'Please don't go. I need you.' Her voice rose in pitch. 'Take me with you.'

I almost laughed at that, and I swung around, unable to see her expression in the darkness now, even from just a few metres away.

'I can't even look after myself,' I said. 'Just look behind you.' I waved an arm at the glow from the upstairs window in the distance. The faint wail of sirens reached us across the fields.

'But where are you going?' Her voice rose in pitch. 'You're going to see Jonas, aren't you?'

My heart squeezed with sympathy for her, but what choice did I have? 'You know you can't come with me, Nina.' I began to slip-slide away from her again. 'Go back to your parents.'

This time, there was no sound of her attempting to follow, and for once I was grateful for Leonora's rules. I veered away from the island slightly, no longer believing Jonas might be there waiting for me – he'd have joined me by now. Instead, I planned to skirt around the island, cross the lake, and walk up past Milner's Drain to the main road. I'd lived at Raven Hall for eighteen months, I felt confident I could find my way in the dark – perhaps Markus was right about me becoming a proper Fens girl. While the fire engines battled the blaze in my Raven Hall bedroom, I'd be marching down to the village to seek refuge with Jonas.

But then a shout flew across the frozen lake: 'Girls!' It was Markus' voice from somewhere near the dock. 'Nina! Beth! Where are you?'

I hesitated, and in that moment, I heard Nina's breaths, short and sharp, moving towards me again. I swung around, trying to make out her shape in the darkness.

'Go back, Nina!'

'No!' She crashed into me and grabbed my hands in her icy fingers. 'I'm coming with you.'

Markus' voice boomed out again, and it sounded closer. 'Girls! Please! Where are you? Come back!'

'Let go of me.' I freed my hands from her grip and stumbled away, no longer sure of my bearings.

'Wait!' she called out. 'Hang on. Dad drilled his holes on this side. He said we mustn't skate beyond the island.'

Nice try, Nina, I thought. 'I'm not skating.'

She was still coming closer. 'But it might not be strong enough—'

'Well, go back then!' I turned in a circle and caught her outline in my peripheral vision. 'I'm trying to get away from *you*, too – can't you understand that?'

And that's when it happened. A loud snap, like the crack of a whip. A strange, slow-motion shift of the ice beneath my feet. And we were both slipping and tipping. And no matter how far I clawed my fingers on to the ice in front of me, my feet and calves and thighs slid down, down, down into the cold, deadly water. I couldn't breathe. And I couldn't move. The world closed in around me.

Sadie

JANUARY 2019

'What's your mother's name?'

Joe's question hangs in the frosty air between them, and Sadie stares at him as if she doesn't understand it. Eventually, she clears her throat.

'Perhaps you could tell me exactly who *you* are, first.'

Joe looks startled, but he gives her a small, apologetic nod. 'Yes, of course. I'm Jonas Blake. I grew up in the village, my mum still runs the B&B there. I used to be friends with ...' His gaze slides towards the lake, as if the rest of his sentence has been sucked away across the black water.

She waits for a couple of seconds. 'Friends with who?'

'There were two girls who used to live here. Nina and Beth.'

Sadie's heart is a drum. Is she finally going to hear the story her mother would never tell her?

'What happened to them?' she whispers.

He eyes her warily. 'Surely you'd know that, if you're Beth's daughter?'

She shakes her head. 'Mum never told me anything about

215

her childhood. Seriously, virtually nothing. I mean, I know that her parents and her brother, Ricky, died in a road accident, but apart from that . . . '

Jonas' pupils are enormous in the torch light. 'You didn't know she lived here?'

'No. How old was she then?'

'Fourteen, fifteen. Didn't she mention the family, even? Leonora and Markus and Nina?'

'No, I told you. I wasn't allowed to ask her anything. Little things could set her off. If she was reminded of the past, she'd withdraw from everything, shut herself away, didn't want to talk about it. So in the end, I stopped asking.'

Jonas looks horrified. 'I tried to find her, afterwards, but she literally . . . ' He swings the torch in a helpless gesture. 'Disappeared.'

Sadie thinks of the charity her mother always insisted on supporting. 'She was homeless for a while. I don't know much more than that. She lived on the streets till she got pregnant with me, and then she got some support, and things got a bit better.'

'Good grief.' Jonas shakes his head heavily. 'I'm so sorry.'

'Just tell me what happened here. Please.'

'It was an accident,' he says slowly. 'There was a fire, in the house. And while they were waiting for help to arrive, Beth and Nina went out on to the frozen lake, and they—'

'What?' Sadie says.

'The ice broke. They fell through. Into the water . . . '

Sadie hugs herself, thinking of all the times she complained of her mother's heating being turned up too high, and her mother saying it's what her cold bones needed.

'The fire brigade had just got here,' Jonas continues. 'They managed to pull both girls out, but ...'

Sadie remembers the line from the ramblers' group blog: *Raven Hall has been abandoned and uncared for since a tragedy befell a local family in the late 1980s.* She takes a step backwards and glances at the gentle glow from the drawing-room window, no longer wanting to hear the rest of the story. What if her mother was responsible for the other girl's death? Is that what happened? Beth and Nina went out on to the ice, but only Beth came back?

Jonas catches at her sleeve, and his voice cracks. 'It was my fault, that's the trouble. I promised Beth I'd meet her on the island, but I wasn't there – I was still at home, I hadn't even set off. If I'd been here ...' He gives Sadie a pleading look. 'Where is she now? I'd love to see her again, to explain ...'

Sadie gives a short laugh. 'That'll be tricky.'

'Why?' His eyes widen. 'She's not ...'

'Dead?' Sadie pulls a face. 'No, but she's not exactly easy to get hold of. She quit her job a few months ago, gave away all her stuff, left me to sort out the tedious bits while she went off to join some cult in the wilderness.'

'Cult?' Jonas says.

'Well, they call it a retreat. It's in the Scottish Highlands. They do talking therapies, that kind of thing, and she's convinced it'll help her, but they're really strict. No phones allowed, no visitors for the first six months, only one letter a month, things like that. She just went and joined them. I couldn't talk her out of it.'

'It does sound a bit cultish.'

'That's what I told her.' Beth drops her gaze, and she sighs. 'But she thought I'd be better off if she left for a while. She thought I was too dependent on her, that because we saw each other all the time, she was stopping me from taking responsibility for myself . . . '

Jonas hesitates. 'And was that true?'

'No!' Sadie looks out over the black water. 'At least, well . . . I did use to go round there a lot and let her go through the job adverts for me, you know, and cook me meals and stuff, but . . . ' She shakes her head. 'I miss her.'

'So . . . ' Jonas sounds confused. 'How did you get invited here tonight if . . . ?'

'I don't know.' Sadie rubs her arms. She pictures her mother falling through the ice with that other girl, Nina, and a thought slams into her, sending a shiver from her fingertips all the way up to her neck. *What if I wasn't picked for this job at random? What if someone invited me here because of the connection between this house and my mother?*

Back in the drawing room, Sadie and Jonas describe the footprints they saw heading down the driveway. The relief in the remaining guests' voices is clear.

'It makes sense,' Zach says. 'It's not that long a walk to the B&B. I'm quite tempted myself.'

'Thought she was too good for us,' Everett grumbles.

'Oh, I wouldn't go that far,' Nazleen says.

Sadie is still reeling from the discovery that her mother once lived in this house, and she eyes the other guests curiously. So, Jonas was once a friend of her mother's, but what about the others? Everett would have been in his forties back then, she guesses, and Zach just a small child.

'Have you been here before?' she asks Nazleen abruptly.

'To this house?' Nazleen frowns. 'No. Why do you ask?'

Sadie shakes her head. 'No reason.'

But if Sadie's presence here isn't a coincidence – if someone at the company knows that her mother used to live here – why did they invite her here without explaining the connection? And who are they, anyway? Sadie frowns, thinking of the other names Jonas mentioned outside – Leonora and Markus. Could it be one of them?

'Well, I'm going to bed.' Zach hauls himself up off the sofa. 'Remind me not to do this sort of thing again, Dad, won't you?'

Sadie wanders across to the window, wanting one last look outside before she too heads up. She feels self-conscious as she parts the curtains – imagine if Genevieve was back out there on the dock, smoking another cigarette, laughing at them. But it's something far stranger – Sadie blinks and turns her head from side to side, trying to catch it in her peripheral vision. Tiny bluish lights flicker and jump in the darkness; with nothing else visible, it's impossible to judge how far away they are.

'There's something . . .' she says, and she can hear the fear in her voice, but she can't hide it. The others hurry towards her – even Everett, who a moment ago was heaving himself out of his chair as if he barely had the energy to stand. They crowd round her, peering into the black night.

'There are tiny lights – look.' She turns a stricken face to Jonas. 'You don't think Genevieve ... ?'

The others watch for a moment, and then Zach laughs.

'They're will-o'-the-wisps,' he says. 'Have you never seen them before?'

'It's just marsh gas,' Jonas says to Sadie, more kindly. 'It's a natural phenomenon. Nothing to do with Genevieve.'

'Oh.' Sadie lets the curtain drop back.

'Perfectly normal to see them ... ' Everett begins.

'In the Fens.' Nazleen sounds weary. 'We know, we know. Well, it's lucky we've seen them tonight, 'cause I, for one, certainly won't be coming back.'

Sadie grinds her teeth against the thought that she ever contemplated trying to get the hostess job here for herself. Certainly not one of her better ideas. Especially now she knows of the connection between this house and her mother's painful past.

The guests exchange muted goodnights at the top of the stairs, and as soon as Sadie is alone in her room, she kicks off her shoes and collapses with a groan on to the bed. Her eyes close instantly, and she's tempted to sleep where she is, fully dressed – but a worried thought gnaws at the edge of her consciousness. She shouldn't be feeling *this* tired; it's not even midnight yet ...

She hauls herself up and prepares for bed properly, trudging down the corridor to the bathroom to brush her teeth, relieved to get back to her room without bumping into any of her fellow guests. Her thoughts are sluggish, as if her mind is operating under water. What was she thinking as she climbed the stairs, again? Something about the job. The hostess job ...

She flips back the sheet and blankets, and she frowns as a new idea occurs to her. What if Nazleen's wrong? What if there is no long-term hostess job? What if ... ? Sadie forces herself to stay on her feet, determined to think this through before she sinks on to the soft mattress and allows her head to touch that oh-so-tempting pillow. *What if this evening's event is a one-off, designed to gather the seven of us together?*

Sadie sways, a hint of her earlier nausea returning. She should have left when she had the chance. She should have volunteered to follow Genevieve's footsteps. She could be tucked up safely in the cosy B&B by now, instead of being stuck here in this huge house with five complete strangers ...

She lifts her gaze to the door. There's a keyhole, but she hasn't seen a key. She plods barefoot to the big cheval mirror and drags it across to just in front of the door, standing back to assess the effect. Anyone could force their way in, still, but at least she'd have a warning now.

When she finally falls into bed, she pulls the sheet and blankets right up to her chin and holds them there, while images slide through her kaleidoscope mind. Blue, looping handwriting: *Hendrik will appreciate your support.* The fair-haired old man in the portrait, looming over them. That dead fish-eye, like a circular, stagnant pool. The black, ominous surface of the lake, rippling, rippling . . .

Sadie doesn't so much fall into sleep; she's sucked down under its surface.

She dreams of her mother. Arms-crossed, warning frown. *I've told you, Sadie. It's not something I can talk about.* A long, sickly yellow hospital corridor, a playroom full of childish plastic toys, while her mother talks to a little tortoise of a woman behind a blue door covered in peeling posters.

I'm okay, Sadie, I promise you.

I don't want you to go, Mum.

She wakes cold and clammy, the blankets thrown aside, her heart pounding as if she's just heard something terrifying. The lamp is still on, and she half sits, feeling dizzy. Her gaze jumps to the door; it's still blocked by the mirror. She lets her head fall back to the pillow. *Thank God.* But there it is again – the noise that woke her: a sharp crack-crack on the window.

Perhaps she's still dreaming. She slides out of the bed and curls her toes into the soft rug. It feels real.

Crack! Another rattle at the window. And it's the strangest thing, but she really does think she can hear her mother's voice calling her.

She drags back the curtains, and by the light from the outside lamps, she can just make out a car on the driveway – a Mini. This is good news, isn't it? Has someone come to check on them?

'Sadie!' There it is again – her name being called, and

someone *is* down there. A woman in a huge coat, standing back, craning her neck to peer at the upstairs windows. Her arm jerks back and upwards, and a flurry of stones – gravel? – hits the window of the room next door. Sadie tries to lift the sash window to get a better look at the woman, but it's locked, so she presses her face closer to the glass and waits for the light to catch the woman full in the face.

It doesn't seem possible. Sadie rubs her eyes and peers again. It really *does* look like her mother down there. And then two things happen at the same time. Sadie inhales through her nose and catches a faint scent of smoke. And the woman on the driveway shouts a single word that slices through the glass and sets Sadie's heart pounding.

'Fire!'

PART TWO

PART TWO

Beth

JANUARY 2019

I hurl another handful of gravel at the window.

What am I doing here?

I vowed I'd never come back. It's painful to remember what happened here thirty years ago. But when Sadie's dutiful monthly letter arrived at the retreat earlier today, a string of words flew out at me like a flock of panicked geese: *I've got an amazing job lined up, a sort of game, at a place called Raven Hall . . .*

I've driven for hours. Too many to count. Red warning lights flashing on the dashboard of the hastily borrowed car, a dreadful grating noise from the engine for the last few miles. I thought Sadie might grow up a bit if I put some distance between us. I never dreamt that in my absence she'd be in danger from my past.

The doors are locked, as are the downstairs windows. Flames glow menacingly behind the glass above the front door. There's no response to my hammering. No signal on my phone. I think frantically: there are no other cars on the driveway – might the house be empty after all?

227

I can't risk it.

I hurl more stones at the upstairs windows, and I work my way along, shouting my daughter's name as loudly as I can.

'Sadie! Are you in there? There's a fire! You have to get out!'

Sadie

Sadie drags the cheval mirror aside and lurches out of her bedroom into a haze of throat-tightening smoke, lit by fierce orange flames somewhere near the stairs. She holds her arm across her face and stumbles closer, her eyes stinging. It's on the staircase. The fire is on the staircase.

'Fire!' she yells.

She hammers on each door in turn, unable to remember in that moment which guest should be in which room.

'Wake up! There's a fire!' She opens the door next to hers and finds herself face to face with Nazleen.

'What do we do?' Sadie says. 'Where's the fire exit? Where are the … the …' She gestures wildly, thinking of smoke alarms and sprinklers and extinguishers. Surely the company has a legal obligation … ?

'Oh my God,' Nazleen says. 'Oh my God, oh my God.'

Sadie swings away and crashes into someone else. It's a dazed-looking Zach.

'How did this happen?' he says. 'We need to get out. What's Jonas doing?'

Sadie turns to watch Jonas creeping closer to the flames, as if he's looking for a way through them. Sparks shoot past his head, and he pats frantically at something on his shoulder and stumbles backwards.

Everett's voice booms over Sadie's shoulder: 'What in the name of all that's holy ... ?'

Sadie tries desperately to think. 'My window's locked. Can any of you get yours open?' She looks from one guest to another. 'Where's Mrs Shrew?'

For a moment, they stare at each other blankly, and then they all hurry into different rooms, and Sadie's left feeling dizzy. What should she do first? Look for Mrs Shrew? Try other windows? Help Jonas?

'Sadie!' It's Jonas, right in front of her. She struggles to lift her gaze from a singed patch of fabric on his shoulder. He takes her by the arm and steers her out of the worst of the smoke, into the nearest bedroom – Nazleen's. He tries the window, but just like in Sadie's room, it won't open. Jonas peers through the glass, then swivels to face her.

'Who's the woman out there?'

She stares at him. 'I thought it was my mum, but ... '

He nods, seeming less surprised by the suggestion than she is.

'She'll go for help,' he says, 'won't she? She's got a car. She'll drive to the village and raise the alarm ... ' He sounds as though he's trying to convince himself more than anything.

Sadie curls her fists, frustrated by the fogginess in her

head – she'd blame it on the smoke, if it hadn't started hours earlier, around the dinner table. She feels as if she's been drugged.

'All the windows are locked.' It's Nazleen, breathless. Sadie turns to look at her, wondering if they'll all wake up from this nightmare in a minute.

Zach stumbles in, and his words are punctuated by coughing. 'I can't find Mrs Shrew. Dad won't stop trying his phone, even though I keep telling him there's no signal. Is there another set of stairs up the far end?'

Sadie remembers the spiral staircase she climbed earlier. She shakes her head.

'It only goes up, to the top of the tower. Not down.'

'Well . . . ' Zach looks taken aback. 'How do we get out, then?'

Sadie's surprised at how calm her voice sounds. 'We'll have to put the fire out, won't we?' She turns to Jonas. 'We'll need water.'

Jonas squeezes the bridge of his nose. 'Okay, yeah. There's debris on the stairs – it looks like someone piled up wood or something, to get it started. It's spreading up the carpet, and the banister's starting to burn. But,' he gives Sadie a wide-eyed look, 'if we can smother it with blankets – wet blankets . . . '

'Everyone,' Sadie says, 'get the bedding off the beds. Curtains, anything you can find. Run the baths to soak them.'

'Will it work?' Zach says.

For a split second, Sadie feels paralysed by his doubtful expression. Her head buzzes with a host of other questions: can that really be her mum outside? Who started the fire? Where's Mrs Shrew?

'For God's sake,' Nazleen snaps at Zach, 'we've got to try something. Go and fill the baths.'

They form a ragged human chain along the corridor, passing sodden sheets and blankets along, and then they surge forwards – all but old Everett, who's still punching numbers uselessly into his phone. They take it in turns to dash closer and hurl the dripping items over the flames. It takes almost every item of bedding from eight bedrooms, but the fire is gradually dampened until they can tackle the final patches with less panic.

'I think we've done it,' Nazleen says.

But Jonas urges caution. 'As long as the staircase can still take our weight.'

Sadie is the first to make her way down the stairs, her feet squelching on the still-smoking blankets. She runs to the front door and pulls back the lower bolt, but her hands are sore from getting too close to the flames, and the upper bolt is stiff and repeatedly slips in her grasp.

'Who locked us in?' she says, her voice high-pitched, as Everett reaches the ground floor, puffing loudly.

Halfway down the stairs, Nazleen holds up a big bunch of keys with a confused expression. 'Not me. But I do have keys . . . '

'It's the bolt that's stuck.' Sadie tries it again, panic rising in her chest like boiling water in a pan. 'It's too stiff. Can someone help?'

Zach springs down the last few stairs behind Nazleen, and Jonas is close behind him, but as they move towards

Sadie, a door creaks open further down the hall and they all swing around. A figure hovers in the study doorway, her pale blue dressing gown lending her a ghostly appearance in the dim light.

'What's going on?' she says peevishly. 'You woke me up.' It's Mrs Shrew.

Sadie presses a hand over her heart. 'What are you doing down here?'

'I couldn't sleep in that room . . . ' Mrs Shrew's voice falters as she peers up the staircase. 'What on earth . . . ?'

'There's been a fire,' Jonas says, and he sounds almost apologetic.

Sadie grabs Zach's arm. 'Just get the door open. Please.'

Zach yanks back the bolt and tries the handle. It isn't locked, and the door swings wide open. Sadie is the first to run out into the freezing night air. Her attention is immediately caught by the metallic grinding of a car engine turning over and over and failing to catch. A moment later, the woman in the big coat hurtles out of the Mini and sprints towards Sadie.

'Mum?' Sadie says. She falls straight into the woman's arms.

'Oh, Sadie,' her mum cries. 'I thought I'd lost you.'

Sadie presses her face into her mum's coat and hugs her hard, utterly speechless. But from somewhere behind, she hears the wonder in Joe's voice as he greets her mother.

'Beth, is that really you?'

Sadie's mum sounds equally amazed. 'Jonas?'

And Joe's words trip over each other then. 'I thought I'd never see you again. I looked for you for months, Beth, I tried everything I could think of ... And then tonight ... what are you doing here? You woke us up.' His voice takes on a new tone of wonder. 'You saved our lives.'

Sadie pulls away from her mum and studies her face. 'You were throwing stones at the windows. But how did you know?'

'Your last letter,' Beth says. She sounds exhausted. 'I tried ringing you from the retreat before I set off, but you didn't answer. I drove all the way down to your flat – I've still got my key. I saw the invitation on the table ...' Her gaze slips over Beth's shoulder, past Jonas, and on to the other guests, and suddenly she rocks backwards as if she's been slapped.

'You,' she says. 'I should have known. This is all *your* doing, isn't it?'

Leonora sways gently from side to side, soothing the baby that's wrapped against her chest. For the hundredth time, she leans forward and peers around the corner of the stable block, but nothing has changed. The front door still yawns open; the chauffeur continues to leaf through his newspaper, oblivious to her presence. She's tempted – so tempted – to shuffle back a few metres, to let her knees unlock, to sink into the warm, damp grass and close her eyes . . . She hasn't slept for more than two hours at a time since the baby was born. But the one thing she desires even more than sleep is to see Hendrik leave Raven Hall for good.

Finally, voices float from the hall, and here is Hendrik stepping out, closely followed by Markus. Hendrik's chauffeur springs up the steps to take a box from Hendrik's arms, and all three men descend to the gravel with sombre faces.

She shrinks back against the sun-warmed wall, unseen, but listening intently.

'I'll keep the job open for you, anyway,' Hendrik says. 'For when you change your mind.'

'Dad.' Markus sounds weary. 'Will you stop staying that? I want to live here . . .'

Hendrik makes a scathing noise. 'She wants to live here, you mean.' His voice softens. 'She's taking advantage of you, Son, can't you see that?'

'Dad, stop it, please. I love her. I told you.'

235

The silence stretches. She stands very still. When the baby stirs, she kisses the top of her head softly. Stay asleep a little longer, Nina.

'Well, like I said . . .' *The clunk of the car door opening, and Hendrik's voice grows muffled.* 'You can join me as soon as you're ready.'

It takes all her will-power to stay hidden until the engine noise has faded beyond the top of the driveway. When she finally emerges, Hendrik's car is out of sight, and Markus is already on the top step, about to retreat indoors.

'Leonora!' *He's shocked; he thought she was staying at her lodgings until tomorrow.* 'Is Nina okay? What are you doing here?'

For one awful moment, she's convinced he's been persuaded by Hendrik's words after all; he's changed his mind; she's come this close and now she's going to have to leave again. But he hurries down to her with his arms wide open, his eyes glowing with concern.

'I couldn't stay away,' *she says.* 'I had to come . . . I couldn't bear to be away for even one more night.'

He pulls her into his arms, the baby sandwiched between them. 'I'm glad you came. I couldn't bear to be away from you, either – either of you.' *They stand like that, the three of them locked in an embrace, until the baby begins to wriggle.*

Then, as he leads her up the steps and into the house, she dips her head and whispers into her daughter's hair. 'This is your home, Nina. This is where you belong. I'll do whatever it takes to make sure it's yours for ever.'

Beth

I stare at the silver-haired woman in the pale blue dressing gown. It's almost thirty years since I saw last her, but her eyes glitter just as brightly now, in the freezing night air, as they did that long-ago summer's day when I first arrived at Raven Hall.

'Leonora.' I say. 'My God. I should have known.'

Her eyes widen, and she pulls her flimsy dressing gown closer around herself. 'Beth? Is that really you?'

I pull Sadie tighter against me. What the hell did Leonora want with my daughter? I'd disappeared, changed my name, done everything I could to leave this place behind. I thought I'd be free of Raven Hall for ever, so long as I never mentioned it again; I had no reason to suspect that Leonora might track me down – why would she? But it seems I've been so focused on burying the past, and on trying to ensure Sadie's life turns out better than my own, that I've deprived Sadie of the very knowledge that might have kept her safe.

Leonora lured me here once and made me play her game. How could I have gone away and left Sadie so vulnerable?

My eyes are gritty with exhaustion. My knuckles are bleeding from hammering on windows and doors. My limbs are weak from the adrenalin that's been pumping through my arteries for too long. But Leonora's expression of faux innocence drives all this from my mind and replaces it with a cold, sharp-edged fury.

I give Sadie one last squeeze and let her go, moving around her on the gravel to advance on Leonora.

'What's *wrong* with you?' As I move towards her, Leonora retreats up the stone steps. I pause, still on the gravel, and I curl my fists. 'I don't know what kind of sick game you're playing this time, but I won't let you get away with it again, I promise you. My daughter could have been *killed* in there.'

Leonora shakes her head with that same wounded expression. 'Your daughter?' Her gaze slides to Sadie. 'I had no idea she was your daughter.'

My laugh hurts my throat. 'Really.'

'No!' Incredibly, Leonora manages to look tearful. 'We were introduced as Miss Lamb and ...' She gestures to herself. 'Mrs Shrew. If I'd known she was your daughter ...'

I want to accuse her of lying, but the guilt that's gnawed away at me for twenty-nine years dries the words in my throat. I'm not blameless here, I can't forget that.

I shake my head sharply. 'Well, it's a remarkable coincidence.' I indicate the open front door behind her, the ruined staircase beyond. 'I suppose this fire was just an accident too?' I turn to Jonas. 'Has someone rung the police? I don't have a signal ...'

Jonas shakes his head. 'The landline's not connected. And,

Beth,' he glances around at the other shivering guests, 'we're all frozen. We need to get coats on, and then a couple of us can drive to the village for help.'

I realise he's gesturing to the ancient Mini, its driver's door still hanging open. I shake my head.

'It overheated, I can't get it to start again. I was lucky to get here at all – I'd have gone for help if I could.' I peer into the surrounding darkness, but I had a view of the driveway in my headlights as I pulled up, and I know there are no other cars here. 'We'll have to walk ...' Turning back, I see Leonora has retreated to the top step. 'Don't let her back in the house!'

Leonora holds up her hands and her tone is plaintive. 'I was only going to get my coat.'

'I'll get them,' another voice says, and for the first time I look properly at the three other guests who came bursting out of Raven Hall behind Sadie. The woman hurrying past Leonora into the hall to fetch the coats is a few years older than Sadie, wild-haired and anxious-looking. The skinny, dark-haired man standing next to Jonas is rubbing his arms and staring at Leonora. The elderly man has gone to sit on the steps to one side; he's partially turned away from us, peering at his phone. I don't recognise any of them.

The wild-haired woman returns with an armful of coats.

'Thanks, Nazleen,' Sadie says, as she takes a coat at random from the woman. I help Sadie put it on.

'Someone will have to walk to the village, then,' I say, 'if there's no other way.' I look at Jonas. 'Do you think you could ... ?'

'Of course.' Jonas drops his voice as he comes closer. 'But be careful while I'm gone.'

'I lived with Leonora for a year and a half,' I say curtly. 'Don't worry. I know what she's capable of.'

The rest of the group stops murmuring, and I realise they all heard me.

I look into Sadie's eyes, and I know exactly what she's thinking. *Tell me, Mum. Don't hide the past any longer. Tell me.* And I don't know whether it's the therapy I've been practising at the retreat, or the shock of seeing Leonora again after all these years, or just the pleading expression in my daughter's eyes, but I feel a sudden surge of strength, as if I'm drawing courage directly from the earth beneath my feet.

'Certain things happened here when I was a child.' I look pointedly at Leonora. 'Not just the fire. Other things, too. Nina was poisoned here.'

There's a collective intake of breath.

Nazleen glances at Leonora, then back to me. 'Who's Nina?'

'Nina was—' For a moment, I don't think I can go on. But Sadie reaches out and catches my hand in hers, and it gives me courage. 'Nina was Leonora's daughter,' I say. 'She was four months younger than me. My best friend.' I squeeze Sadie's hand tighter. 'And Leonora made her sick, deliberately. I'm convinced of it. Not just once. Three times, at least.'

On the top step, Leonora shakes her head, but her expression is fearful.

The skinny man pipes up. 'Wait. I felt sick this evening. Several of us did, didn't we?' He calls out to the old man sitting on the steps. 'You did too, didn't you, Dad? And you said you felt really tired, like you'd been drugged or something.'

Nazleen says, 'Yeah, me too. I felt nauseous, and then dizzy, like I couldn't think straight.'

At my side, Sadie nods. 'Me too. Actually, I don't think it's worn off yet. My head still feels hollow. And, Joe, didn't you say ...?'

Jonas shuffles his feet. 'Yeah, I haven't been feeling that great either.'

As we lift our gazes back to Leonora, she lurches towards the open door.

'Stop her!' I shout.

The skinny man throws himself in front of her, blocking her retreat into the house.

'Well done, Zach,' Nazleen says.

Leonora pokes the man called Zach in the chest. 'Let me pass.' Her voice trembles. 'This is *my* house ...'

I move up the steps behind her. 'You say that, Leonora, but it's not true, is it? This was never really your house.'

She turns to glare at me. 'How dare you! I took you in when you had nobody. I was only ever kind to you ...'

'You made me lie,' I say. 'You made me pretend to be Nina. You poisoned your own daughter, you started that fire in my bedroom ... Why? It was all to do with the house, I know, but *why* ...?'

Leonora presses her lips together and shakes her head.

'Okay,' Jonas says cautiously. 'Look, we need to get the police out here. You lot go back inside. I'll grab a torch and run to the village.'

Nazleen crosses her arms. 'There's no way I'm sitting in a room with *her*.' She jerks her chin at Leonora. 'Not if she just tried to kill us.'

'How about,' Sadie says, 'we lock her in the study? There's a key in the door. Can we get on with it? I'm freezing.'

Zach stands aside, and Leonora casts a disdainful look over us all.

'Oh, for goodness' sake,' she says, but she marches into the house and shuts herself in the study without another word. Zach strides to the door and turns the key. Jonas retrieves a torch from the hall table, but he pauses on the top step next to me as he comes out again.

'I'll be as quick as I can.' He searches my gaze. 'It really is good to see you again, you know.'

For a moment, despite my exhaustion, I consider offering to go with him. Anything to avoid setting foot in Raven Hall again. But the sight of Sadie's shivering figure stops me. She needs me to stay here with her; I'm not leaving her again.

I nod at Jonas. 'Just hurry.'

He sets off down the driveway at a jog, quickly swallowed by the darkness, only the bouncing beam of his torch showing his progress as he heads towards the road.

The old man, who up until now hasn't said a word, hauls himself up from his position on the steps, and he shuffles towards us with a sour expression.

'Come on then, let's get back inside,' he says. 'One of you girls put the kettle on, will you? I'm frozen half to death here. This bloody house.'

Sadie

The interior of the house is chilly, the air tainted with lingering, acrid smoke. When Sadie thinks of how warm and welcoming the place felt on her arrival, mere hours ago, it makes her feel off balance. Let alone the discovery that her mother used to live here with Mrs Shrew, of all people, who apparently tried to burn them in their beds tonight. Sadie has a thousand questions churning in her mind, and no idea where to start.

She glances at her mother, sensing this isn't the best time to ask her for more information. Beth is pale, wide-eyed; she stands just inside the threshold and wraps her arms around herself as her gaze jumps around the dimly lit hall. The other guests have gone straight through to the drawing room, and Sadie can hear Nazleen and Zach arguing over whether to light a fire in the grate. A moment later, Nazleen reappears in the hall, closing the drawing-room door softly behind her.

'Zach's lighting a fire,' she says, with an artificial brightness. 'I'll make some tea.' Her gaze comes to rest on Beth's hands, and she frowns. 'Are you hurt?'

Beth holds her hands out in front of her and stares at her bleeding knuckles as if they're not hers. 'I was knocking on the windows so hard . . .'

Nazleen's tone softens. 'Go and sit down. I'm sure Joe won't be long. We'll be out of here soon.'

Beth doesn't reply. Nazleen hurries off in the direction of the kitchen, and as soon as she's gone, Beth turns to Sadie.

'I've got to talk to Leonora. I need to know why she did it, why she brought you here. Honestly, Sadie, if I'd had any idea . . .'

'I know, Mum.' Sadie gives Beth's hand a gentle squeeze, taking care not to hurt her. 'Okay, let's do it, we'll go and talk to her together.'

But Beth still doesn't move, and Sadie feels a familiar stir of frustration. This is what she remembers, growing up: this closed, fearful expression on her mum's face. At the first mention of the past – or any other emotionally difficult topic – Beth would retreat into herself, refuse to engage.

With effort, Sadie keeps her voice gentle. 'You can't run away from things for ever, Mum . . .'

'I know.' Beth nods tightly. 'You're right.' But she trudges towards the study as if she's been summoned there; as if it wasn't her own idea at all.

Beth unlocks the door and walks in. Sadie hangs back in the doorway, watching Beth approach the green-topped desk. Leonora sits on the far side of it, her expression one of haughty contempt.

'What do you want?' Leonora snaps.

Beth's voice is strained. 'Why did you bring my daughter here? I know you blame me for what happened, but to take it out on my daughter . . .'

Sadie frowns; what's this about blame? What did her mother *do* here, all those years ago?

'I've already told you.' Leonora's reply is icy. 'I didn't know she was your daughter until just now.'

Beth draws in a shaky breath. 'What happened to Markus . . . it wasn't my fault . . .'

A loud bang in the hall sends Sadie spinning around, heart pounding. Someone's knocking at the front door, but it's too soon to be Joe returning with the police, surely? She glances back at Beth and Leonora, but they both seem as startled as she is. Nazleen is still in the kitchen, and the drawing-room door is closed, so when the door knocker crashes again, Sadie hurries to answer it.

A woman stands on the top step, her dark hair hanging in front of her shoulders like limp curtains, her face sallow in the yellowish light from the overhead lamps. She stumbles over her words, and Sadie can't tell whether it's from cold or from fear.

'Is everyone okay?' the woman says. 'I saw fire, from across the fields, and I was worried.' She glances beyond Sadie, into the hall, and her tone softens. 'Oh, I see you're all right . . .'

Bemused, Sadie turns around. Leonora is approaching, her hands outstretched to the woman as if she's half angry to see her, half pleading with her to go away.

'Yes, we're all fine,' Leonora says. 'You didn't need to come. You should go now.'

But the woman is no longer looking at Leonora. Her gaze has moved past her to fix on Beth, and her eyes are enormous, her face slack with astonishment.

'Beth?'

Beth

And in an instant, I'm back floundering under the ice.

It's her voice that does it. Despite her stranger's face – harshly lined, bordering on gaunt in the wash of sickly yellow light from above the front door – I know it's her from the way she says my name with such wounded disbelief.

Nina.

I haven't seen her in almost three decades. My last memory of her is hazy – rough hands tugging me to the surface, Nina's dark eyes reflecting my own shock, staring at me, as we're each carried away towards the swirl of blue lights on Raven Hall's drive . . .

I suck in a deep breath. 'Nina.' My voice is a croak.

Somehow, I close the gap between us, but my heart is pounding, because – what will she say to me? I ran away from the hospital the next day; I never went back. I left her there, with Leonora. I didn't take her with me.

I stop in front of her, and we gaze at each other.

'Is it really you?' she whispers.

I try to smile. 'How are you?'

Something flickers in her expression, and I prepare myself for an accusation, but instead she reaches out tentatively for me.

'Oh, Beth.' She touches me lightly, as if to check I'm real, and then she flings her arms around me. 'It really is you. I'm so happy to see you.'

I return her hug, feeling dizzy. 'What are you doing here?'

Finally, she lets go of me, and she steps back, and then she gives a small laugh. 'I might ask the same of you. What's going on?' She glances at Leonora, and then at the fire-ravaged staircase. 'Seriously. What happened? Is anyone hurt? Have you called the police?'

'Someone's gone for help on foot,' Sadie says cautiously, as if she's not quite sure whether she believes her own words. 'They'll call the police when they get to the village.'

I reach for my daughter's hand. 'Sadie, this is Nina. She was . . .' I hesitate, weighing my delight at being reunited with Nina against my long-term sense of guilt at leaving her behind. 'She was like a sister to me . . .'

Sadie says nothing, merely stares at Nina. I don't notice Leonora drawing closer until her voice cuts across us.

'A sister?' Leonora snaps. 'How dare you. After what you did to our family. After what you did to Markus . . .'

My chest tightens. 'That wasn't my fault.'

'Mum?' Sadie says.

Leonora spits her words out at me. 'You took Nina out on to the ice that night. You knew Markus would follow. You knew the risks, but you lured him out there anyway . . .'

'No,' I say. 'It wasn't like that . . .'

'He was trying to save you,' she says. 'And when he fell through—' Her voice cracks. 'They couldn't save *him*.'

And suddenly I'm back there, in the lake, and I can't breathe. Fingertips clawing at the edge of the ice, fire roaring in my chest ... When I finally haul my face up into the air, there's a single yell from Markus, somewhere close by. Next to me in the dark, Nina's gasping, coughing. Somewhere in the distance, Leonora is screaming.

And then I'm waking in the hospital, Leonora looming over me, her face gaunt. *This was all your fault, Beth. Markus died because of you* ...

I shake my head, forcing myself to return to the present, blinking back tears. 'I didn't know the ice would break ...'

Nina is frowning at Leonora. 'Mum, you can't keep blaming Beth. We went out on to the ice together that night; she didn't drag me out there. I followed her, even after she told me to go back.'

I shoot Nina a grateful look. It's true. That *is* what happened. I want Nina to say more, to explain to my daughter that I'm not the terrible person Leonora is accusing me of being. But a door creaks at the back of the house, and a moment later Nazleen comes into view, carrying a tea tray, looking at us in mild astonishment.

'What's going on?' She raises her eyebrows at Nina. 'Oh, it's you.'

Nina draws herself up, as if waking from a dream. 'Oh, you've made tea, what a good idea. Shall we go and ... ?' She indicates the drawing-room door.

Sadie and Nazleen look pointedly at me, and I summon my courage.

'Nina, we ... actually ...' I grimace. 'We asked Leonora to wait in the study until the police get here. We think she ...' I glance at the blackened staircase. 'We're concerned that she might be responsible for the fire.'

Nina begins to smile, and then she seems to realise I'm being serious.

'No way.' Her eyes widen, and she turns to Leonora and studies her as if seeing her in a new light. 'No, come on. There must be another explanation ...' But we can all hear the doubt in her voice. Leonora's expression remains closed, tight-lipped.

'She was downstairs,' Sadie explains to Nina, 'when the fire started. While we were asleep in our beds.'

'And someone drugged us,' Nazleen adds. 'We've all felt ill tonight, and ...' She glances at me. 'Well, Beth told us that Leonora poisoned her own daughter, years ago, so we think ...'

Nina draws her breath in sharply.

'I'm sorry,' I say softly to Nina, acutely aware that Nazleen has no idea Nina *is* Leonora's daughter. Images I've tried to suppress for years are crowding into my mind: the blue checked dress, the oily residue in the mug, Leonora accusing me of starting the fire in my bedroom when I knew it wasn't me ...

Nina's voice is faint. 'How much longer do you think the police will be?'

'Not long,' I say.

There's a pause, and then Nina makes a gesture of defeat.

'Well, okay then. Put her back in the study, if you have to. I'll come and wait with you, until the police get here.'

Leonora stalks away and shuts herself in the study again. Nazleen turns the key on her this time, and the tension in my shoulders eases slightly as I follow Nina into the once-familiar drawing room, where Zach and the old man are huddled by a modest fire in the grate.

Sadie is safe. The police are on their way. And not only is Nina here, she's chosen to come with me rather than wait with Leonora. Despite everything, Nina still trusts me.

Leonora rarely visits their local market town – they have everything they need delivered to Raven Hall, after all – but she does enjoy these occasional trips out. Perhaps she should do this more often.

She buys herself a necklace that catches her fancy. A new shirt for Markus. A Cabbage Patch doll for Nina's upcoming ninth birthday. Then she pauses in front of the bakery window and eyes up the cakes. She'll buy three doughnuts. Markus and Nina will be waiting for her to return home for lunch. They can eat these out on the veranda afterwards, where Nina can scatter sugar to her heart's content.

Tucking the paper bag in with her other purchases, she strolls back to the car park, and that's when she sees it: the mink-blue Ford Capri.

Outwardly, she freezes, but inside her heart is pounding, her muscles tense and ready to run. She scans the car park twice, three times. There's no sign of the Capri's owner. A young couple pass her, casting her wary looks, and she darts across to her own car, to start the engine with trembling fingers.

She needs to get home. She needs to get back to the safety of Raven Hall. Her shopping lies forgotten in the car park as she escapes the town.

When she reaches the village, she presses her sunglasses more firmly against her nose, and she keeps her gaze fixed on the road ahead, her fingers rigid on the steering wheel, until she emerges on

252

the other side. And then, out on the lane, a good few hundred yards from the top of Raven Hall's driveway, she sees Nina whizzing towards her on her little blue bike. Leonora slams on her brakes. She leaps out, into the middle of the road.

'What are you doing?' She grabs her daughter by the arm, shoves her into the back seat of the car.

'Mummy, my bike—'

'You mustn't leave Raven Hall,' she shouts at her. 'You must never come this far, not by yourself.'

'But I was coming to meet you.'

'What if someone saw you?' She shakes Nina's arm to make sure she's listening. 'Do you hear me? You stay close to home, okay? You mustn't come this far again.'

By the time they pull up outside the house, Nina is sobbing hysterically. Markus gives Leonora a despairing look.

'Did you have to be so hard on her?'

She reaches out and tries to stroke her daughter's hair, but Nina flinches away from her.

'Daddy will go back and get your bike,' she says, her voice soft now with guilt. 'I'm sorry, Nina. I was frightened. You could have been hit by a car, anything could have happened . . .'

Markus scoops the little girl out of the back seat. 'It's okay, sweetie, Mummy didn't mean to scare you.'

Leonora reaches out to touch Nina again as Markus carries her up the steps in his arms, and this time Nina doesn't turn away. She gazes back at Leonora, watching her shut the front door firmly behind them, watching her lean back against it with a sigh of relief. Even after Markus has set Nina down and wiped her tear-stained cheeks and gone to fetch her a chocolate biscuit, her eyes are still fixed on her mother.

'You just have to remember,' Leonora tells her, as gently as she can. 'It's very important, Nina. You must never leave Raven Hall without us. It isn't safe.'

Sadie

Sadie still has that hollow feeling in her head, but she's convinced there's something else wrong with her too. Her body is on full alert, as if an invisible threat is constantly behind her, ducking out of sight each time she glances over her shoulder. She frowns at the back of Beth's head as she follows her into the drawing room.

Zach gazes at Nina as they take their seats, and his expression slides from bemusement to surprise.

'Oh, hi,' he says to Nina. 'I thought you'd left?'

Sadie knows she's missed something. She was so thrown to discover the stranger at the door was Nina – the woman her mother describes as once being like a *sister* to her – that she'd barely registered that Nina looked vaguely familiar too. She studies her now, trying to work out where she's seen her before.

Nina accepts a cup of tea from Nazleen, and she smiles at Zach.

'Yeah, I went home to bed, but I had a bad dream, and when

I got up for a glass of water, I looked out the window and I saw smoke . . . '

Finally, Sadie remembers. 'You were the photographer last night, weren't you?' Her gaze roams over Nina's hair and face. 'You look different. I guess your hair was covered . . . '

'Keeps it out the way of the lens.' Nina gives Sadie a puzzled look. 'Didn't you recognise me when you opened the door just now?'

Sadie shakes her head, frustrated by the sluggishness of her thoughts. 'Did you drive back?' she asks. 'Maybe we could overtake Joe, bring help back sooner . . . '

But Nina sighs. 'No, I had a drink when I got back. It helps me sleep, you know. I get nightmares sometimes . . . '

She looks distressed for a moment, and Beth reaches across and squeezes her hand. Sadie's surprised to feel a twinge of jealousy. She's never had to share her mother with anyone before.

'So I walked back,' Nina says.

'You live that close?'

'Not usually, no. I'm just staying there tonight, for the photography job, you know. The thing is, when I . . .when we got the chance . . . Well, it's strange but . . . suddenly I really wanted to come back and see the place.' She glances at Beth again.

Sadie nods slowly. 'How did they hire you? Did you meet the owner?' She looks around at the other guests. 'Who *is* the owner of the murder mystery company? Does anyone know?'

She's met with blank expressions.

'Do you think . . . ?' Nazleen says hesitantly. 'I mean, if it was Mrs Shrew who started the fire . . . '

Zach's eyes widen. 'You don't think *she's* the owner, do you? The one who invited us here. I mean, why would she . . . ?'

Sadie feels nauseous again. *Yes, why would Leonora want to hurt them?*

Everett's voice rumbles from the depths of his armchair. 'Because she's deranged, that's why. The woman needs locking up.'

Nina ducks her head, but not before Sadie catches a flash of emotion in her eyes, and suddenly Sadie feels desperately sorry for her. The others clearly don't know that Nina is Leonora's daughter, and whatever Leonora has done, it isn't Nina's fault. Does Nina think Leonora is capable of it? Sadie rubs her temples. Her thoughts are like darting fish, sparking across her mind, slipping out of reach. Despite the hot tea and the flames in the grate, she still feels cold all over.

Nina gets to her feet. 'I need something stronger than tea. Anyone else? I saw whiskey in the pantry earlier.' The others sit in silence while she's gone, but she returns quickly, with a bottle tucked under her arm and a stack of crystal glasses.

Everett leans forward eagerly. 'Good girl.'

'Yes,' Nazleen says, smiling. 'This might warm us up a bit.'

Nina clatters the glasses on to the coffee table, and she sloshes generous servings of whiskey into each of them. As Sadie watches, she finally catches hold of one of the questions that have been niggling at her. She takes the glass offered and sits back.

'If you saw the fire,' she says to Nina, 'from your window . . . why didn't you call the fire brigade?'

Nina's condescending expression reminds Sadie so strongly of Leonora, it's almost amusing. 'Well, I tried to, obviously, but you know how the phones can be, out here in the Fens ... Cheers.' Nina knocks back the contents of her glass, tucks her chin into her neck and shivers. 'Gosh, that's good.' She nudges Beth's arm next to her. 'Drink up.'

Sadie is frowning. 'But the landline, surely ...'

Nina's tone has a distinct coldness in it now. 'Well, yes ... That's a funny story, actually ...'

Sadie makes eye contact with Beth. *Something's not right here.* But Beth lowers her gaze and stares down into her glass, and Sadie's heart sinks. Yet again, her mother seems to be withdrawing, refusing to engage.

'So, I'll tell it to you from the beginning,' Nina says, refilling her glass. 'Anyone for a top-up?'

The guests murmur politely and shake their heads: they haven't started on their first servings yet. They settle back in their seats to hear Nina's story, lifting the glasses of golden liquid to their lips.

Beth

'No!' It's out of my mouth almost before I know I'm going to say it. 'Don't drink it!'

The others stare at me, their mouths hanging open, and slowly they lower their glasses. All except Everett, who tuts and tips his glass back to swig from it anyway. I spring towards him and knock the glass from his hand, sending it hurtling through the air to smash against the black marble fireplace in an explosion of glittering, ice-like shards.

'What the hell are you playing at?' Everett barks.

I'm not sure exactly when I knew something was wrong – perhaps when Sadie's worried gaze hit mine, or when I saw a coldness in Nina's eyes that wasn't there thirty years ago – but I'm as certain as I can be that there is something in that whiskey.

I ignore Everett and swing around to check on Sadie. She looks so young, suddenly. She gives me that same trusting smile she always used to when she was a child, and then she peers down into her own glass.

'There's definitely something in it that shouldn't be there,' she says, swirling the contents gently. 'Something oily ...'

Everett is all bluster. 'What's going on? Are you saying that Averell woman is trying to poison us, now that she's failed to burn us in our beds?'

I turn to Nina, who's just swallowed a whole glass of the stuff. I'm concerned for her, but I can't help thinking, *How could she not have had something to do with this?* I desperately want to believe, like Everett, that Leonora is wholly responsible. But Leonora is locked in the study, and how would she have known we'd end up drinking the whiskey?

'You just drank it ...' I say to her, stupidly.

She gazes back at me. 'You were right, you know,' she says eventually. 'About Mum poisoning me when I was a child.'

The room is utterly silent as the other guests absorb this revelation that the photographer is, in fact, Nina, Leonora's daughter.

Nina gives a heavy sigh. 'I made Mum admit it. After – you know – after Markus died. She said it was,' she mimics Leonora's voice, *'Just a gentle herbal preparation, that's all.* Just enough to keep me out the way when my grandfather visited.' Nina's face crumples. 'Can you imagine how that *feels*?'

I swallow hard. 'But what about now?' I gesture at the whiskey bottle. 'How did *this* happen?' I search her gaze, and there's plenty of emotion there – anger, frustration, self-pity – but no surprise; no shock or anxiety at having drunk another dose of her mother's poison. And suddenly I'm thinking of the last time I was in this house; of the horror and fear on

Leonora's face before she ran up into the smoke to look for Nina . . .

'My God,' I say. 'I always thought it was your mum who started the fire in my bedroom. I was sure I hadn't left anything on, I thought maybe she was creating an excuse to get rid of me, but—' I shake my head. 'Leonora loves this house. Too much. Definitely too much to risk burning it down – either then or now. Whereas you . . .'

Nina doesn't take her eyes off me. She says nothing, but even after all these years, I can still read her – her wounded air of always being in the right, no matter what.

I step closer to her, my heart pounding painfully. 'You did this, didn't you? Brought these people here. Put something in their food to make them sleepy. Started the fire . . . It was you, wasn't it?'

She shakes her head and laughs softly. 'Oh, Beth. You're being ridiculous. You must be exhausted.' She sits forward, as if that's an end to the conversation, and she pulls a white scrunchie hairband from her pocket, scoops up her hair, gathers and twists it until it's captured in a bun on the back of her head.

Deflated, I glance around at the others. Is Nina right? Is this my exhaustion talking? I'm hoping that Sadie, at least, might offer me some reassurance, but she's staring at Nina with a fascinated expression, and when she blurts out a question of her own, I genuinely believe I've lost my grip on the whole situation.

'What time is it, Nina?' Sadie says, enunciating her words with care.

Nina raises her eyebrows, then draws back the cuff of her coat. 'Ten past four.'

'Your watch . . .' Sadie says. I follow her gaze to Nina's white sports watch. Sadie sounds both amazed and triumphant. 'You've been sitting in your car outside Mum's house, haven't you? These past few weeks. In a dark grey Audi . . .'

I look from Sadie to Nina, my bewilderment greater than ever. 'Is that true? Why? Why would you do that?'

Suddenly, Nina's face collapses into a childlike expression – hurt and resentful, as if she's been the victim of a cruel trick. She glares at me as though it's all my fault, and she can't seem to resist bouncing the blame back on to me.

'It took me months to track you down, I had to persuade someone who works with Caroline . . . And then, when I rang your workplace, they just said you didn't work there any more. They wouldn't tell me anything else. I watched your house for *hours*, Beth. You never went in or out. All I saw was this sad daughter, and people carting away your furniture . . .' She shakes her head, as if the whole world has conspired against her. 'You never answered your invitation. You made me think you were dead.'

Sadie

Sadie scans her memory. All that post of her mother's that she scooped up and dropped unopened into the cardboard box in the hall ... Beth had assured her, before she left for the retreat, that all her bills were settled, there'd be nothing that needed Sadie's attention. And, of course, Sadie had believed her; she'd barely glanced at anything in that box. How easily an invitation to a murder mystery weekend might have been lost among the pizza leaflets and charity letters and free newspapers ...

Beth stares at Nina and her voice is faint. 'You really thought I was dead?'

Nina presses her lips together, and Sadie suspects she's regretting her outburst.

'So it was you who sent the invitations,' Sadie says to her. 'But I saw you watching Mum's house weeks before I got my invite. Was I ... ' She glances at Beth. 'Did you invite me here as a replacement for my mum?'

Nina ignores her. She looks utterly exhausted now; she

slumps back on the sofa, and her next words are quiet and directed only at Beth.

'What does it matter, now, anyway?' she says. 'The whole thing has failed, hasn't it? I concede defeat, Beth – congratulations. You win again.'

Leonora watches Markus and Nina from the kitchen window. They're playing croquet on the lawn, mallets clacking, Nina shrieking indignantly every time Markus knocks one of her balls out of place. It's a joyful, vicious game.

She glances at the clock; she wishes she could be as relaxed as they are.

It's been three weeks since Stephanie's phone call. 'Sorry, Leonora, I thought I should let you know, I've just taken a booking for a Mr Hendrik Meyer for next month, and his secretary said she was booking an appointment with the local estate agent, too . . .'

At first, Leonora had felt hopeless. This was it: Hendrik was coming back to put an end to all her dreams. He'd sell the house, throw them out . . . Markus tried to reassure her, but she had to face the truth: their chances of persuading Hendrik to let them stay at Raven Hall were virtually nil. But then Markus – her wonderful, kind-hearted, clever Markus – had come up with a plan . . .

She glances at the clock again. Their guest will be here in a few minutes. She raps on the kitchen window to summon Markus and Nina in.

By the time the car draws up on the gravel, the three of them are lined up on the top step, and Leonora shoots a quick look at Markus over Nina's head: can they really pull this off? Are they making a mistake? Is it too late to change their minds?

The car door opens, and out steps the child: blonde-haired,

round-cheeked, her face a mask of self-protection that Leonora rec-
ognises only too well: the face of a survivor, the face of an orphan.
Leonora's heart squeezes with a painful mix of sympathy and terror.
This girl is their best chance – their only chance.

Leonora hurries down the steps to greet her.

Beth

'This isn't a game, Nina!' I shake her by the arms, trying to make her look at me. 'Why did you do it?'

Nina's expression is closed now, she turns her head away. Sadie moves to the window, to the gap in the curtains, and the relief in her voice makes my heart ache.

'The police are here.'

I'm shocked to feel tears welling up. Jonas has called for help. We're going to be okay. I turn back to Nina, but still she refuses to look at me, and I feel my anger rising.

'What was this all *for*?' I gesture at Sadie and the other guests huddled in their dressing gowns and overcoats; at the abandoned whiskey glasses; at the door that hides the blackened staircase beyond. 'Just tell me, will you?'

'Yes, tell us.' Nazleen's voice is indignant. 'You don't even know me. Why would you want to hurt me?'

Yeah,' Zach chimes in plaintively. 'What did we ever to do you?'

Finally, Nina meets my gaze – only for a fraction of a second, but it's enough to make my blood freeze. I stumble backwards, away from her, away from the ice-cold fury in her eyes. *I know what some of us did to her.*

Leonora made her sick, hid her from the world and from her own grandfather. Jonas switched his attentions to me when I came on the scene. And as for me, I took her place, pretended to be her, stole her only friend away from her . . .

'There's no point looking for a rational reason,' Everett growls from his armchair. 'She's a criminal. She needs locking up.'

Nina gets to her feet. Blue light slices through the window and washes over her face. She moves closer to the armchair by the fire.

'Dr Everett,' she says. 'I notice *you* haven't asked me why I invited you here.'

Everett's tone is aggrieved. 'I've never met you before, either.' He glances around the room nervously. 'I had no idea that woman was your mother until just now.'

'*That woman,*' Nina says, 'has a name. Leonora Averell. Do you remember her? Please tell me you haven't forgotten driving her back to your house, years ago, when she was alone and vulnerable.'

Everett's dark eyes widen, and Nina nods as something tightens in his expression.

'I see you do remember,' she says.

Blue light fills the room now. Car doors slam outside, boots pound across the gravel.

Everett barks at Zach. 'Get them in here, quick. They need to take her away, lock her up.'

Nina tilts her head, and she looks him straight in the eye. 'Dr Roy Everett. We haven't properly met. I'm Nina Averell. And I'm your daughter.'

Sadie

For a long, breath-holding moment, no one says a word. Nina stares down at Everett, and Everett gazes back at her with mounting horror.

'It's not true, Dad,' Zach says, 'is it?'

Everett is saved from having to reply. The front door crashes open in the hall, and a woman's voice shouts, 'Police!' Beth leaps to her feet, and Sadie moves to stand next to her.

Two uniformed officers burst into the drawing room, firing questions at the guests, and more than one trembling hand rises to point directly at Nina. The officers converge on her, and they take her to one side to talk.

'I don't understand,' Sadie murmurs to Beth after a few minutes have passed. 'How did you live with this family for so long? The mother poisoning the daughter, the daughter setting the house on fire. It all sounds . . .'

'It wasn't like that.' Beth pulls a face. 'I mean, okay, those bits weren't good, but apart from that – most of the time – it was a pretty wonderful place to live . . .'

Sadie remains unconvinced. 'But you said they made you pretend to be Nina – why?'

Beth answers slowly. 'It was to do with the house. Leonora didn't want to lose the house.'

'Well, that turned out well.' Sadie mulls it over, frowning. 'Do you think they dreamt this up together then, Nina and Leonora?'

For a long moment, Beth doesn't reply. They both watch as Nina repeatedly shakes her head in response to the police officers' questions, and Sadie thinks perhaps Beth doesn't think it's fair to speculate.

But eventually, Beth sighs. 'I just can't imagine Leonora agreeing to anything that would damage this house.'

Sadie catches hold of Beth's hand, then. '*We're* going to be okay, Mum, aren't we?' She searches Beth's gaze, feeling like a child again, desperate for her mother's reassurance. 'Aren't we?'

'Oh, Sadie.' Beth draws her into her arms, and she holds her tight. 'Of course we are. We've got each other, haven't we? We're definitely going to be okay.'

Beth

I hold Sadie close to me as I watch the police officers caution Nina and arrest her.

My poor, damaged friend, Nina.

Nina isn't Markus' daughter. She's the local doctor's daughter. I can hardly believe it. And yet . . . I glance from Nina's slim frame to Zach's; from Zach's fine, dark hair back to Nina's. Although her half-brother must be a good few years younger than her, the genetic link between them seems suddenly, glaringly clear.

Finally, after thirty years, the bizarre rules of Nina's childhood begin to make sense. Leonora kept Nina hidden, not just from the village doctor himself, but from anyone local who knew him, who might have put two and two together. Nina looked nothing like Markus, and all it would take would be one nosy neighbour to remark on her similarity to Dr Everett or his son, and the secret might escape . . . *And what if that secret found its way to Hendrik?*

There was no love lost between Leonora and Hendrik – I'd seen that right from Hendrik's first visit. Would Hendrik have allowed Markus to continue living at Raven Hall with Leonora and Nina for as long as he did, if he'd known the truth? Would he have been happy with the idea of Nina eventually inheriting the house? I think not.

It's entirely inappropriate, but I feel a sudden urge to laugh. Anyone else in Leonora's position, wanting to hide the paternity of their baby, would have had an easy option: they'd have moved away from where the father lived. But Leonora's obsession with Raven Hall made that solution impossible.

Then my anger returns. It was one thing for Leonora to hide Nina away from her biological father and the other locals, quite another for her to scour children's homes for a more convincing granddaughter for Hendrik. Whatever terrible things Nina has done here tonight, the ultimate blame lies with Leonora; of that, I'm certain.

Perhaps Nina catches a flash of sympathy in my eyes, because she calls out to me suddenly.

'My mother always loved this house more than she loved me; you know that, don't you?' She looks desperately sorry for herself. 'I'm not obsessed with Raven Hall like them. All I wanted was a tiny bit of justice.'

I say nothing in reply. My mind is still reeling. She tried to kill my daughter this evening. But she used to be my best friend – how will I ever come to terms with this?

As the officers lead Nina towards the door, she looks over her shoulder and locks her gaze on mine.

'I just hope the fire did enough damage,' she says bitterly. 'I hope they have to tear this whole place down.'

And then she's gone, led out to an ambulance that spills blue light over the gravel driveway. I'm glad, of course, that she's been taken into custody. But I can't help agreeing with her final words: *I hope they have to tear this whole place down.*

Sadie

Sadie watches her mother.

Beth has been sitting by the drawing-room window ever since the police led Nina out to the ambulance, and she's barely taken her gaze off the ambulance doors. She says she just wants to know where Nina will be taken – to the hospital or to a police cell? But Sadie knows she's struggling to process the fact that the woman she was once so close to tried to kill several people tonight.

Including Sadie.

If Mum was emotionally reticent before, what will she be like after this?

The police have been through the drawing room, collecting samples and asking more questions. The guests aren't allowed to leave yet, but, a few minutes ago, a pair of officers offered to escort them back up the damaged staircase to their bedrooms, so they could change out of their nightclothes and pack their bags.

'Do you want to come with me?' Sadie had asked Beth.

Beth shook her head. 'Not till I know what they're doing with Nina.'

Sadie turned back to the officers. 'I'll wait here a bit longer, if that's okay. I don't want to leave my mum alone.'

Outside, the darkness is finally giving way to sunrise. Beyond the band of reeds, the surface of Avermere glints with reflected oranges and pinks and golds. Beth leans closer to the glass and breathes out an 'Oh'.

Sadie goes to join her, and she peers beyond the emergency vehicles to a civilian car, and a man standing next to it.

'Who's that?' Sadie says. 'Is it Joe?'

A moment later, he turns, and she sees that is Joe. He walks around to the passenger side and helps a second person climb out of the car – an elderly man, white-haired and slow-moving. The old man doesn't straighten fully once he's out on the gravel. He leans on a stick as he walks, his tall frame stooped, his gait uncertain.

Beth is no longer watching the ambulance; she seems transfixed by the spectacle of Joe and the old man approaching the house.

'Come on,' Sadie says, aware that her bright tone sounds false. 'Let's go and see if Joe's got any news.'

She sets off for the hall, half-expecting Beth to stay by the window, but, after a short delay, Beth does follow her. They wait on the top step as the two men approach at the old man's slow pace. When Joe looks across and spots them, his whole face lights up.

'Wow, Mum,' Sadie murmurs, 'he sure looks pleased to see

you.' She's only ever known her mum single; Beth always maintained she wasn't interested in finding a partner while Sadie was growing up. Sadie's pondering her feelings about this when her attention is caught by the old man again – something about his face as he glances up ...

'Woah,' Sadie says. 'That man looks like ...' She turns to Beth. 'He looks like the man in the portrait in the dining room.'

Beth doesn't reply. The men reach the bottom of the steps, and the old man leans more heavily on Joe's arm as they begin to climb.

Joe looks up at Beth. 'How are you?' Belatedly, he tears his gaze from her and smiles at Sadie too. 'And how're you feeling? The police just told us they found sleeping tablets ground up in the pantry, alongside an empty bottle of herbal stuff. I guess that accounts for how dopey we've all been feeling ...' His smile has disappeared now. 'And they told us it was Nina ...'

The old man coughs heavily into his fist, and even with his face tilted down, Sadie can see he looks utterly miserable. She catches Joe's eye and looks pointedly back at the old man.

'Oh, yes, sorry,' Joe says. 'This is Hendrik Meyer. He owns Raven Hall; he was staying at the B&B last night ... Hendrik, this is Beth and Sadie.'

Hendrik barely looks at them, but indicates they should all move inside. They make their way into the still-chilly drawing room, and Joe guides Hendrik to the armchair that Roy Everett was sitting in not so long ago. Sadie adds a couple more logs to the fire, and then she joins Joe on the sofa opposite Hendrik. For the first time, she feels self-conscious that she's wearing nightclothes under her borrowed coat. Amazing how such trivial worries creep right back in as soon as your life's no longer in danger.

Beth returns to the window, to resume her watch over the ambulance.

Sadie studies Hendrik covertly, strangely entranced by the washed-out blue of his age-clouded eyes. He peers around the room and his gaze comes to rest on the glass fragments scattered over the black marble hearth. *It looked much nicer in here earlier*, Sadie wants to tell him. *It was quite glamorous and welcoming back then.* But she worries it would sound odd for her to try to cheer up this old man, when she's never met him before. So she stays quiet.

Joe shifts his position to look at Beth. 'The police said we've just got to be patient . . .'

Finally, Sadie remembers what she wanted to ask him. 'Was Genevieve there, at the B&B?'

'Yes.' He gives her a relieved smile. 'She was. After all that panic. Mum said she knocked just after eleven – a young woman with dark hair in a red dress, fur coat. She told Mum she'd been at a house party but got fed up with the other guests – can you believe it?'

Even in her least responsible moments, Sadie would never have walked out of a job leaving people to worry over her like that. Still, she's relieved they didn't find Genevieve's body at the bottom of the lake . . . With a jolt, she remembers what happened to Hendrik's son, Markus.

'So, yeah,' Joe says, 'I jogged back to the B&B and rang the police. And I found Hendrik still up. I knew he was on his way from the airport when I set off to come here – it was him I tried to ring during dinner, to give him an update . . . Anyway, there he was, in the lounge, wide awake and having a drink, so . . .'

'Eight-hour time difference,' Hendrik says gloomily. 'It doesn't get any easier as you get older, I tell you.'

'I emailed Hendrik a few weeks ago,' Joe explains. 'I kept seeing vehicles coming and going from Raven Hall – carpenters' vans, department store lorries. I thought maybe Hendrik was getting the place tidied up to sell, but he said—'

'I thought it was squatters,' Hendrik says. 'And I said not to worry, I wanted to come over for one last visit anyway, sort through some stuff here and get the place on the market. But then, when Joe said he'd been invited to an event here, I asked him to go along and see who was behind it.' He turns his head away to cough, then turns back. 'I suppose, before I called the police, I wanted to make sure it wasn't Nina, come back to her old home. But I never imagined . . .'

'That this is what she had planned,' Sadie says.

'Exactly.' Hendrik shakes his head morosely. 'I'd have let her live here, you know – I'd have given her the house if she wanted it. I did try to stay in touch, after Markus . . .' He pauses, waiting for his throat to settle. 'But Leonora cut me off, refused all my offers of money for the child. She took Nina away – to the south coast somewhere.'

'I'm sorry,' Sadie says. 'That must have been difficult.'

Hendrik sighs. 'I should have tried harder to contact her once she was an adult and out of Leonora's clutches. That's the other reason I flew over. I suppose I was hoping, if I could find Nina, we might talk face to face. I've no doubt her mother poisoned her against me, but still – she *is* my granddaughter.'

Sadie holds her breath. *He doesn't know yet.* She glances at Joe, but he wasn't there to hear Nina's final revelation either. And over by the window, Beth remains silent. Should Sadie leave it to the police to tell Hendrik eventually, or would it be kinder to break the news to him herself?

'Oh, Mr Meyer,' she says gently. 'I'm so sorry. Right before the police arrived, Nina told us . . .' She hesitates. She has no idea how he's going to take the news; will he be devastated – or might he even be relieved?

'What is it?' Joe says.

Sadie swallows. 'I'm afraid Nina said she'd found out she wasn't Markus' biological daughter. Roy Everett is her father . . .'

She keeps her eyes trained on the hunched old man in the armchair. He lifts his head and stares straight back at her. He looks neither angry nor surprised, merely confused.

'Come closer, will you?' he says. 'What did you say your name was?'

Warily, she approaches his chair and, at a gesture from him, she crouches so that he can get a good look at her face. His brow lowers, and his gaze grows sharper.

'All right,' he says. 'Enough. Is this some sort of game?' And then he looks up, and Sadie realises that Beth has come to stand beside her.

'Hendrik,' Beth says, 'there's a lot more you don't know, I'm afraid.'

Hendrik's eyes widen. 'Nina? Is that you? But the police said ...'

Beth shakes her head. 'I'm not Nina. I never was. They found me in a children's home, and they brought me here and asked me to play a game, to act the part of Nina, to try to fool you. I suppose it was because she didn't look like Markus ... Oh, Hendrik, I'm so, so sorry.'

Sadie looks in shock from her mother back to Hendrik. He screws up his eyes, and Beth reaches out and touches him tentatively on the shoulder. For an awful moment, Sadie thinks he's about to cry, but when he opens his eyes again, she realises he's laughing – bewildered, strained laughter, but laughter, nonetheless.

'Let me show you something,' he says. 'Jonas, help me up ...'

Jonas eases Hendrik to his feet, and Hendrik fumbles around in his pockets, eventually pulling out a battered leather wallet.

'Here it is.' Hendrik sits back down with a huff, and then he slides a photo from the wallet. It's in colour, but faded. He passes it to Sadie.

Sadie frowns. 'When was this taken?' She peers at it more closely, her heart knocking strangely. *I don't remember sitting for this.* It looks so old fashioned – was it for an audition? No, there's nothing familiar about it – not the garden setting, not the blue checked dress, not the plaits ...

She passes the photo to Beth and frowns at Hendrik. 'It's not me. Who *is* it?'

'She was my wife,' Hendrik says. 'Anneliese, Markus' mother. This was taken when she was sixteen, when I first met her. And you're her spitting image, my dear. You look even more like her than your mother did.' He eases back in the chair and switches his gaze to Beth. 'Now, tell me again about this so-called game.'

With every minute that Hendrik is in the house, Leonora feels Raven Hall slipping from her grasp. The way he looks at her with those piercing-blue eyes. The way he looks at Beth . . .

'I'm Nina, Sir,' Beth told him when he arrived. And now she's playing her violin for him. But Leonora can barely breathe; she's waiting for Hendrik to leap up, to declare the whole performance a sham, to banish them all from this place for ever.

She curls her fingers tightly in her lap, so Hendrik won't see them shaking. Why did she let Markus talk her into trying this? But then again . . . what other option did they have?

Beth lowers her violin, and – is it possible? Hendrik is crying. He's genuinely crying.

'That was beautiful, my child,' he says. 'You remind me so much of your grandmother, Anneliese.'

Slowly, slowly, Leonora uncurls her fingers. Against all the odds, it seems their little game might just have worked.

Beth

I can't tear my eyes from the photo of Anneliese. The blue checked dress … the ribbons at the end of her plaits … and her face – so eerily similar to Sadie's. But how can this be? What does it mean?

I'm barely aware of Hendrik rising from his chair again. It's not until he grasps my hand that I finally let the photo fall.

'Look at me,' he says, his voice raspy. 'You remember the first time we met?'

I expect to see anger or disgust in his eyes, but it's something else entirely – a mixture of confusion and concern. I can't find my voice, but I nod.

'I recognised your outfit,' he says. 'Markus had a copy of this photo, so Leonora would have seen it. I thought she must be trying to unsettle me, by dressing you up to look like Anneliese. It felt like a cruel trick.'

I shake my head. 'That wasn't the trick.'

'But you want me to believe – what? That you were a stranger? That she picked you at random from a children's home? A

284

blonde, musical child, who might just pass as Anneliese's granddaughter?'

'Yes, so you wouldn't kick them out,' I say, 'and sell Raven Hall. And it worked, didn't it?'

He stares at me, and then we both drop our gaze to the hearth, where the photo of Anneliese lies surrounded by splinters of glass. I can feel my whole history trembling.

'What does it mean?' I say.

Hendrik shakes his head, frowning. 'I don't know. We must be missing something.'

'Well, come on, then.' Sadie steps forward and picks up the photo. 'There's only one person who might be able to explain this. And the way I see it, her daughter nearly killed me a few hours ago, and she, at best, took advantage of you when you were a child, Mum.' She looks from me to Hendrik, and her eyes glow with determination. 'Leonora owes us some answers.'

'Why should I tell you anything?' Leonora snaps.

She sits with her arm touching one of the dining-room curtains, in an unsettling mirror image of my earlier position at the drawing-room window, and my heart contracts with unexpected sympathy as I follow her gaze through the glass to the ambulance that still hasn't moved from the driveway. Despite everything Nina's done, Leonora still loves her. I'm not convinced Nina loves her back, but my own feelings about the pair of them are too complicated for me to analyse their relationship right now.

'I'm sure if Nina wasn't okay,' I say gently, 'they'd have taken her to hospital by now.'

Leonora gives a tiny nod of acknowledgement.

'It's just,' I say, 'I know about Nina's biological father now. But still – I'd really like to understand my part in the ... in the game. Why you asked me to pretend to be Nina.' I study her closed expression. 'You gave me a very happy home here, Leonora.' I cross my fingers behind my back before I realise what I'm doing. It's as if asking a favour of Leonora has made me revert to being a child again.

To my surprise, tears well up in her eyes. 'I did try ...'

'Oh, you did.' Hurriedly, I drag across another of the heavy dining chairs and seat myself next to her. 'You were always extremely kind to me.'

She searches my gaze. 'I never meant to hurt you, Beth. We were desperate, that's all. When Stephanie told us Hendrik was coming back ...'

'Stephanie, Jonas' mum?' I manage not to glance towards the half-open door, behind which Sadie, Jonas and Hendrik are hiding, listening to every word. Thankfully, Leonora was still being questioned by the police in the study when Hendrik arrived, so she has no idea he's even in the house.

'Stephanie was the only other person who knew about Nina,' Leonora says. 'She saw me get into Roy Everett's car once, and that was the evening he ...' She shakes her head, as if it's not something she can bear to remember. 'And she was the one who helped Markus and I get back together, a couple of months later. So when Nina was born

286

only seven months after that, and what with her looks and everything . . . '

'Ah.' I let this sink in. 'But surely Hendrik did the maths, too?'

'He couldn't have been sure, though. Markus and I had been seeing each other beforehand, so for all Hendrik knew, we might have been sleeping together then. And he never saw Nina as a baby.'

For a second, my sense of injustice overwhelms my caution. 'But it was none of Hendrik's business, anyway! Nina *was* Markus' daughter – okay, not in the biological sense, but in every other sense.' It takes all my effort not to glare across at the door. 'Why couldn't Hendrik just accept you and Nina as part of his family?'

Leonora gives me a tired look, as if I'm missing the point. 'He'd have accepted us if we'd all moved to the States, like he wanted, I'm sure. It wasn't about acceptance. He just . . . he always suspected my motives for staying in this house. If he found out for sure that Nina wasn't Markus' daughter, I was afraid he might . . . '

'What?' I stare at her. 'Oh. You thought it would destroy Nina's chances of inheriting the house, is that what you mean?'

She presses her lips together and turns away. I've clearly stumbled into dangerous territory. Frantically, I try to pull the conversation back.

'So, when Stephanie told you Hendrik was coming . . . '

She relaxes slightly and sighs. 'We guessed that he wanted to sell the house, to force us to follow him to the States. But we thought . . . if we could just show him how much Nina needed to stay here ... Except to do that he'd need to believe she *was* his granddaughter. And we couldn't change the way she looked, of course. But Markus had this crazy idea that we could get her intensive music lessons and take advantage of Hendrik's weak spot, because Anneliese used to play the cello. Markus said he'd ask a client of his, a journalist who'd mentioned she played the violin ... '

I sit up straighter. 'Caroline?'

'Exactly.' Leonora pulls a face. 'But of course, Caroline said Markus was being ridiculous. Nina had no hope of learning enough in three weeks to impress anyone. Caroline told him her own niece had been playing the violin for seven years, and she was still constantly learning and improving ... '

I swallow hard. *That was me.*

Leonora gazes through the window, lost in her memories now. 'But apparently, during this conversation, Caroline mentioned she was trying to adopt her niece. And when Markus got home, he said she'd shown him a photo. And he said, *It's a shame Nina doesn't look more like Caroline's niece.* He said, *She's plump and blonde and round-faced, just like my mum's side of the family.*'

I can hardly breathe. 'So you thought ... '

'Well, that's when we decided to invite you here. It was only meant to be for a week or so. Enough time to trick Hendrik into believing you were Nina, and then we'd let you go back to the children's home.' Briefly, she meets my gaze, and her expression grows earnest. 'But we liked having you here, Beth. *Nina* liked you. And Markus always wanted her to have a brother or sister – he was the one who suggested you stay until Caroline was ready for you ...'

'But Caroline never was ready for me,' I say faintly.

'No.' She turns back to the window. 'No, Caroline turned out to have been playing a game of her own.'

I stare at her, and it takes me a moment to respond. 'What do you mean?'

But she's lost in her thoughts now. As the silence stretches, my hope stretches with it, like a strand of toffee about to snap. Then, when she finally begins to talk again, her words come quickly, referring to me in the third person, as if she's forgotten I'm right here next to her. I wonder if the shock of last night has finally caught up with her – and then I forget everything else as I'm drawn into her story.

'Markus said he'd never noticed anything odd about Beth until he got back from his diving trip. But then he saw something, when he was getting his suitcases out of the car. *She looked just like my mother*, he said. Not that he told me at the time.' She frowns. 'No, he kept it quiet. Until Caroline came for her Christmas visit.'

I think back to that last visit of Caroline's – the stilted conversation in the drawing room; Markus suggesting we walk around the lake but leave Leonora at home; Markus suggesting that Nina and I take the rowing boat out for what might be the last time before the lake froze over. Markus and Caroline strolling away along the lake path, then, just the two of them ...

'I watched from the window,' Leonora says. 'They went all the way around, past the tree stump, out of sight. And when they came back, Caroline looked angry, she left straightaway, but,' her voice turns bitter, 'Markus was in a great mood. He wanted to tell the girls the news straightaway, he said, but luckily I made him tell me first, and then I begged him to wait . . .'

I lean closer. 'Tell the girls what news?'

She doesn't seem to hear me. 'And then he wanted to buy them matching bracelets . . .'

'What news, Leonora? What was it?'

'Caroline wasn't his *client*.' She spits out the word. 'She was his ex-girlfriend. I'd seen her years earlier, from a distance, but she wasn't a hard-faced journalist back then, she was all long hair and denim shorts and orange crop top . . . She used to call herself Kat.'

Something stirs in my memory, like sludge shifting at the bottom of the lake. My brother, Ricky, calling our rarely seen Aunt Caroline 'Aunty Kat'. As if he'd once had a closer relationship with her, before I came on the scene.

Leonora's voice drops. 'He said he made Caroline tell him the truth on that walk around the lake. That after they broke up, she found out she was pregnant. She was going to get rid of the baby. But her sister persuaded her . . .'

'No,' I whisper.

'Because her sister's son had cystic fibrosis, and she was desperate for another child, but she was scared of it having the same condition . . . So the sister took on Kat's baby.'

I shake my head. 'No!'

'Markus said it made Nina and Beth practically sisters.' She screws up her face in anger. 'But that wasn't true! And everything I'd ever planned—'

I stumble to my feet, and Leonora's attention snaps back to the present. She looks horrified for a moment, and then she glares at me accusingly.

'Get out!' She, too, springs to her feet, her voice rising to a shriek. 'What are you doing in here? Get out of my house!'

I run from her. But I can't run from the truth.

I'm Markus and Caroline's daughter.

Sadie

Sadie stumbles backwards into the hall as Beth flees the dining room.

Beth is white-faced, horrified. She repeats the same words over and over: 'I'm not ... I'm not ... I'm not ...' When Sadie tries to go to her, to comfort her, Beth bats her away as if she doesn't recognise her.

Sadie's still struggling to make sense of Leonora's words herself. She barely knows her Great-aunt Caroline ... *My grandmother, Caroline*, she thinks with a jolt. But one thing's for sure: Beth has never coped well with even trivial emotional subjects. How can she possibly cope with a revelation of this magnitude?

'Beth, look at me.' Somehow, Joe's voice cuts through Beth's panic. 'You're going to be okay,' he tells her. 'Everything's going to be fine, I promise.'

Beth's breathing gradually slows. 'I'm not ... I'm not who I thought I was ...'

'You're still my mum, though,' Sadie says, and this time

she manages to catch hold of Beth's hands. 'It doesn't change *us*, does it?'

Beth stares back at her. 'I wish I hadn't asked . . . Everything I ever thought . . . I wish I didn't know . . .'

Sadie's heart contracts with guilt, because it was her who sent Beth to talk to Leonora in the first place.

'I'm so sorry,' Sadie says. 'I'm really sorry, Mum.'

Beth

I'm Markus and Caroline's daughter.

It hits me repeatedly, like waves battering a shore.

Sadie doesn't take her eyes off me. 'I'm so sorry, Mum.' I want to comfort her, but I don't know how to comfort myself.

'Everything's going to be fine,' Jonas says again.

I close my eyes. I'm not the person I thought I was. And on top of that, my biological mother is still alive. But she kept our connection hidden, not just when I had parents who loved me, but after I believed myself orphaned, when I was at my most vulnerable. I'm torn between wanting an explanation from her, and wanting never to see her again. What kind of a mother is she?

And then another question occurs to me. Am I like her? *Am I like Caroline?*

My eyes snap open, and I see the tears on Sadie's cheeks.

'I should never have suggested you talk to Leonora,' Sadie says. 'I'm so, so sorry.'

'No.' I draw myself up, and I try to smile at her. 'I was

wrong when I said I'd rather not know. Of course it's better to know . . .'

'Really?' she says.

'Really.'

I draw her into my arms then, my precious daughter.

I'm nothing like Caroline.

Sadie

A police officer interrupts them to tell them Nina has been given the all-clear by the paramedics. She's been charged with attempted murder, and they're taking her to the police station. The rest of them are free to leave.

Beth feels faint, and Joe guides her to a chair in the hall where she sits with her head hanging, breathing deeply. After a minute, she glances up at Sadie and smiles weakly.

'It's lack of sleep, that's all. I'll be fine, honestly.'

Sadie leaves her with Joe, and she goes to talk to Hendrik. He's the only one of them who continues to look unruffled by Leonora's revelation – reassured, even.

'Well, well,' he says. 'So, now we know. It all makes sense.' He beams at Sadie, and finally she feels a flicker of something like gladness in her heart. She studies him with renewed curiosity.

'So ... you're my great-grandfather, then?'

'It's marvellous, isn't it?' He grasps her hand. 'To find each other, after all this time. But you've got a decision to make now, young lady.'

Sadie can't help but smile; anyone else calling her young lady, she'd bite their head off, but somehow, coming from her very own, newly discovered great-grandfather . . .

'What decision?' she says.

'Do you want the house?' Hendrik glances across to Beth, then back to Sadie. 'I can't imagine your mother wants it. I was going to sell it, get rid of it once and for all. But if you want it, Sadie . . . well, Raven Hall is yours.'

Beth

Caroline's email said she'd only be back in London for a quick forty-eight-hour turnaround, but if it really was that important, she could spare us ten minutes. Outside the apartment, Sadie gives me an encouraging smile. I press the doorbell and step back, my heart pounding.

The door jerks open almost immediately, and I'm not sure what I was expecting but it wasn't this. Caroline stands there, glaring at us, and she's holding a piece of card at arm's length, dangled between finger and thumb, as if she's revolted by it.

'If you're here because of this, I'm not interested. It's going straight in the bin, and I don't have time for chitchat.'

I stare at her, bemused, and then my gaze slides along her arm to the card: it's another of Nina's invitations.

'Can I see it?' Sadie asks, and she virtually snatches the card from Caroline's hand. She scans it quickly, then gives me a shocked look. 'Nina invited Caroline, too.'

'I've literally just opened it,' Caroline snaps. 'I've been away for three months, there's no point sending me things like this in the post.'

Gingerly, I take the card from Sadie, and I read the blue looping handwriting on the back: *We'd love to see you there!*

'I guess now we know why Genevieve was hired at the last minute,' Sadie says to me. 'A substitute for Caroline when she didn't reply.'

Caroline makes an impatient noise. 'Look, could you tell me what this is about? I'm really very busy.'

'I know.' I say.

She frowns. 'What?'

'Everything. About Leonora's game. About Markus. About . . . you. I know you're my mother.'

She rocks back on her heels. After a few seconds of shock, her expression softens into something that looks like regret, and for a moment I glimpse tears in her eyes. But when she finally speaks, her voice is calm and controlled.

'Who told you?'

No happy relief that the truth is finally out. Just that sharp question, as if she wants the answer for one of her articles.

'Leonora,' I say. 'She told me everything.'

Caroline's shoulders sag. Sadie and I are barely across the threshold, the door still wide open behind us. I shift uncomfortably, waiting for her to say something, although I don't know what I'm hoping for. What could she possibly say that would make me feel better? I almost wish I hadn't come, but Sadie takes my hand and her touch reminds me of my new resolutions. To face the past. To be more open about my feelings.

'I was an idiot,' Caroline says eventually, quietly. She looks directly at me. 'I thought sending you off to Raven Hall would solve all our problems – mine, yours *and* theirs. I never thought anyone would guess . . .'

I stare at her. 'But what about . . . before that? When Mum and Dad died, the accident. Didn't you think then . . . ?'

She shakes her head. 'It was too late, by then, to tell you. How could I? And anyway, my work . . .'

Sadie makes a scathing noise, but I squeeze her hand to hush her. I want to hear everything Caroline has to say before we leave. Because I know we're going to leave, and soon.

'Look, I'm sorry, Beth,' Caroline says. 'I don't know what else you want me to say. Your parents loved you. They're the ones who wanted you. I tried, honestly, but I never could . . .' She drops her gaze. 'I'm sorry.'

The silence stretches. Eventually I look at my watch.

'Well, we'll leave you to it,' I say.

Sadie gives Caroline a strange, penetrating look. 'I feel sorry for you, Caroline.'

We leave then, Sadie and I. We walk back out of the apartment, hand in hand. I'm glad I faced Caroline, my mother. But I'm even more glad to be going home with my daughter now.

Sadie

JULY 2019

Sadie turned down Hendrik's offer of Raven Hall.

There were too many arguments against it. Not least, the horror on her mother's face when Hendrik first suggested the idea. But also, the awkwardness of accepting such an immense gift from a ninety-year-old great-grandfather she'd only just met; and the responsibilities and lifestyle changes that taking on a house like Raven Hall would entail . . .

'I still think you should have grabbed it with both hands,' Wendy says. Sadie has met her former agent for coffee, and they're weaving between tables in a café overlooking the high street, heading for their favourite seats. 'God, Sadie, you could have sold it straight on if you didn't want it, kept the money. You'd be a millionaire by now.'

Sadie laughs. 'It's not like that, though. Hendrik would buy me a different house, if I asked him – he even says he'll find me a job in his company, if I want it. But weirdly, it makes me realise . . . '

Wendy pulls a face as she sits down. 'Oh, please. Don't start with the *love is more powerful than money* stuff.'

'No, honestly, it's just a weird situation to be in. I want to take my time, that's all. I actually quite like my life as it is . . . '

'How can you say that? You've already changed loads.'

'Yeah, but that was nothing to do with Hendrik,' Sadie says. 'That was me.'

After their ordeal at Raven Hall, Beth finally opened up to Sadie about her past. As well as telling Sadie about her time at Raven Hall, Beth described the months she spent sleeping on the streets afterwards, and the homeless charity that helped her – the same charity that she in turn has tried to support ever since. When Sadie spotted the charity's name on a job advert in the local newspaper a few weeks later, she drew a circle around it and rang the number straightaway.

'So, when do you start?' Wendy asks her.

'In three weeks.' Sadie can't disguise her excitement. 'They'll be training me at first, of course, and I know it'll be hard but . . . I really can't wait. To actually feel like I'm making a difference to people . . . '

Wendy sighs. 'So, no more mermaid auditions?'

'Nope,' Sadie says with a grin. 'Not for the time being, anyway.'

'Oh, well.' Wendy sips her coffee and tips in a sachet of sugar. 'At least your mum sounds happier now. How's her new man working out?'

'Jonas? Yeah, pretty well, actually.' Sadie smiles. 'I mean, he's not that new but . . . yeah, I think he's good for her. I really like him.'

'Oh, it's no good.' Wendy gets to her feet. 'I've got to have some of that carrot cake. It's calling to me.'

Sadie thinks about Jonas as Wendy heads back to the counter. Jonas was horrified when he discovered Nina had been their photographer that evening; embarrassed that he'd been so focused on the other guests he'd barely glanced at the staff. But Beth had reminded him that that was Nina's intention, and Sadie had smiled to see Beth's determined expression as she reassured him. Beth no longer changes the subject when tricky emotions are brought up. She really has changed.

Sadie twists the charm bracelet on her wrist. After years of hardly ever wearing it, she decided to put it on this morning; she enjoys the sense of connection it gives her to her grandfather, Markus.

Wendy returns with her cake. 'So, fill me in, then. Is there a date for the trial? Have you seen any of the other guests? What's the latest?'

Sadie sighs. She's not supposed to talk about the case, but that doesn't stop everyone asking her for details. There's been plenty of information in the press, though, so she sticks to this and pretends it's all she knows.

'They're still collating evidence,' she says. 'There's no date yet.'

'And Nina Averell's still locked up?'

'Yep.'

Wendy's eyes are enormous. 'I can't believe your mum was friends with a *murderer*.'

'Attempted,' Sadie says weakly.

'I know, but Nina was so devious, wasn't she? Hiring those people to refurbish the house, and they all believed her when she said she was the owner ... And knocking back the poisoned gin herself, to try and make the rest of you drink it ...'

'It was whiskey, actually. And the active compound had broken down, so it didn't have much effect, anyway.'

'Still.' Wendy's eyes shine with admiration. 'You're lucky to be alive. I was saying that to— Actually, do you know what, you could step straight into that mermaid commercial now, if you still wanted it. I'd just need to make one call ...'

Sadie laughs. 'No, thanks – and listen. Don't go around talking about this too much, will you?'

'Gosh no, don't worry.' Wendy nods seriously. 'My lips are sealed.'

They sip their coffees. Sadie closes her eyes for a moment, relishing the buzz of happy chatter all around them in the café. In fact, there have been two major developments in Nina's case – neither of which Sadie can share with Wendy.

Shortly after Nina learnt the truth, in jail, about Beth being Markus' biological daughter, Beth was called back to the police station to be interviewed about a new accusation that Nina had levelled against Leonora. Nina is now claiming that Leonora sent Markus out on to the ice deliberately, knowing it was likely that he would fall through.

'My mother knew I wouldn't have carried on following Beth,' Nina had stated to her solicitor. 'She knew I'd have turned around and gone back to the house – I wasn't allowed to leave Raven Hall or go into the village. So there was no need for her to send Dad out after me. But she sent him anyway, because she knew the ice was weakening, and she was desperate to silence him. She wanted to protect my fraudulent inheritance of Raven Hall.'

Sadie and Beth can't agree on whether they think this is even remotely possible.

'Leonora *loved* Markus,' Beth said to Sadie afterwards. 'He meant everything to her. He was the love of her life.'

'Was he?' Sadie replied. 'Or did he always come second to Raven Hall?'

Beth had frowned. 'Well, there's no way she could have known he'd fall through, anyway . . . No. Much as I'm happy to believe a lot of bad things about Leonora, I can't believe she'd stoop that low.'

Sadie wants to believe her mum is right, but she still finds the very suggestion unsettling. While Nina awaits her trial in a cell, Leonora is out on bail for the historic poisoning of her daughter; she's still, as far as Sadie's aware, holed up in her little seaside cottage, brooding on the loss of her ancestral home. And in an ironic twist, Leonora is providing evidence for the other major development in the far-reaching investigation.

When the police collected the game cards that the dinner guests had been given, they noticed that the comments on them were uniquely personal. Sadie can still remember the gist of hers: *You must have been a great disappointment to your mother, unable to hold down a job . . .*

But in among the other mean-spirited jibes, one guest's card – its gravy-stained quarters carefully pieced back together – stood out for the specific and serious nature of its accusations. Nina's attempt to unsettle her guests and prick their consciences has resulted in a fierce spotlight being turned on to Roy Everett.

At the same time that the police began investigating the thinly veiled accusations on Roy Everett's card, several women who'd seen him on news footage of the incident at Raven Hall came forward to put on record that he'd behaved inappropriately towards them. Some of the allegations are worse, but Sadie and Beth aren't privy to the details. However, Roy Everett will be facing his own trial in due course, and Sadie trusts that justice will be served.

'Okay,' Wendy says, dabbing crumbs from around her mouth. 'I can see your mind's on other things. Have a brilliant time in America, won't you? Give me a ring when you get back.'

Sadie gives her a quick hug goodbye. Hendrik has bought tickets for Sadie and Beth to fly out tomorrow, to visit him for a couple of weeks. Beth nearly declined the offer – not least, Sadie suspects, because she doesn't like the idea of being away from Jonas for that long. But Sadie talked her into accepting it; the timing is perfect – they'll be back just in time for Sadie to start her new job. And she's looking forward to seeing her great-grandfather again in person. They Skype every few days, but it isn't the same.

But before they fly out, there's one more invitation that Sadie has talked Beth into accepting. The new owner of Raven Hall – a Mr El Daly, former investment banker and inventor of an encryption process that made him a fortune – has offered to show them around the newly repaired and refurbished Raven

Hall. Beth was hesitant at first, but she surprised Sadie by warming to the idea.

'I think it might help, actually,' Beth had said, once she'd thought about it. 'I'm done with trying to block out the past. This might make it easier to move on.'

Sadie knows that Jonas has played a large role in Beth's new-found positivity. Beth has been staying with Sadie in Sadie's flat for the last few months, but the arrangement will come to an end soon, because Beth and Jonas are going travelling. They've planned a six-month round-the-world-trip together, making up for the years they lost. It makes Sadie smile every time she thinks of it.

As she climbs into her car, Sadie's mind drifts back to Wendy's other question: *Have you seen any of the other guests?*

She did, in fact, meet up with Nazleen and her wife for drinks a couple of months ago. They skirted around the subject of Raven Hall, and they made vague promises to meet again, but she's not convinced they'll follow through.

Genevieve, she saw in the distance at the police station a few weeks ago, when she and Beth went in to discuss their statements. Sadie pointed Genevieve out to Beth, but the young woman was too far away for them to attract her attention and say hello.

Zach, Sadie hasn't seen at all. Even Jonas commented that the doctor's son has been lying low since the accusations against his father began to rumble around the village.

Sadie finds it sad that, after those intense few hours they spent together at Raven Hall, Nina's seven intended victims have been scattered apart. Of course, Sadie and Jonas are connected now, by Beth, so they have each other to talk to when they need to offload about the events of that night. But Sadie worries about the other innocent guests – Nazleen, Genevieve and Zach. The police told her about Nina's daisy notebook, filled with observations Nina had made when she was spying on Beth's house and Sadie's flat; and on Everett and Jonas, too. Is it worse to be a targeted victim, like they were, or to be collateral damage, like the others?

Sadie puts all such questions out of her mind as she arrives at her flat to pick up Beth. It's time to return to Raven Hall.

Leonora

She follows the same routine every morning. Takes a brisk walk to the beach and back. Makes a black coffee. Fires up the laptop she bought at great expense from the softly spoken man in the computer shop. Checks the day's news headlines. Then she types in her usual search word: Raven Hall.

After weeks of pulling up the same old news reports and photos, today a new article appears at the top of the list. Her heart beats faster as she clicks on the link and waits for her feeble broadband to respond to her command. She's only sixty-four, but her joints are aching today, despite all the ginger tea she's been drinking and her frequent dips in the sea.

Finally, the article loads.

'Take an exclusive peek at the magnificent interior of newly refurbished Raven Hall,' it says. 'Mr El Daly, 37, shows us the grand new staircase and the luxuriously refitted reception rooms, all completed with carefully sourced materials and ethically produced furniture to delight any guest.'

She winces as she scrolls down.

'Following the devastating fire and near loss of life at Raven Hall a mere six months ago, many locals feared the house would once again fall into ruin and disrepair. But under the meticulous guidance of its proud new owner, the transformation is truly remarkable.'

Leonora's smile is sour as she scrolls through the photos. How has it come to this? Nina, her only daughter, is languishing in a prison cell. And this stranger is now the legal owner of Raven Hall.

Leonora knows how hard Nina will be finding her loss of freedom. After Markus died, Nina never did settle at the seaside cottage. She moved out as soon as she turned sixteen, and she led an itinerant lifestyle for years: travelling with a loose group of friends, picking up ad hoc work, visiting Leonora only when it happened to suit her.

Sometimes, on those unannounced visits, Nina would bring gifts that hinted at where she might be living – punnets of strawberries, baskets of apples, trugs of parsnips with the soil still clinging to them. Occasionally, she brought people with her, and Leonora would feed them all a hearty meal while sneaking glances at their matted hair and unwashed clothes. On one memorable occasion, Nina set down an apple basket in the hall as she came in, and it took Leonora twenty minutes to realise there was a baby inside it. Leonora dashed to the shop for formula milk, and the infant guzzled it as if it hadn't been fed for days.

Leonora still had the bulk of her Averell inheritance – the money left over after Raven Hall was sold to clear her late father's debts. Hoping to encourage Nina to settle down, she transferred a hefty *chunk of it into Nina's bank account. But if Nina ever spent more than a bare minimum of it on herself, Leonora saw no evidence of it. Nina continued to disappear for months at a time.*

Until last year.

Perhaps it was Leonora's relief at seeing Nina on her doorstep that made her drop her guard, last summer. She had no one else to share her secrets with, after all, but this time she went too far. She mentioned her ongoing, desperate hope that Nina would one day inherit Raven Hall, and Nina's face had instantly hardened. Leonora kicked herself; Nina had accused her more than once of loving the house more than she loved Nina – Raven Hall was always a sensitive subject between them.

So, Leonora had resigned herself to not seeing Nina for another few months after that. But to her surprise, Nina returned a few days later, and she carried on visiting weekly. She began to ask Leonora endless questions about her childhood, scrawling notes in her old daisy notebook, until Leonora felt decidedly uneasy.

'I've decided how I want to spend my inheritance,' Nina announced one afternoon. 'And you're going to help me, Mother – don't look at me like that. By the end of it, Raven Hall will belong to us again . . .'

Leonora should never have trusted her. But Nina was her daughter; what else could she do?

She still doesn't understand where she went wrong with Nina. Despite all the terrible things that happened to Leonora when she was younger, she never sought revenge – not on Roy Everett, not on Hendrik, not on anyone. All she wanted was to see Raven Hall returned to the Averell family. She's not even sure what caused her more pain – Nina's attempt to kill her or Nina's attempt to destroy Raven Hall.

Raven Hall will always belong to the Averells, whatever the lawyers say. It seems unlikely, now, that Nina will ever set foot in it again, but Leonora hasn't lost all hope – quite the opposite. Her dreams about Raven Hall are stronger now than they've ever been.

She reaches out a trembling finger and touches the image of the house on the screen.

'Hold on a little longer,' she whispers. 'You will be ours again soon, I promise.'

Beth

Raven Hall's grey façade gleams, untarnished, in the gentle Fenland sunlight. As Sadie brings her car to a halt on the gravel, I can't help thinking of Caroline: the way she drove me here on that first day, fully aware I was her daughter, unmoved by the fact that neither Markus nor I had the faintest idea we were related.

A stocky man with a broad smile bounds down the stone steps – Mr El Daly, the new owner. And suddenly this visit feels absolutely right.

'You go and look around inside,' I say to Sadie, 'but I want to stay out here.' I glance at the lake, thinking of Markus. 'I'd like to be by myself, to say goodbye.'

So, Sadie and Mr El Daly head into the house, and I stroll down the grassy incline, remembering all the times I ran down here with Nina and Jonas. I smile when I think of Jonas; after a lifetime of masking my feelings, I've discovered the power of talking, and Jonas is a patient listener. Only this morning, I rang him about an odd phrase of Nina's that was niggling at me: *I'm not obsessed with Raven Hall like them.*

'Why did she say *them*?' I asked Jonas. 'Why not *her*? As in, Leonora.'

Jonas had given it some thought. 'She must have meant Markus, I guess – who else could have been as obsessed with Raven Hall as Leonora?'

I'm not convinced, but perhaps that's because I like to think better of Markus. As I approach the dock, sunlight dazzles on the water, and my eyes sting at the injustice of not knowing Markus was my father while he was alive. But I remind myself that the future is bright.

A noise up by the house makes me turn, and I see a dark-haired young woman slipping out through the front door. She trots down the steps, and when she notices me watching her, she presses a hand over her heart and gives a startled laugh. I hurry up the grass towards her.

'Sorry!' I call out. 'I didn't mean to make you jump.'

She frowns as I come closer. 'Are you from the hot tub company? Only we weren't expecting you till three ...'

'No, I was just ...' A glint of jewellery catches my attention, and, without intending to, I reach out. 'Do you mind ... can I see?'

Her guarded expression gives way to delight, and she springs forward with her hand outstretched to show off a glittering diamond ring. 'It's a beauty, isn't it? We're getting married next week. Just a small wedding – my grandmother on my side, and his parents on his . . . And then I'll be Mrs El Daly of Raven Hall.'

But it's not her ring I'm gazing at. 'No, where did you get your bracelet from?'

'Oh, this?' She hooks up the delicate gold chain. 'From my mum – it's the only thing she ever gave me. We're not close. I mean, she left me with my gran when I was a baby – in an apple basket, of all things. Gran brought me up. But my mum did show that she cares about me, in her own way, a few months ago. She dragged me in to some crazy plan she'd dreamt up, but then she warned me to leave before it got too dangerous . . .'

She twists the bracelet around to show me the charms.

'Flag iris,' I murmur, trying to hide my astonishment while my mind races to understand the implication of her words. 'Greylag goose. Reed warbler.' Jonas' question resounds in my ears – Who else could have been as obsessed with Raven Hall as Leonora? – and my heart pounds with the suspicion that the answer is standing right here in front of me.

'Do you know what I really like about it?' The young woman is still twisting the bracelet, gazing down at it, oblivious to my unease. Her faraway tone is so familiar, I feel I might have stepped thirty-one years into the past, to when I stood talking to Leonora in this very spot.

I shake my head, speechless.

'My gran loves the thought of me wearing this here. She always says this is where we both belong.' She lifts her gaze to my face and blinks a few times, as if she's emerging from a trance. 'Anyway, it's lovely to meet you . . .'

As her hand reaches for mine, I finally find my voice again. 'Beth.'

'I'm Genevieve.' She smiles warmly at me. 'Welcome to Raven Hall.'

Acknowledgements

This book wouldn't exist if it wasn't for my two brilliant editors, Emma Beswetherick at Piatkus and Amanda Bergeron at Berkley. Thank you both for everything, not least your kindness and patience.

I'm also enormously grateful to Eleanor Russell, Kate Hibbert, Andy Hine, Helena Doree, Sareer Khader, Jin Yu, Diana Franco and Danielle Keir. Thank you for helping my books reach so many readers.

Rebecca Ritchie of AM Heath is the best literary agent an author could wish for, and I'm ridiculously lucky to be represented by her. Thank you for believing in my writing, Becky.

I'm grateful to everyone who shared their knowledge with me for this book, even though the changes I made to the manuscript meant that some details were no longer needed. Particular thanks to Danielle Feasby, Colin Issitt, Claire Daniel, Anita Faul and Sam Foord for being so generous with your expertise.

A special mention to the Mrs H crew – Suzanne Harrison,

Helen Richards, Susannah Jennings, Helen Harrison, Sylvie Martin, Val Watson and Claire Thorne – who keep me sane on a near-daily basis.

And thank you to all my family, especially Brian, Will, Ed and Arthur, for your unconditional support, as ever.

If you'd like to read about one family's mission to set up a small nature reserve in the East Anglian Fens, please take a look at the Facebook page for Madeleine's Patch (facebook.com/madeleinespatch).

THE
PERFECT
GUESTS

Reading Guide

Reading Group Questions

1. In the early stages of Leonora's relationship with Markus, she worries that she's a bad person, and she hopes that Markus might help her 'to change, to improve, to become more like him'. Do you think Leonora's desire to be a good person counts for anything? Is it fair to say that, in the end, it's Markus who becomes more like her?

2. Who was responsible for the cracks that formed in Beth and Nina's friendship? Do you think it was inevitable that things would go wrong?

3. Nina tells Beth, 'My mother always loved this house more than she loved me.' Do you think that's true? Does it fit with Leonora's behaviour when she ignores Markus' instruction to phone the fire brigade and rushes upstairs into thick smoke to search for Nina?

4. Stephanie tried to be a good friend to Leonora, protecting Nina's identity and warning Leonora about Hendrik's visits. Do you think Stephanie did the right thing? If she'd decided not to keep Leonora's secrets, might the outcome have been better for Nina?

5. Do you feel Leonora and Markus bear equal responsibility for the initial 'game'? Was it reasonable for them to assume it would be harmless to Beth?

6. If you could explore the life of one of the minor characters, which would you choose?

7. How do you feel about the choices Caroline made, both before Beth was born and afterwards? Do feel any sympathy for her?

8. In the aftermath of the 2019 events at Raven Hall, Beth says about her childhood there: 'Most of the time – it was a pretty wonderful place to live'. Does this statement surprise you?

9. Near the end, Sadie wonders whether it's worse to be a targeted victim of a crime, or to be thought of as collateral damage. What do you think?

10. What would you like to see happen at Raven Hall in the days and weeks following the final chapter?

Behind the Book

A question for the author: what inspired you to choose the Fens as the setting for *The Perfect Guests*?

When I graduated from vet school back in 1997, I began working for a friendly veterinary practice in Huntingdon, in the East of England. It wasn't long before they sent me to cover a shift at their smallest branch surgery, which they described as being 'out in the Fens', in a little town called Ramsey. The vet nurses had already discovered from accompanying me on home visits that I had no sense of direction, so they sketched me a map on the back of a lab results fax and assured me the route was quite straightforward. I flung my stethoscope and drugs formulary onto the passenger seat of my battered old Volvo, and off I set.

I soon found myself in distinctively wide-open countryside. Long, straight roads. Flat fields of crops stretching to a featureless horizon. A huge dome of washed-out blue above. And on all sides – in ditches, in reed-lined channels, in silvery sheets on the fields themselves – the glint of water.

I got lost, of course. In my defence, there aren't many obvious landmarks when you're a newcomer driving between endlessly similar fields. In any case, I'm perfectly used to being lost, so it didn't trouble me; instead it gave me a chance to appreciate the striking sense of space and solitude offered by the rural Fens. I paused at signposted junctions and studied village names that hinted at a preoccupation with the contours of the land: Ramsey Heights, Ramsey Hollow, Ramsey Mereside, Ramsey Forty Foot (which I later learnt took its name from the Forty Foot Drain).

In the end, by approaching Ramsey from the 'wrong' direction, I found myself driving in on the very road I was aiming for, which bore the rather intriguing name, 'Great Whyte'. Even with my new-graduate brain distracted by the imminent prospect of meeting new colleagues and clients, I was surprised by just how wide the Great Whyte was – a remarkably broad street in this otherwise small and unassuming market town; twice as wide as the roads I was used to back in Huntingdon and Cambridge.

I was even more startled when I discovered what lay beneath the Great Whyte. But to explain that, it helps to know a little of the history of the Fens.

The term 'the Fens' is used to describe a low-lying region of around 1,500 square miles in the East of England, encompassing parts of Lincolnshire, Cambridgeshire, Norfolk and Suffolk, with its easternmost boundary along the coast. Once covered by ancient forest, it was reduced to peat bogs and marshland when the sea began to encroach upon it, and for a long time these wetlands were deemed inhospitable by all but the hardiest of folk. Those tough few inhabitants built their homes on scattered 'islands' of slightly raised ground and travelled in boats through shifting marsh channels and across lakes, which they called meres. They lived primarily off the abundant fish and waterfowl – pike and eel, crane and heron, bittern and egret, and many more.

Then came a profound discovery: that the peat-rich earth lying just beneath the shallow waters was impressively fertile. And so began a series of attempts to drain the Fens.

The Romans made a start on it. Efforts continued through the Middle Ages. In 1620, King James I called in the expertise of Dutch engineers, including Cornelius Vermuyden. Water channels were dug and widened, coastal walls were built, and – despite bitter resistance from local residents – slowly but surely, wind-powered pumps drained the marshes to expose a vast plain of rich agricultural land. In later centuries, the wind pumps were replaced by Victorian steam technology, then diesel-fuelled engines, and finally modern electric pumps. Meanwhile, the crops that thrived on the black, peaty soil earnt the Fens the nickname 'the bread basket of England'.

As I drove my beloved Volvo down the surprisingly wide Great Whyte in Ramsey that day, I was only vaguely aware of this watery Fenland history. And it was a fair while longer before I discovered that the word 'Whyte' here is believed to come from the Anglo-Saxon 'Waite', meaning dock.

Before the Fens were drained, Ramsey was one of these 'islands' that could only be reached by boat, either via channels through the marshes or along a river called the Bury Brook. In medieval times, the town of Ramsey flourished, not least due to the Benedictine Ramsey Abbey which was founded there in AD 969. Goods were delivered to the townspeople along the Bury Brook, and the section of the river where the boats docked was called the Great Whyte. But when the drainage of the Fens began in earnest in the seventeenth century, the very shape of the land and water courses changed.

As the land area increased, the town of Ramsey was able to expand, and the Great Whyte now flowed not along the edge of an island but down the centre of a broad street. Road links sprang up across the region. The 'island towns' in the Fens were no longer wholly dependent on their waterways. And by the mid-nineteenth century, with the additional promise of the railway soon to come to Ramsey, the much-reduced Great Whyte had fallen into redundancy.

So in 1852, engineers built a set of brick tunnels to enclose the water that flowed down the middle of the street and conceal it underground. After that, the townspeople no longer needed a bridge to cross the Great Whyte; they could stroll back and forth between shops, banks, public houses (with names like the Boat Inn, the White Swan, and the still-open-today Jolly Sailor) and eventually, of course, the veterinary surgery.

I continued to work at that surgery on Great Whyte, on and off, until 2016 when I left veterinary practice to start writing fiction. During that time, I learnt about some of the other side-effects of Fenland drainage, both on the region's threatened wildlife and on the land itself. Year upon year, as the water continues to be drawn out, the peaty soil shrinks and the land itself sinks still further.

In recent years, I've taken my children to Holme Fen to visit the lowest point in Great Britain, where a four-metre-high iron post marks the fall in land level between 1851 and now. I've explored some of the nature reserves in the region, and I've read about schemes to re-flood parts of the Fens in winter months, not least to lock carbon into the peat to prevent its release contributing to global warming. I've even tried a bit of wild swimming in the chilly Fenland waters.

Little wonder that when I started mulling over ideas for the setting of *The Perfect Guests*, it was a patch of Fenland that sprang to mind: an isolated house next to a remnant of what was once a great lake, surrounded by fields and water channels in every direction. Here, a child could grow up roaming freely but still be hidden away from the world. Here, no one could approach without fear of being spotted. Here, a fire could take hold without alerting the neighbours . . .

Raven Hall is a fictitious house set in a very real landscape. I hope, if you haven't already, you might one day get the chance to visit the Fens – to marvel at the richness of its wildlife and its wonderful conservation projects, to catch a fascinating glimpse of its history, and most of all to soak up the glorious sense of open space under that huge dome of a Fenland sky.

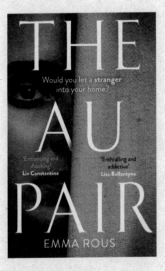